Elizabeth Barrett Browning

Poems of Elizabeth Barrett

Volume I

Elizabeth Barrett Browning

Poems of Elizabeth Barrett
Volume I

ISBN/EAN: 9783337206765

Printed in Europe, USA, Canada, Australia, Japan

Cover: Foto ©Andreas Hilbeck / pixelio.de

More available books at **www.hansebooks.com**

THE

POEMS

OF

ELIZABETH BARRETT BROWNING.

Complete in Three Volumes.

CORRECTED BY THE LAST LONDON EDITION   WITH AN INTRODUCTORY
ESSAY BY H. T. TUCKERMAN.

VOLUME I.

NEW YORK:

JAMES MILLER, 647 BROADWAY,

(SUCCESSOR TO C. S. FRANCIS & CO.)

1869.

CONTENTS.

VOL. I.

TRANSLATIONS.

THE POETRY

OF

ELIZABETH BARRETT BROWNING.

BY H. T. TUCKERMAN.*

GENUINE verse is an excellent safety-valve. I once heard the publication of a lady's effusions regretted by one of her sex, on the ground that she had " printed her soul." The objection is not without significance to a refined nature, but its force is much diminished by the fact that poetry is " caviare to the general." It is the few alone who possess any native relish for the muse, and a still more select audience who can trace the limits between fancy and the actual, or discover the separate fruits of personal experience and mere observation. Those capable of thus identifying the emanations of the mind with traits of character, and recognizing the innate desires or peculiar affections of a writer, and plucking out the heart of his mystery, will be the very ones to reverence his secret, or at least to treat it with delicacy. The truth is, no one can reach the fountains of emotion in another, except through sympathy—and

---

* Taken, by permission of the Author, from "Thoughts on the Poets."

1

there is a freemasonry, an instinctive mutual understanding thus awakened, which makes the revelation sacred. Accordingly there is little danger of a compromise of self-respect in uttering to the world our inward life, if any proper degree of tact and dignity is observed. The lovers of poetry are thus gratified; the deeper sentiments and higher aspirations of the universal heart are confirmed; solace is afforded the unhappy by confessions of kindred sorrow—and all the while, the privacy of the individual is uninvaded. At the same time, let us acknowledge that authorship, as a career, is undesirable for a woman. Only when duty lends her sanction, or pre-eminent gifts seem almost to anticipate destiny, can the most brilliant exhibition of talent add to the intrinsic graces or true influence of the sex. There are circumstances, however, which not only justify but ennoble publicity. There are situations in life which in a manner evoke from retirement those whose tastes are all for seclusion. If we look narrowly into the history of those with whose thoughts and feelings literature has made us most intimate, it will often appear that in them there was combined a degree of sensibility and reflection which absolutely, by the very law of the soul, must find a voice, and that it was the pressure of some outward necessity, or the pain of some inward void that made that voice—(fain to pour itself out in low and earnest tones) —audible to all mankind. Some one has said that fame is love disguised. The points of a writer are usually those wherein he has been most alone; and they owe their effect to the vividness of expression which always results from conscious self-reliance. Literary vanity is a frequent subject of ridicule; but many confound a thirst for recognition with a desire for praise. The former is a manly as well as a natural sentiment. Indeed there is something noble in the feeling which leads an ardent mind—looking in vain for a response to its oracles among the fellow-creatures amid which its lot is cast—to appeal to a wider circle and send its messages abroad on the wings of the press, in the hope and faith that some heart will leap at the tidings and accept them as its own. I am persuaded that this truly human craving for sympathy and intelligent communion, is frequently mistaken for a weaker and more selfish appetite—the morbid love of fame. High-toned and sensitive beings invariably find their most native aliment in personal associations. They are sufficiently aware that notoriety profanes, that the nooks, and not the arena of life, afford the best refreshment. It is usually because poverty, ill-health, domestic trial, political tyranny, or misplaced affection, has deprived their hearts of a complete sanctuary, that they seek for usefulness and honor in the fields of the world.

"My poems," says Mrs. Browning, "while full of faults, as I go forward to my critics and confess, have my soul and life in them." We gather from other hints in the preface and especially from her poetry itself, that the life of which it is "the completest expression" attainable, has been one of unusual physical suffering, frequent loneliness and great study. As a natural result there is a remarkable predominance of thought and learning, even in the most inartificial overflow of her muse. Continually we are met by allusions which indicate familiarity with classic lore. Her reveries are imbued with the spirit of antique models. The scholar is everywhere co-evident with the poet. In this respect Mrs. Browning differs from Mrs. Hemans and Mrs. Norton, in whose effusions enthusiasm gives the tone and color. In each we perceive a sense of beauty and the pathos born of grief, but in the former these have a statuesque, and in the two latter a glowing development. The cheerfulness of Mrs. Browning appears the fruit of philosophy and faith. She labors to reconcile herself to life through wisdom and her religious creed, and justifies tenderness by reason. This is a rather masculine process. The intellect is the main agent in realizing such an end. Yet discipline and isolation explain it readily; and the poetess doubtless speaks from consciousness when she declares the object of her art "to vindicate the necessary relation of genius to suffering and self-sacrifice." The defect of poetry thus conceived is the absence of spontaneous, artless and exuberant feeling. There is a certain hardness and formality, a want of *abandon* of manner, a lack of gushing melody, such as takes the sympathies captive at once. We are conscious, indeed—painfully conscious—that strong feeling is here at work, but it is restrained, high-strung and profound. The human seems to find no natural repose, and strives, with a tragic vigor that excites admiration, to anticipate its spiritual destiny even while arrayed in mortal habiliments. Without subscribing to her theology we respect her piety. "Angelic patience" is the lesson she teaches with skill and eloquence. She would have the soul ever "*nobler than its mood.*" In her isolation and pain she communed with bards and sages, and found in their noble features, encouragement such as petty joys failed to give. She learned to delight in the ideals of humanity, and gaze with awe and love on their

> Sublime significance of mouth,
> Dilated nostrils full of youth,
> *And forehead royal with the truth.*

In her view,

> Life treads on life and heart on heart—
> We press too close in church and mart,
> To keep a dream or grave apart.

And from all this she turns to herself, and cherishes her individuality with a kind of holy pride. She seeks in the ardent cultivation of her intellectual resources a solace for the wounds and privations of life. She reflects intensely—traces the footsteps of heroes—endeavors to make the wisdom of the Past and the truths of God her own—and finds a high consolation in embodying the fruits of this experience in verse :

> *In my large joy of sight and touch,*
> *Beyond what others count as such,*
> *I am content to suffer much.*

It would argue a strange insensibility not to recognize a redeeming beauty in such an example. Mrs. Browning is an honor to her sex, and no member thereof can fail to derive advantage from the spirit of her muse. It speaks words of " heroic cheer," and suggests thoughtful courage, sublime resignation, and exalted hope. At the same time, we cannot but feel her incompleteness. We incline to, and have faith in less systematic phases of woman's character. There is a native tenderness and grace, a child-like play of emotion, a simple utterance, that brings more genial refreshment. We do not deprecate Mrs. Browning's lofty spirit and brave scholarship. They are alike honorable and efficient; but sometimes they overlay nature and formalize emotion, making the pathway to the heart rather too long and coldly elegant for quick and entire sympathy. Yet this very blending of sense and sensibility, learning and love, reason and emotion, will do much, and has already done much. (as we can perceive by recent criticisms,) to vindicate true sentiment and a genuine devotion to the beautiful. These glorious instincts are sternly rebuked every day under the name of enthusiasm, imagination and romance, as vain and absurd, by those who have intelligent but wholly practical minds

2

The sound and vigorous thought visible in Mrs. Browning's poetry, and the self-dependence she inculcates, will command the respect and win the attention of a class who sneer at Tennyson as fantastic, and Keats as lack-a-daisical. They may thus come to realize how the most kindling fancies and earnest love, ay, the very gentleness and idealism which they deem so false and weak, may co-exist with firm will, rare judgment, conscientiousness and truth, lending them both fire and grace, and educing from actual and inevitable ill, thoughts of comfort like these :

> Think!—the shadow on the dial
>   For the nature most undone,
> Marks the passing of the trial,
>   *Proves the presence of the sun !*
> Look!—look up, in starry passion,
>   To the throne above the spheres,
> Learn!—the spirit's gravitation
>   Still must differ from the tear's.
> Hope!—with all the strength thou usest
>   In embracing thy despair;
> Love!—*the earthly love thou losest*
>   *Shall return to thee more fair ;*
> Work!—make clear the forest tangling
>   Of the wildest stranger land ;
> Trust!—the blessed deathly angels
>   Whisper "Sabbath hours at hand."

Mrs. Browning's imagery is often Dantesque and Miltonic. She evinces a certain distrust of her own originality ; but her tastes, both natural and acquired, obviously ally her to the more thoughtful and rhetorical poets. In the " Drama of Exile " are numerous passages, born of the same earnest contemplations which give such grave import to the language of the sightless bard of England. and the father of Italian song. The following are examples to the purpose :

> . . . . As the pine,
> In Norland forests, drops its weight of sorrows
> By a night's growth, so growing towards my ends
> I drop thy counsel.
> *   *   *   *   *
> Drawing together her large globes of eyes,
> The light of which is throbbing in and out,
> Around their continuity of gaze.

Adam, as he wanders from Paradise, exclaims .

> How doth the wide and melancholy earth
> Gather her hills around us gray and ghast,
> And stare *with blank significance of loss*
> Right in our faces.

Lucifer narrates an incident with singular vividness :

> Dost thou remember, Adam, when the curse
> Took us from Eden? On a mountain peak
> Half-sheathed in primal woods, and glittering
> In spasms of awful sunshine, at that hour
> A lion couched—part raised upon his paws,
> With his calm, massive face turned full on thine,
> *And his mane listening.* When the ended curse
> Left silence in the world, right suddenly
> He sprang up rampant, and stood straight and stiff,
> As if the new reality of death
> Were dashed against his eyes—and roared so fierce,
> (Such thick, carniverous passion in his throat
> Tearing a passage through the wrath and fear.)
> And roared so wild, and smote from all the hills
> Such fast, keen echoes, crumbling down the oaks,
> To distant silence, that the forest beasts,
> One after one, did mutter a response
> In savage and in sorrowful complaint,
> Which trailed along the gorges. Then at once
> He fell back, and rolled crashing from the height.
> Hid by the dark-orbed pines.

Lucifer's curse is a grand specimen of blank verse. As instances of terse and meaning language, take the two brief stanzas descriptive of Petrarch and Byron The phrase "forlornly brave," applied to the latter, is very significant:

Who from his *brain-lit heart* hath thrown
A thousand thoughts beneath the sun,
All perfumed with the name of one,

   *   .   .   .   .   .*

And poor, proud Byron, sad as grave,
And salt as life, forlornly brave,
And grieving with the dart he drave.

"The Rhyme of the Duchess May" and "Bertha in
the Lane" are by no means perfect, artistically speaking,
but they have genuine pathos. "To Flush, my Dog"
is apt as a piece of familiar verse. "Cowper's Grave"
and "Sleep" have a low, sad music, at once real and
affecting; while many of the lines in "Geraldine" ring
nobly and sweet; and in "The Crowned and Wedded,"
"The Lady's Yes," and other minor pieces, the true
dignity of her sex is admirably illustrated. While thus
giving Mrs. Browning due credit for her versatile talent,
we repeat that, in our view, the most interesting phase
of her genius is her sincere recognition of that loyalty
and tenderness—that "strong necessity of loving," and
that divine reality of the heart, which are essential to
all that is moving in poetry and all that is winsome in
experience. Could we not trace the woman beneath
attainment and reflection, our admiration might be excited, but our sympathies would not awaken.

The most beautiful passages of the 'Drama," to our
thinking, are such as these :

Adam.   God! I render back
    Strong benediction and perpetual praise
    From mortal, feeble lips (as incense smoke
    Out of a little censer may fill heaven)
    That thou in striking my benumbed hands,
    And forcing them to drop all other boons
    Of beauty, and dominion and delight,
    Hast left this well-beloved Eve—this life
    Within life, this best gift between their palms
    In gracious compensation!

       .   .   .   .   .

O my God!

!n standing here between the glory and dark--
The glory of thy wrath projected forth
From Eden's wall ; the dark of our distress
Which settles a step off in the drear world—
Lift up to thee the hands from whence have fallen
Only Creation's sceptre, thanking thee
That rather thou hast cast me out with *her*
Than left me lorn of her in Paradise,
With angel looks and angel songs around,
To show the absence of her eyes and voice,
And make society full desertness
Without the uses of her comforting
·   ·   ·   ·   ·   ·

. . . . Because with her I stand
Upright as far as can be in the fall,
And look away from heaven, which doth accuse me.
And look up from the earth which doth convict me,
Into her face ; and *crown my discrowned brow*,
Out of her love ; and put the thoughts of her
Around me for an Eden full of birds ;
And lift her body up—thus—to my heart ;
And with my lips upon her lips thus, thus—
Do quicken and sublimate my mortal breath,
Which cannot climb against the grave's steep sides
But overtops this grief. . . . .

The essence of all beauty I call love,
The attribute, the evidence and end,
The consummation to the inward sense
Of beauty apprehended from without
I still call love. . . . .

. . . . Mother of the world,
Take heart before his presence.   Rise, aspire
Unto the calms and magnanimities,
The lofty uses and the noble ends,
The sanctified devotion and full work,
To which thou art elect forevermore.
First woman, wife and mother!

What we have thus far written of Elizabeth Barrett
Browning, refers to her first volumes and that period of

her life when, confined to her apartments in London, by what was deemed an incurable disease, parental devotion surrounded her with every outward means of intellectual delight: culture, companionship and suffering, then and there, disciplined and developed her mind; and the severity of her muse, the preponderance of learning and thought over sentiment and sympathy, was the natural result of this isolation and study. But it was reserved for this most highly endowed of modern Englishwomen, to enlarge and deepen her experience of life, and become inspired thereby to a scope of expression, which endeared her to national and personal affinities, by virtue of a more adequate and authentic utterance thereof, than has elsewhere found expression in our times. The happy experience of a wife and a mother and a sojourn in Italy, at the epoch of the civic regeneration of that land of Art and Song, awakened a more vital earnestness and tender music in her verse. To the poems suggested by classic themes, mediæval legends, or Scriptural history, wherein the scholar was coevident with the woman, were now added the more personal and passionate element of love, and a sympathy with the rise and progress of Italian freedom and unity, only possible to a comprehensive and ardent soul: "Sonnets from the Portuguese" embalm and embody the one, and "Casa Guidi Windows" chronicle the other; the former are the most complete and exquisite, the noblest and most eloquent memorials of woman's love ever written by one of the sex; the latter, the most vivid and gracious picture and plea which the revolution in Italy has evoked. In these we trace the promise and the power recognized in the "Seraphim," the "Drama of Exile," "Romaunt of the Page," and other early poems, carried into spheres more akin to

universal sympathies: there is the same originality in
metaphor, the same vigor of language, the same evidence of a mind familiar with the treasures of ancient
and modern learning; but there is also greater freedom
and flow; humanity is not so overlaid with erudition,
grace with discipline: now we are thrilled by the devotion, and now softened by the meekness of the sentiment;
here the grand integrity and there the comprehensive
grasp of her thought, delights us; vigorous Saxon
words or felicitous historical reference, challenge admiration: the pathos of "The Cry of the Human," "Cowper's Grave," and "He Giveth His Beloved Sleep"—the
sublimities of "Prometheus Bound," and the noble grace
of "Lady Geraldine's Courtship"—qualities so prophetic
of the advent of a true poet, in these more mature and
elaborate poems, seem transferred from the realm of
fancy to that of fact: love in her bosom finds a more
direct and therefore more human expression than when
objectively described, and the wrongs and prowess of
Italy, as seen and felt, are interpreted with a realism not
attainable through fancy and fable. If ever the life of
a gifted woman was ordained by Providence to discipline
and develop her genius, such was the case with Eliza
beth Barrett Browning. Isolated in early youth from
the pleasures and the cares that attend upon health and
fortune, deprived of the common incentives to vanity
and amusement, yet furnished with rare opportunities for
the most thorough education; weaned from the world
by suffering, won to reflection and knowledge by a kind
of moral necessity, when this process and privation had
wrought out a strong, wise, and aspiring mind, the
frail body was renewed, the most endeared human
relations entered upon, and the most interesting country
of civilized Europe visited at the moment of its political

enfranchisement. It is almost impossible to imagine an experience better fitted to educate and inspire a woman of genius. Born in London in 1809, at the age of ten she became a writer; in 1833 appeared "Prometheus Bound;" then followed a season of illness, retirement and study, deeply overshadowed by her first great sorrow —the loss of her brother, under the most painful circumstances; in 1846 she married Robert Browning; in 1861 she died at Florence. What she learned, suffered, enjoyed, believed, and accomplished during those years may be found in her Poems; and we shall vainly search the records of literature for a nobler or more earnest and touching memorial of a woman's life, love, and faith. She was not a consummate artist: there is often a ruggedness and an involved construction, a crude and careless utterance in her verse, especially in her later political effusions; sometimes a want of simplicity and often a want of melody detracts from the charm; but the spirit of her writings is so high and humane, the grandeur and beauty of her expression so full and frequent, the purity of her soul and the generosity of her sympathies so eloquent, and the original power of her verse so prevalent, that it seems ungracious to criticise the *form* when the *substance* is so profound and precious. Her genius was not dramatic; and it is easy to discover errors of judgment and of taste in her longest didactic poem; but the sentiment, the argument and the imagery thereof, would furnish with the most select materials of the divine art scores of popular minstrels. There are prosaic interludes and homely expressions in "Aurora Leigh," at which verbal critics will carp; but it is a real poem, vital, earnest, eloquent and brave. Nowhere have we read a more clear, significant, better sustained exposition of the heart and mystery,

the problems and the conventionalism of her century, of
society, and of life; nowhere a more just and beautiful
plea for Art. There are famous poets of the other sex,
now living, unequal to the grasp of this high argument.
There is a freshness and freedom, a distinctness and a
courage, a feeling and a reason in "Aurora Leigh,"
which at once wins the mind and stirs the heart.

It defines and illustrates with marvellous eloquence
the difference between *intellect* and *soul*, the ideal and
the commonplace—poetry and the world, and vindi-
cates love. It dissects the fallacies of modern philan-
thropy. We hear a woman's voice, but it is wise and
deep, chartered with lore and chastened by grief, and
tender with sympathy, and commanding from the most
elevated plane of consciousness, whence the sibyl looks
forth upon life. The book has pictures of everlasting
nature and of modern life, exquisitely and bitterly true.
We have never read a poem so full of original and
striking, yet natural and appropriate metaphors. In
attempting to note them we found the white margin of
each page half lined. Sometimes Mrs. Browning weaves
a phrase Dantesque in its terse meaning, Shakesperian
in its felicitous wording. No female writer has ever so
firmly and comprehensively dealt with the English
tongue. There are passages of condensed thought and
eloquent significance equal to the best which Charles
Lamb gleaned from the old dramatists. These alternate,
however, with the most colloquial and prosaic sentences,
and this juxtaposition of the familar and the sublime is
one of the remarkable, and perhaps inauspicious, traits
of the poem.

It is pleasant and memorable to feel, as we lament
the departure of this endeared child of song, that the
earliest if not the most earnest recognition of her merits

2

came from this side of the Atlantic : her readers in America far outnumber those in England : among our countrymen and countrywomen she found attached friends, gained through personal intercourse in Italy, and by correspondence.   It is remarkable that the uniform testimony of the former gives evidence that the interest of Mrs. Browning's character transcended that of her writings ; the woman charmed and cheered even more than the author ;   or rather the " daily beauty" of her life made those who enjoyed her intimacy attach a value and an interest to her personal influence more endearing than fame or genius.   There was something so genuine, earnest, candid, and humane in her manners, aspect, and conversation, that people of every class, calibre, and nationality, found in her the truth, the love, and the faith which her verse proclaims and celebrates.

Although so long an invalid, Mrs. Browning's death was unexpected at the time.   Those who recognize in her remarkable life a providential experience, will feel the same benign coincidences in the circumstances of her departure : feeble, and, for some time, undecided as to her place of sojourn for the summer, she greatly enjoyed the return to Florence, and to the dwelling which had witnessed so many happy hours of domestic love and social communion—where some of her best poetry was written, and her child was born.   Her spirits revived at the sight of this endeared home abroad.   She looked cheerfully upon the old tapestry and paintings, the effigies of her favorite poets, the familiar chair and table, around which, as around a heart-reared throne, her friends used to gather ; she went out in the summer twilight, leaning upon her husband's arm, upon the pleasant balcony, with its clustering shrubs and flowers, and greeted the dim, but familiar walls of the old

Church of Santo Felice opposite—talking gratefully the while, of Italy, of mutual friends, and of future plans: her mind and affections were never more strong and vivid; but nature was already yielding in an organization of marvellous delicacy; and that slight figure, with the large, deep and tender eyes, and clustering brown hair, was about to vanish from the scene it had made so precious and hallowed. Early on the morning of the 29th of June, 1861, with pleasant words on her lips, unconscious that the sleep that stole over her senses was that of death, this gifted and gracious woman peacefully expired. In the English burying-ground, without the gates of Florence, accompanied by her terribly bereaved husband and boy, and a few friends, the remains of Mrs. Browning were laid in earth; and her grave is already the shrine of pilgrims from both sides of the sea. The city where she so long dwelt, and whose struggle for freedom she so memorably sang— according to an old but rarely revived mediæval custom—placed on Casa Guidi this inscription of love and honor to her memory:

> Qui scrisse e morì
> ELIZABETH BARRETT BROWNING,
> Che in cuore di Donna seppe unire
> Saprenza de Dotto, e Facondia di Poeta;
> Fece del suo aureo verso, ancilo,
> Fra Italia e Inghilterra.
> Pose questa memoria
> Firenze grata.
> A. D. 1861

Which may be rendered thus:

> Here wrote and died,
> ELIZABETH BARRETT BROWNING,
> Who in her woman's heart united
> The wisdom of a sage, and the eloquence of a Poet;
> With her golden verse she linked Italy to England.
> Florence grateful placed
> This memorial
> A. D. 1861.

DEDICATION.

TO MY FATHER

WHEN your eyes fall upon this page of dedication, and you start to see to whom it is inscribed, your first thought will be of the time far off when I was a child and wrote verses, and when I dedicated them to you, who were my public and my critic. Of all that such a recollection implies of saddest and sweetest to both of us, it would become neither of us to speak before the world: nor would it be possible for us to speak of it to one another, with voices that did not falter. Enough, that what is in my heart when I write thus, will be fully known to yours.

And my desire is that *you*, who are a witness how if this art of poetry had been a less earnest object to me, it must have fallen from exhausted hands before this day,—that *you*, who have shared with me in things bitter and sweet, softening or enhancing them every day——that *you*, who hold with me over all sense of loss and transciency, one hope by one Name,—may accept the inscription of these volumes, the exponents of a few years of an existence which has been sustained and comforted by you as well as given. Somewhat more faint-hearted than I used to be, it is my fancy thus to seem to return to a visible personal dependence on you, as if indeed I were a child again; to conjure your beloved image between myself and the public, so as to be sure of one smile,—and to satisfy my heart while I sanctify my ambition, by associating with the great pursuit of my life, its tenderest and holiest affection.

Your

E. B. B.

ADVERTISEMENT.

Tıɪs edition, including my earlier and later writings, I have endeavoured to render as little unworthy as possible of the indulgence of the public. Several poems I would willingly have withdrawn, if it were not almost impossible to extricate what has been once caught and involved in the machinery of the press. The alternative is a request to the generous reader that he may use the weakness of those earlier verses which no subsequent revision has succeeded in strengthening, less as a reproach to the writer, than as a means of marking some progress in her other attempts.

E. B. B.

THE SERAPHIM.

I look for Angels' songs, and hear Him cry.

GILES FLETCHER.

THE SERAPHIM.

PART THE FIRST.

It is the time of the Crucifixion; and the angels of heaven have departed towards the earth, except the two Seraphim, Ador the Strong and Zerah the Bright One.

The place is the outer side of the shut heavenly gate.

Ador.   O SERAPH, pause no more!
Beside this gate of Heaven we stand alone.
  Zerah.   Of Heaven!
  Ador.   Our brother hosts are gone—
  Zerah. Are gone before.
  Ador. And the golden harps the angels bore
           To help the songs of their desire,
           Still burning from their hands of fire,
           Lie without touch or tone
             Upon the glass-sea shore.
  Zerah. Silent upon the glass-sea shore!

Ador. There the Shadow from the throne—
    Formless with infinity,
    Hovers o'er the crystal sea ;
      Awfuller than light derived,
  And red with those primæval heats
    Whereby all life has lived.
Zerah. Our visible God, our heavenly seats !
Ador. Beneath us sinks the pomp angelical,
    Cherub and seraph, powers and virtues, all,—
      The roar of whose descent has died
    To a still sound, as thunder into rain.
      Immeasurable space spreads magnified
    With that thick life, along the plane
    The worlds slid out on. What a fall
      And eddy of wings innumerous, crossed
      By trailing curls that have not lost
      The glitter of the God-smile shed
      On every prostrate angel's head !
      What gleaming up of hands that fling
      Their homage in retorted rays,
      From high instinct of worshipping,
        And habitude of praise.
Zerah. Rapidly they drop below us.
      Pointed palm and wing and hair,
      Indistinguishable show us
      Only pulses in the air
      Throbbing with a fiery beat,
      As if a new creation heard
    Some divine and plastic word,
      And trembling at its new found being,
        Awakened at our feet.

Ador.   Zerah, do not wait for seeing.
　　His voice, it is, that thrills us so
　　As we our harpstrings, uttered *Go,*
　　Behold the Holy in his woe—
　　And all are gone, save thee and—
Zerah.   Thee!
Ador.   I stood the nearest to the throne
　　In hierarchical degree,
　　What time the Voice said *Go.*
　　And whether I was moved alone
　　By the storm-pathos of the tone
Which swept through Heaven the alien name of *woe,*
　　Or whether the subtle glory broke
　　Through my strong and shielding wings,
　　Bearing to my finite essence
　　Incapacious of their presence,
　　　Infinite imaginings,
None knoweth save the Throned who spoke;
But I, who, at creation, stood upright
　　And heard the God-Breath move
Shaping the words that lightened, 'Be there light,'
　　Nor trembled but with love,
　　Now fell down shudderingly,
My face upon the pavement whence I had towered,
As if in mine immortal overpowered
　　By God's eternity.
Zerah.   Let me wait!—let me wait!—
Ador.   Nay, gaze not backward through the gate.
God fills our heaven with God's own solitude
　　Till all the pavements glow:
His Godhead being no more subdued

8

By itself, to glories low
    Which seraphs can sustain,
What if thou, in gazing so,
Should behold but only one
Attribute, the veil undone—
And that to which we dare to press
    Nearest, for its gentleness—
        Ay, His love!
How the deep ecstatic pain
Thy being's strength would capture!
Without language for the rapture,
    Without music strong to come
        And set the adoration free,
    For ever, ever, wouldst thou be
    Amid the general chorus dumb,
God-stricken to seraphic agony!——
    Or, brother, what if on thine eyes
        In vision bare should rise
The life-fount whence His hand did gather
        With solitary force
        Our immortalities!
Straightway how thine own would wither,
        Falter like a human breath,
        And shrink into a point like death.
        By gazing on its source!
        My words have imaged dread.
    Meekly hast thou bent thine head,
    And dropt thy wings in languishment
    Overclouding foot and face;
    As if God's throne were eminent
        Before thee, in the place.

Yet not—not so,
O loving spirit and meek, dost thou fulfil
The Supreme Will,
Not for obeisance but obedience,
Give motion to thy wings.   Depart from hence
  The voice said ' Go.'
 Zerah.   Beloved, I depart.
His will is as a spirit within my spirit,
A portion of the being I inherit.
His will is mine obedience.   I resemble
A flame all undefilèd though it tremble ;
I go and tremble.   Love me, O beloved !
  O thou, who stronger art,
And standest ever near the Infinite,
Pale with the light of Light !
Love me, beloved ! me, more newly made,
  More feeble, more afraid ;
And let me hear with mine thy pinions moved,
As close and gentle as the loving are,
That love being near, heaven may not seem so far.
 Ador.   I am near thee, and I love thee.
  Were I loveless, from thee gone,
  Love is round, beneath, above thee,
  God, the omnipresent One.
  Spread the wing, and lift the brow.
  Well-beloved, what fearest thou ?
 Zerah.   I fear, I fear—
 Ador.   What fear ?

Zerah.   The fear of earth.

Ador.   Of earth, the God-created and God-praised
In the hour of birth?
Where every night, the moon in light
Doth lead the waters, silver-faced?
Where every day, the sun doth lay
A rapture to the heart of all
      The leafy and reeded pastoral,
As if the joyous shout which burst
      From angel lips to see him first,
Had left a silent echo in his ray?

   Zerah.   Of earth—the God-created and God-curst,
      Where man is, and the thorn.
      Where sun and moon have borne,
      No light to souls forlorn.
Where Eden's tree of life no more uprears
Its spiral leaves and fruitage, but instead
The yew-tree bows its melancholy head,
And all the undergrasses kills and seres.

   Ador.   Of earth the weak,
Made and unmade,
Where men that faint, do strive for crowns that
      fade?
Where, having won the profit which they seek,
They lie beside the sceptre and the gold
With fleshless hands that cannot wield or hold,
And the stars shine in their unwinking eyes?

   Zerah.   Of earth the bold:

Where the blind matter wrings
An awful potence out of impotence,
Bowing the spiritual things
    To the things of sense.
Where the human will replies
With ay and no,
Because the human pulse is quick or slow.
Where Love succumbs to Change,
With only his own memories, for revenge.
And the fearful mystery—

    Ador.   Called Death?
   Zerah.   Nay, death is fearful,—but who saith
    'To die,' is comprehensible.
    What's fearfuller, thou knowest well,
    Though the utterance be not for thee,
    Lest it blanch thy lips from glory—
    Ay! the cursed thing that moved
    A shadow of ill, long times ago,
    Across our heaven's own shining floor,
    And when it vanished, some who were
    On thrones of holy empire there,
    Did reign—were seen—were—never more.
      Come nearer, O beloved!
   Ador.   I am near thee.   Didst thou bear thee
    Ever to this earth?
   Zerah.   Before.
    When thrilling from His hand along
    Its lustrous path with spheric song,

    3*

The earth was deathless, sorrowless.
Unfearing, then, pure feet might press
The grasses brightening with their feet,
For God's own voice did mix its sound
In a solemn confluence oft
With the rivers' flowing round
And the life-tree's waving soft.
Beautiful new earth, and strange!

Ador.   Hast thou seen it since—the change?

Zerah.   Nay, or wherefore should I fear
        To look upon it now?
I have beheld the ruined things
Only in depicturings
Of angels from an earthly mission,—
Strong one, even upon thy brow,
When, with task completed, given
Back to us in that transition,
I have beheld thee silent stand,
Abstracted in the seraph band,
        Without a smile in heaven.

Ador.   Then thou wert not one of those
Whom the loving Father chose
In visionary pomp to sweep
O'er Judæa's grassy places,
O'er the shepherds and the sheep,
Though thou art so tender?—dimming
All the stars except one star,
With their brighter kinder faces,
And using heaven's own tune in hymning,

While deep response from earth's own mountains
    ran,
  ' Peace upon earth—goodwill to man '
  Zerah.   " Glory to God !"—I said Amen afar.
And those who from that earthly mission are,
    Within mine ears have told
That the seven everlasting Spirits did hold
With such a sweet and prodigal constraint,
The meaning yet the mystery of the song,
What time they sang it, on their natures strong;
That, gazing down on earth's dark steadfastness,
And speaking the new peace in promises,
The love and pity made their voices faint
Into the low and tender music, keeping
The place in heaven, of what on earth is weeping.
  Ador. Peace upon earth ! Come down to it.
  Zerah.   Ah me!
I hear thereof uncomprehendingly.
Peace where the tempest—where the sighing is—
And worship of the idol, 'stead of His ?
  Ador. Yea, peace, where *He* is.
  Zerah.   *He !*
Say it again.
  Ador.   Where *He* is.
  Zerah.   Can it be
That earth retains a tree
Whose leaves, like Eden foliage, can be swayed
By the breathing of His voice, nor shrink and fade ?
  Ador. There is a tree !—it hath no leaf nor root ;
Upon it hangs a curse for all its fruit:
    Its shadow on His head is laid.

For He, the crowned Son,
Has left his crown and throne,
Walks earth in Adam's clay,
Eve's snake to bruise and slay—
Zerah.   Walks earth in clay?
Ador.   And walking in the clay which He created,
He through it shall touch death.
What do I utter? what, conceive?   Did breath
Of demon howl it in a blasphemy?
Or was it mine own voice, informed, dilated
By the seven confluent Spirits?—Speak—answer
me!
Who said man's victim was his deity?
Zerah.   Beloved, beloved, the word came forth
from *thee.*
Thine eyes are rolling a tempestuous light
Above, below, around,
As putting thunder-questions without cloud,
Reverberate without sound,
To universal nature's depth and height.
The tremor of an inexpressive thought
Too self-amazed to shape itself aloud,
O'erruns the awful curving of thy lips:
And while thine hands are stretched above
As newly they had caught   [Lord
Some lightning from the Throne—or showed the
Some retributive sword—
Thy brows do alternate with wild eclipse
And radiance—with contrasted wrath and love—
As God had called thee to a seraph's part,
With a man's quailing heart.

Ador. O heart—O heart of man!
  O ta'en from human clay,
 To be no seraph's but Jehovah's own!
  Made holy in the taking,
  And yet unseparate
 From death's perpetual ban,
And human feelings sad and passionate!
Still subject to the treacherous forsaking
Of other hearts, and its own steadfast pain.
O heart of man—of God! which God hath ta'en
From out the dust, with its humanity
Mournful and weak yet innocent around it,
And bade its many pulses beating lie
Beside that incommunicable stir
Of Deity wherewith He interwound it.
O man! and is thy nature so defiled,
That all that holy Heart's devout law-keeping,
And low pathetic beat in deserts wild,
And gushings pitiful of tender weeping
For traitors who consigned it to such woe—
That all could cleanse thee not—without the flow
Of blood—the life-blood—*His*—and streaming *so?*
O earth the thundercleft, windshaken!—where
The louder voice of "blood and blood" doth rise—
Hast thou an altar for this sacrifice?
  O heaven—O vacant throne!
O crowned hierarchies, that wear your crown
  When His is put away!
Are ye unshamed, that ye cannot dim
Your alien brightness to be liker Him,—
Assume a human passion—and down-lay

       C

Your sweet secureness for congenial fears—
And teach your cloudless ever-burning eyes
   The mystery of His tears!
 Zerah. I am strong, I am strong!
  Were I never to see my heaven again,
  I would wheel to earth like the tempest rain
  Which sweeps there with an exultant sound
  To lose its life as it reaches the ground.
  I am strong, I am strong!
  Away from mine inward vision swim
  The shining seats of my heavenly birth—
  I see but His, I see but Him—
  The Maker's steps on His cruel earth.
  Will the bitter herbs of earth grow sweet
  To me, as trodden by His feet?
  Will the vexed, accurst humanity,
  As worn by Him, begin to be
  A blessed, yea, a sacred thing,
  For love, and awe, and ministering?
   I am strong, I am strong!
  By our angel ken shall we survey
  His loving smile through his woeful clay?
   I am swift, I am strong—
  The love is bearing me along.
 Ador. One love is bearing us along.

PART THE SECOND.

Mid-air, above Judæa. Ador and Zerah are a little apart from the visible Angelic Hosts.

Ador.　BELOVED! dost thou see?—
Zerah.　　　Thee,—thee.
　　Thy burning eyes already are
　　Grown wild and mournful as a star
　　Whose occupation is for aye
　　To look upon the place of clay
　　　Whereon thou lookest now!
　　The crown is fainting on thy brow
　　To the likeness of a cloud—
　　The forehead's self a little bowed
　　From its aspect high and holy,
　　As it would in meekness meet
　　Some seraphic melancholy.
　　Thy very wings that lately flung
　　An outline clear, do flicker here,
　　And wear to each a shadow hung,
　　　Dropped across thy feet.
　　In these strange contrasting glooms,
　　Stagnant with the scent of tombs,
　　Seraph faces, O my brother,
　　Show awfully to one another.
　Ador.　Dost thou see?
　Zerah.　　　　Even so—I see
Our empyreal company;

Alone the memory of their brightness
   Left in them, as in thee;
The circle upon circle, tier on tier—
   Piling earth's hemisphere
   With heavenly infiniteness;
     Above us and around,
Straining the blue horizon like a bow:
Their songful lips divorced from all sound;
A darkness gliding down their silvery glances,—
Bowing their steadfast solemn countenances,
As if they heard God speak, and could not glow.
  Ador. Look downward! dost thou see?
  Zerah. And wouldst thou press *that* vision on
   my words?
Doth not Earth speak enough
Of change and of undoing,
Without a seraph's witness? Oceans rough
With tempest, pastoral swards
Displaced by fiery deserts, mountains ruing
The bolt fallen yesterday,
That shake their piney heads, as who would say
  'We are too beautiful for our decay'—
Shall seraphs speak of these things? Let alone
   Earth, to her earthly moan.
Voice of all things. Is there no moan but hers?
Ador. Hearest thou the attestation
   Of the roused Universe,
   Like a desert lion shaking
   Dews of silence from its mane?
   With an irrepressive passion
    Uprising at once,

Rising up and forsaking
Its solemn state in the circle of suns
   To attest the pain
Of Him who stands (O patience sweet!)
In his own hand-prints of creation,
   With human feet?
Voice of all things.   Is there no moan but ours?
Zerah.   Forms, Spaces, Motions wide,
   O meek, insensate things,
O congregated matters! who inherit
   Instead of vital powers,
   Impulsions, God-supplied;
   Instead of influent spirit,
   A clear informing beauty—
   Instead of creature-duty,
   Submission calm as rest!
   Lights, without feet or wings,
   In golden courses sliding!
   Glooms, stagnantly subsiding,
Whose lustrous heart away was prest
   Into the argent stars!
   Ye crystal, firmamental bars,
   That hold the skyey waters free
   From tide or tempest's ecstasy!
   Airs universal! thunders lorn,
   That wait your lightnings in cloud-cave
   Hewn out by the winds!   O brave
   And subtle Elements! the Holy
   Hath charged me by your voice with folly.*

* "His angels He charged with folly."—*Job*, iv. 18.

4

Enough, the mystic arrow leaves its wound.
Return ye to your silences inborn,
Or to your inarticulated sound!

   Ador.   Zerah.

   Zerah.   Wilt *thou* rebuke?
God hath rebuked me, brother.—I am weak.

   Ador.   Zerah, my brother Zerah!—could I speak
Of thee, 'twould be of love to thee.

   Zerah.   Thy look
Is fixed on earth, as mine upon thy face!
Where shall I seek *Him?*—

                    I have thrown
    One look upon earth—but one—
    Over the blue mountain-lines,
    Over the forests of palms and pines;
    Over the harvest-lands golden;
    Over the valleys that fold in
    The gardens and vines—
      He is not there!
    All these are unworthy
    His footsteps to bear,
      Before which, bowing down
I would fain quench the stars of my crown
      In the dark of the earthy
    Where shall I seek Him?

                No reply?
    Hath language left thy lips, to place
      Its vocal in thine eye?
    Ador, Ador! are we come
    To a double portent, that
    Dumb matter grows articulate

And songful spirits dumb?
. Ador, Ador!
Ador.   I constrain
   The passion of my silence.   None
   Of those places gazed upon
   Are gloomy enow to fit His pain.
   Unto Him, whose forming word
   Gave to Nature flower and sward,
   She hath given back again,
      For the myrtle, the thorn;
For the sylvan calm, the human scorn.
Still, still, reluctant Seraph, gaze beneath!
There is a city——
   Zerah.   Temple and tower,
Palace and purple would droop like a flower,
      (Or a cloud at our breath)
      If He neared in His state
      The outermost gate.
   Ador.   Ah me, not so
In the state of a King, did the victim go!
And Thou who hangest mute of speech
      'Twixt heaven and earth, with forehead yet
      Stained by the bloody sweat——
God! man! Thou hast forgone thy throne in each!
   Zerah.   Thine eyes behold Him?
   Ador.   Yea, below.
   Track the gazing of mine eyes,
   Naming God within thine heart
   That its weakness may depart
      And the vision rise.
   Seest thou yet, beloved?

Zerah.   I see

    Beyond the city, crosses three,
    And mortals three that hang thereon,
    'Ghast and silent to the sun :
And round them blacken and welter and press
    Staring multitudes, whose father
    Adam was—whose brows are dark
    With his Cain's corroded mark ;
    Who curse with looks.   Nay—let me rather
    Turn unto the wilderness.

Ador.   Turn not.   God dwells with men.

Zerah.   Above

He dwells with angels; and they love.
Can these love ?   With the living's pride
They stare at those who die,—who hang
In their sight and die.   They bear the streak
Of the crosses' shadow, black not wide,
To fall on their heads, as it swerves aside
      When the victims' pang
      Makes the dry wood creak.

Ador.   The cross—the cross !

Zerah.   A woman kneels

    The mid cross under—
    With white lips asunder,
    And motion on each :
    They throb, as she feels,
    With a spasm, not a speech;
    And her lids, close as sleep,
    Are less calm—for the eyes
    Have made room there to weep
    Drop on drop—

Ador.   Weep ? Weep blood,
        All women, all men !
        He sweated it, He,
        For your pale womanhood
        And base manhood.   Agree,
        That these water-tears, then,
        Are vain, mocking like laughter !
        Weep blood !—Shall the flood
Of salt curses, whose foam is the darkness, on roll
Forward, on, from the strand of the storm-beaten
        years,
And back from the rocks of the horrid hereafter,
And up, in a coil, from the present's wrath-spring,
Yea, down from the windows of Heaven opening,—
Deep calling to deep as they meet on His soul,—
        And men weep only tears ?
    Zerah. Little drops in the lapse !
        And yet, Ador, perhaps
        It is all that they can.
        Tears ! the lovingest man
        Has no better bestowed
        Upon man.
    Ador.   Nor on God.
    Zerah.   Do all-givers need gifts ?
If the Giver said ' Give, ' the first motion would slay
Our Immortals ; the echo would ruin away
The same worlds which He made.   Why, what
        angel uplifts
        Such a music, so clear,
        It may seem in God's ear   [thus,
Worth more than a woman's hoarse weeping ? And

4*

Pity tender as tears, I above thee would speak,
Thou woman that weepest! weep unscorned of us!
I, the tearless and pure, am but loving and weak.

   Ador.   Speak low, my brother, low,—and not
         of love,
Or human or angelic!   Rather stand
Before the throne of that Supreme above,
In whose infinitude the secrecies
Of thine own being lie hid, and lift thine hand
Exultant, saying, 'Lord God I am wise!' —
Than utter *here*, 'I love.'
   Zerah.   And yet thine eyes
Do utter it.   They melt in tender light—
The tears of Heaven.

   Ador.   Of Heaven.   Ah me!
   Zerah.   Ador!
   Ador.   Say on.
   Zerah.   The crucified are three.
Beloved, they are unlike.
   Ador.   Unlike.
   Zerah.   For one
      Is as a man who sinned, and still
      Doth wear the wicked will—
   The hard malign life-energy,
Tossed outward, in the parting soul's disdain,
On brow and lip that cannot change again.
   Ador.   And one—
   Zerah.   Has also sinned.
And yet, (O marvel!) doth the spirit-wind
Blow white those waters?—Death upon his face
   Is rather shine than shade,

A tender shine by looks beloved made.
He seemeth dying in a quiet place,
And less by iron wounds in hands and feet
Than heart-broke by new joy too sudden and sweet.

    Ador. And ONE!—

    Zerah.   And ONE—

    Ador.   Why dost thou pause?

    Zerah.   God! God!

Spirit of my spirit! who movest
Through seraph veins in burning deity,
To light the quenchless pulses!—

    Ador.   But hast trod
The depths of love in Thy peculiar nature;
And not in any Thou hast made and lovest
In narrow seraph hearts!—

    Zerah.   Above, Creator!
Within, Upholder!

    Ador.   And below, below,
The creature's and the upholden's sacrifice!

    Zerah. Why do I pause?——

    Ador.   There is a silentness
        That answers thee enow;
        That, like a brazen sound
Excluding others, doth ensheathe us round:
Hear it! It is not from the visible skies
        Though they are very still,
Unconscious that their own dropped dews express
The light of heaven on every earthly hill.
It is not from the hills; though calm and bare
        They, since the first creation,
Through midnight cloud or morning's glittering air

Or the deep deluge blindness, toward the place
Whence thrilled the mystic word's creative grace,
        And whence again shall come
        The word that uncreates;
Have lift their brows in voiceless expectation.
It is not from the places that entomb
Man's dead—though common Silence there dilates
Her soul to grand proportions, worthily
        To fill life's vacant room.
        Not there—not there!
Not yet within those chambers lieth He,
A dead One in His living world!   His south
And west winds blowing over earth and sea,
And not a breath on that creating Mouth!
        But now,—a silence keeps
        (Not death's, nor sleep's)
        The lips whose whispered word
Might roll the thunders round reverbrated
        Silent art Thou, O my Lord,
        Bowing down Thy stricken head!
        Fearest Thou, a groan of thine
Would make the pulse of thy creation fail
As thine own pulse?—would rend the veil
Of visible things, and let the flood
Of the unseen Light, the essential God,
Rush in to whelm the undivine?—
Thy silence, to my thinking, is as dread!
   Zerah.   O silence!
   Ador.   Doth it say to thee—the NAME,
Slow-learning Seraph?
   Zerah.   I have learnt.

Ador.   The flame
Perishes in thine eyes.
    Zerah.   He opened His—
And looked. I cannot bear—
    Ador.   Their agony?
    Zerah. Their love. God's depth is in them
        From his brows
White, terrible in meekness, didst thou see
        The lifted eyes unclose?
He is God, seraph! Look no more on me,
O God; I am not God.
    Ador.   The loving is
Sublimed within them by the sorrowful.
In heaven we could sustain them.
    Zerah.   Heaven is dull,
Mine Ador, to man's earth. The light that burns
        In fluent, refluent motion,
        Along the crystal ocean;
The springing of the golden harps between
The bowery wings, in fountains of sweet sound;
The winding, wandering music that returns
Upon itself, exultingly self-bound
In the great spheric round
        Of everlasting praises:
The God-thoughts in our midst that intervene,
Visibly flashing from the supreme throne,
        Full in seraphic faces,
Till each astonishes the other, grown
More beautiful with worship and delight!
My heaven! my home of heaven! my infinite
Heaven-choirs! what are ye to this dust and death,

This cloud, this cold, these tears, this failing breath,
Where God's immortal love now issueth
            In this MAN's woe?
   Ador. His eyes are very deep yet calm—
   Zerah.   No more
On *me*, Jehovah-man—
   Ador.   Calm-deep. They show
A passion which is tranquil. They are seeing
No earth, no heaven: no men that slay and curse—
            No seraphs that adore.
Their gaze is on the invisible, the dread—
The things we cannot view or think or speak,
Because we are too happy, or too weak;
The sea of ill, for which the universe
With all its pilèd space, can find no shore,
With all its life, no living foot to tread.
But He, accomplished in Jehovah-being,
            Sustains the gaze adown,
            Conceives the vast despair,
And feels the billowy griefs come up to drown,
Nor fears, nor faints, nor fails till all be finished.
   Zerah. Thus, do I find thee thus? My undimin
            ished
And undiminishable God!—My God!
The echoes are still tremulous along
The heavenly mountains, of the latest song
Thy manifested glory swept abroad
In rushing past our lips! They echo aye
            "Creator, Thou art strong!—
Creator, Thou art blessed over all."
By what new utterance shall I now recall,

Unteaching the heaven-echoes?   Dare I say,
"Creator, Thou art feebler than Thy work!
Creator, Thou art sadder than thy creature!
   A worm, and not a man,
   Yea, no worm—but a curse?"
I dare not, so, mine heavenly phrase reverse.
Albeit the piercing thorn and thistle-fork
   (Whose seed disordered ran
From Eve's hand trembling when the curse did
  reach her)
Be garnered darklier in thy soul! the rod
That smites Thee never blossoming, and Thou,
Grief-bearer for thy world, with unkinged brow—
I leave to men their song of Ichabod!
I have an angel-tongue—I know but praise.
 Ador. Hereafter shall the blood-bought captives
  raise
The passion-song of blood.
 Zerah.   And *we*, extend
Our holy vacant hands towards the Throne,
Crying " We have no music!"
 Ador.   Rather, blend
   Both musics into one!
The sanctities and sanctified above
Shall each to each, with lifted looks serene,
   Their shining faces lean,
   And mix the adoring breath .
And breathe the full thanksgiving.
 Zerah.   But the love—
The love, mine Ador!
 Ador.   Do we love not?

Zerah.   Yea,
But not as man shall! not with life for death,
New-throbbing through the startled being! not
With strange astonished smiles, that ever may
Gush passionate like tears, and fill their place:
Nor yet with speechless memories of what
Earth's winters were, enverduring the green
         Of every heavenly palm
           Whose windless, shadeless calm
Moves only at the breath of the Unseen.
Oh, not with this blood on us—and this face,—
Still, haply, pale with sorrow that it bore
In our behalf, and tender evermore
With nature all our own, upon us gazing!—
Nor yet with these forgiving hands upraising
Their unreproachful wounds, alone to bless!
Alas, Creator! shall we love Thee less
Than mortals shall?

Ador.   Amen! so let it be.
We love in our proportion—to the bound
Thine infinite our finite, set around,
And that is finitely,—Thou, infinite
And worthy infinite love!   And our delight
Is watching the dear love poured out to Thee,
From ever fuller chalice.   Blessed they,
Who love Thee more than we do! blessed we,
Viewing that love which shall exceed even this,
And winning in the sight, a double bliss,
For all so lost in love's supremacy!
The bliss is better.   Only on the sad
      Cold earth there are who say

It seemeth better to be great than glad.
The bliss is better! Love Him more, O man,
     Than sinless seraphs can.
  Zerah. Yea, love Him more.
  Voices of the angelic multitude. Yea, more!
  Ador.   The loving word
Is caught by those from whom we stand apart:
For Silence hath no deepness in her heart
Where love's low name low breathed would not be
     heard
By angels, clear as thunder.
  Angelic voices.   Love him more!
  Ador. Sweet voices, swooning o'er
     The music which ye make!
   Albeit to love there were not ever given
   A mournful sound when uttered out of heaven,
   That angel-sadness ye would fitly take.
   Of love, be silent now! we gaze adown
   Upon the incarnate Love who wears no crown.
  Zerah. No crown! the woe instead
     Is heavy on His head,
     Pressing inward on His brain,
     With a hot and clinging pain,
     Till all tears are prest away,
   And clear and calm His vision may
     Peruse the black abyss.
     No rod, no sceptre is
   Holden in His fingers pale:
   They close instead upon the nail,
     Concealing the sharp dole—
   Never stirring to put by

The fair hair peaked with blood,
Drooping forward from the rood
    Helplessly—heavily—
On the cheek that waxeth colder,
Whiter ever,—and the shoulder
Where the government was laid.
His glory made the Heavens afraid;
Will He not unearth this cross from its hole?
His pity makes His piteous state:
Will He be uncompassionate
    Alone to His proper soul?
    Yea, will He not lift up
    His lips from the bitter cup,
    His brows from the dreary weight,
    His hands from the clenching cross—
Crying, 'My Father, give to me
Again the joy I had with Thee,
Or ere this earth was made for loss?'
    No stir—no sound—
The love and woe being interwound
    He cleaveth to the woe;
And putteth forth heaven's strength below—
    To bear.

Ador.   And that creates His anguish now,
Which made His glory there.

   Zerah.   Shall it indeed be so?
    Awake, thou Earth! behold!
    Thou, uttered forth of old
    In all thy life-emotion,
    In all thy vernal noises;
    In the rollings of thine ocean,

Leaping founts, and rivers running ;
In thy woods' prophetic heaving
Ere the rains a stroke have given ;
In thy winds' exultant voices
When they feel the hills anear :
In the firmamental sunning,
And the tempest which rejoices
Thy full heart with an awful cheer !
Thou, uttered forth of old
And with all thy musics, rolled
In a breath abroad
By the breathing God !
Awake! He is here ! behold !
Even *thou*—

beseems it good
To thy vacant vision dim,
That the deathly ruin should,
For thy sake, encompass Him ?
That the Master-word should lie
A mere silence—while His own
Processive harmony—
The faintest echo of His lightest tone
Is sweeping in a choral triumph by ?
Awake! emit a cry !
And say, albeit used
From Adam's ancient years
To falls of acrid tears,
To frequent sighs unloosed,
Caught back to press again
On bosoms zoned with pain—
To curses still and sullen

The shine and music dulling
With closed eyes and ears
That nothing sweet can enter—
Commoving thee no less
With that forced quietness,
Than the earthquake in thy centre—
Thou hast not learnt to bear
This new divine despair!
These tears that sink into thee,
These dying eyes that view thee,
This dropping blood from lifted rood,
They darken and undo thee!
Thou canst not, presently, sustain this curse!
Cry, cry, thou hast not force!
Cry, thou wouldst fainer keep
Thy hopeless charnels deep—
Thyself a general tomb—
Where the first and the second Death
Sit gazing face to face
And mar each other's breath,
While silent bones through all the place,
'Neath sun and moon do faintly glisten,
And seem to lie and listen
For the tramp of the coming Doom.
Is it not meet
That they who erst the Eden fruit did eat,
Should champ the ashes?
That they who wrapt them in the thunder-cloud,
Should wear it as a shroud,
Perishing by its flashes?
That they who vexed the lion, should be rent?

Cry, cry—'I will sustain my punishment,
The sin being mine! but take away from me
This visioned Dread—this Man—this Deity.'
The Earth.   I have groaned—I have travailed—
  I am weary—
I am blind with mine own grief, and cannot see,
As clear-eyed angels can, His agony :
And what I see I also can sustain,
Because His power protects me from His pain.
I have groaned—I have travailed—I am dreary,
Hearkening the thick sobs of my children's heart :
  And can I say 'Depart'
To that Atoner making calm and free?
  Am I a God as He,
To lay down peace and power as willingly?
 Ador.   He looked for some to pity.   There is
  none.
All pity is within Him, and not for Him;
His earth is iron under Him, and o'er Him
  His skies are brass :
  His seraphs cry 'Alas'
With hallelujah voice that cannot weep;
And man, for whom the dreadful work is done——
 Scornful voices from the Earth.   If verily this *be*
  the Eternal's son—
 Ador.   Thou hearest :—man is grateful!
 Zerah.   Can I hear,
Nor darken into man nor cease for ever
  My seraph-smile to wear?
  Was it for such,
  It pleased Him to overleap
 v*

His glory with His love, and sever
From the God-light and the throne
And all angels bowing down,
From whom His every look did touch
New notes of joy from the unworn string
Of an eternal worshipping!
    For such He left His heaven?
    There, though never bought by blood
And tears, we gave Him gratitude!
We loved Him there, though unforgiven!

Ador.   The light is riven
      Above, around,
And down in lurid fragments flung,
That catch the mountain-peak and stream
      With momentary gleam,
Then perish in the water and the ground.
      River and waterfall,
      Forest and wilderness,
Mountain and city, are together wrung
Into one shape, and that is shapelessness;
      The darkness stands for all.

Zerah. The pathos hath the day undone:
      The death-look of His eyes
      Hath overcome the sun,
And made it sicken in its narrow skies.

Ador. Is it to death? He dieth.

Zerah.   Through the dark,
He still, He only, is discernible—
The naked hands and feet transfixèd stark
The countenance of patient anguish white
      Do make themselves a light

More dreadful than the glooms which round them
      dwell,
And therein do they shine.
   Ador.   God! Father-God!
Perpetual Radiance on the radiant throne!
Uplift the lids of inward Deity,
     Flashing abroad
    Thy burning Infinite!
Light up this dark, where there is nought to see,
Except the unimagined agony
Upon the sinless forehead of the Son.
  Zerah.   God, tarry not! Behold, enow
Hath He wandered as a stranger,
Sorrowed as a victim. Thou
    Appear for Him, O Father!
    Appear for Him, Avenger!
Appear for Him, just One and holy One,
    For He is holy and just!
At once the darkness and dishonour rather
To the ragged jaws of hungry chaos rake,
  And hurl aback to ancient dust
  These mortals that make blasphemies
  With their made breath! this earth and skies
    That only grow a little dim,
    Seeing their curse on Him!
    But Him, of all forsaken,
    Of creature and of brother,
    Never wilt Thou forsake!
Thy living and Thy loving cannot slacken
Their firm essential hold upon each other—
And well Thou dost remember how His part

Was still to lie upon Thy breast, and be
Partaker of the light that dwelt in Thee
    Ere sun or seraph shone ;
And how while silence trembled round the throne,
Thou countedst by the beatings of His heart,
The moments of Thine own eternity !
       Awaken,
O right Hand with the lightnings !   Again gather
His glory to thy glory !   What estranger—
What ill supreme in evil, can be thrust
Between the faithful Father and the Son ?
    Appear for Him, O Father !
    Appear for Him, Avenger !
Appear for Him, just One and holy One !
    For He is holy and just.
  Ador.   Thy face, upturned toward the throne, is
    dark—
Thou hast no answer, Zerah.
  Zerah.   No reply,
O unforsaking Father ?—
  Ador.   Hark !
Instead of downward voice, a cry
    Is uttered from beneath !
  Zerah.   And by a sharper sound than death,
    Mine immortality is riven.
The heavy darkness which doth tent the sky,
Floats backward as by a sudden wind—
    But I see no light behind :
  But I feel the farthest stars are all
    Stricken and shaken,
And I know a shadow sad and broad,

Doth fall—doth fall
On our vacant thrones in heaven.
   Voice from the Cross. My God, my God,
Why hast Thou me forsaken?
   The Earth. Ah me, ah me, ah me! the dreadful
     why!
My sin is on Thee, sinless One! Thou art
God-orphaned, for my burden on Thy head.
Dark sin! white innocence! endurance dread!
Be still, within your shrouds, my buried dead—
Nor work with this quick horror round mine heart!
   Zerah. He hath forsaken *Him!* I perish—
   Ador.   Hold
Upon His name! We perish not. Of old
His will——
   Zerah.   I seek His will. Seek, Seraphim!
My God, my God! where is it? Doth that curse
Reverberate spare us, seraph or universe?
     He hath forsaken *Him.*
   Ador. He cannot fail.
   Angel voices. We faint—we droop—
     Our love doth tremble like fear—
   Voices of Fallen Angels from the earth. Do we
     prevail?
Or are we lost?—Hath not the ill we did
     Been heretofore our good?
Is it not ill that One, all sinless, should
Hang heavy with all curses on a cross?
Nathless, *that cry!*—with huddled faces hid
Within the empty graves which men did scoop
To hold more damnèd dead, we shudder through

What shall exalt us or undo,—
  Our triumph, or—our loss.
Voice from the Cross. It is finished.
Zerah.   Hark, again!
Like a victor, speaks the Slain—
  Angel voices. Finished be the trembling vain!
  Ador. Upward, like a well-loved Son,
    Looketh He, the orphaned One—
  Angel voices. Finished is the mystic pain!
  Voices of Fallen Angels. His deathly forehead
    at the word,
    Gleameth like a seraph sword.
  Angel voices. Finished is the demon reign!
  Ador. His breath, as living God, createth—
    His breath, as dying man, completeth.
  Angel voices. Finished work His hands sustain!
  The Earth. In mine ancient sepulchres
    Where my kings and prophets freeze,
    Adam dead four thousand years,
    Unwakened by the universe's
    Everlasting moan,
    Aye his ghastly silence, mocking—
  Unwakened by his children's knocking
  'At his old sepulchral stone—
  ' Adam, Adam! all this curse is
    Thine and on us yet!' ——
  Unwakened by the ceaseless tears
  Wherewith they made his cerement wet—
    ' Adam, must thy curse remain?'—
  Starts with sudden life, and hears
Through the slow dripping of the caverned eaves,—

Angel voices. Finished is his bane!

Voice from the Cross. FATHER! MY SPIRIT TO
    THINE HANDS IS GIVEN!

    Ador. Hear the wailing winds that be
By wings of unclean Spirits made!
    They, in that last look, surveyed
The love they lost in losing heaven,
      And passionately flee,
With a desolate cry that cleaves
The natural storms—though *they* are lifting
God's strong cedar-roots like leaves;
And the earthquake and the thunder,
Neither keeping neither under,
Roar and hurtle through the glooms,—
And a few pale stars are drifting
Past the Dark, to disappear,
What time, from the splitting tombs,
Gleamingly the Dead arise,
Viewing with their death-calmed eyes,
The elemental strategies,
To witness, victory is the Lord's!
Hear the wail o' the spirits! hear.

    Zerah. I hear alone the memory of His words

THE EPILOGUE.

I.

My song is done!
My voice that long hath faltered shall be still
The mystic darkness drops from Calvary's hill
Into the common light of this day's sun.

II.

I see no more Thy cross, O holy Slain!
I hear no more the horror and the coil
        Of the great world's turmoil,
Feeling thy countenance *too still*,—nor yell
Of demons sweeping past it to their prison.
The skies, that turned to darkness with Thy pain,
        Make now a summer's day,—
And on my changèd ear, that sabbath bell
        Records how CHRIST IS RISEN.

III.

And I—ah! what am I
To counterfeit, with faculty earth-darkened
        Seraphic brows of light
And seraph language never used nor hearkened?
Ah me! what word that Seraphs say, could come
From mouth so used to sighs—so soon to lie
Sighless, because then breathless, in the tomb?

IV.

Bright ministers of God and grace!—of grace
Because of God!—whether ye bow adown
In your own heaven, before the living face
Of Him who died, and deathless wears the crown—
Or whether at this hour, ye haply are
Anear, around me, hiding in the night
Of this permitted ignorance your light,
  This feebleness to spare,—
Forgive me, that mine earthly heart should dare
Shape images of unincarnate spirits,
And lay upon their burning lips a thought
Cold with the weeping which mine earth inherits;
And though ye find in such hoarse music wrought
To copy yours, a cadence all the while
Of sin and sorrow—only pitying smile!—
  Ye know to pity, well.

V.

I too may haply smile another day
At the far recollection of this lay,
When God may call me in your midst to dwell,
To hear your most sweet music's miracle
And see your wondrous faces. May it be,
For His remembered sake, the Slain on rood,
Who rolled His earthly garment red in blood
(Treading the wine-press) that the weak, like me,
Before His heavenly throne should walk in white.

6

THE POET'S VOW.

——— O be wiser thou,
Instructed that true knowledge leads to love.

WORDSWORTH.

THE POET'S VOW.

PART THE FIRST.

SHOWING WHEREFORE THE VOW WAS MADE.

I.

Eve is a twofold mystery—
   The stillness Earth doth keep;
The motion wherewith human hearts
   Do each to either leap,
As if all souls between the poles,
   Felt 'Parting comes in sleep.'

II.

The rowers lift their oars to view
   Each other in the sea;
The landsmen watch the rocking boats,
   In a pleasant company;
While up the hill go gladlier still
   Dear friends by two and three.

6*   E

III.

The peasant's wife hath looked without
  Her cottage door and smiled;
For there the peasant drops his spade
  To clasp his youngest child
Which hath no speech, but its hands can reach
  And stroke his forehead mild.

IV.

A poet sate that eventide
  Within his hall alone,
As silent as its ancient lords
  In the coffined place of stone;   [monk—
When the bat hath shrunk from the praying
  And the praying monk is gone.

V.

Nor wore the dead a stiller face
  Beneath the cerement's roll:
His lips refusing out in words
  Their mystic thoughts to dole,
His steadfast eye burnt inwardly,
  As burning out his soul.

VI.

You would not think that brow could e'er
  Ungentle moods express,
Yet seemed it, in this troubled world,
  Too calm for gentleness:
When the very star, that shines from far,
  Shines trembling ne'ertheless.

VII.

It lacked—all need—the softening light
   Which other brows supply:
We should conjoin the scathëd trunks
   Of our humanity,
That each leafless spray entwining may
   Look softer 'gainst the sky.

VIII.

None gazed within the poet's face—
   The poet gazed in none:
He threw a lonely shadow straight
   Before the moon and sun,
Affronting nature's heaven-dwelling creatures,
   With wrong to nature done.

IX.

Because this poet daringly,
   The nature at his heart,
And that quick tune along his veins
   He could not change by art,
Had vowed his blood of brotherhood
   To a stagnant place apart.

X.

He did not vow in fear, or wrath,
   Or grief's fantastic whim;
But, weights and shows of sensual things
   Too closely crossing him,
On his soul's eyelid the pressure slid
   And made its vision dim.

XI.

And darkening in the dark he strove
    'Twixt earth and sea and sky,
To lose in shadow, wave and cloud,
    His brother's haunting cry.
The winds were welcome as they swept:
God's five-day work he would accept,
    But let the rest go by.

XII.

He cried—' O touching, patient Earth,
    That weepest in thy glee,
Whom God created very good,
    And very mournful, we!
Thy voice of moan doth reach His throne,
    As Abel's rose from thee.

XIII.

' Poor crystal sky, with stars astray;
    Mad winds, that howling go
From east to west; perplexed seas,
    That stagger from their blow!
O motion wild! O wave defiled!
    Our curse hath made you so.

XIV.

' *We!* and *our* curse! Do *I* partake
    The desiccating sin?
Have *I* the apple at my lips?
    The money-lust within?
Do *I* human stand with the wounding hand,
    To the blasting heart akin?

XV.

' Thou solemn pathos of all things,
  For solemn pomp designed!
Behold, submissive to your cause,
  An holy wrath I fmd,
And, for your sake, the bondage break,
  That knits me to my kind.

XVI.

' Hear me forswear man's sympathies,
  His pleasant yea and no—
His riot on the piteous earth
  Whereon his thistles grow!
His changing love—with stars above!
  His pride—with graves below!

XVII.

' Hear me forswear his roof by night,
  His bread and salt by day,
His talkings at the wood-fire hearth,
  His greetings by the way,
His answering looks, his systemed books,
  All man, for aye and aye.

XVIII.

' That so my purged, once human heart,
  From all the human rent,
May gather strength to pledge and drink
  Your wine of wonderment,
While you pardon me, all blessingly,
  The woe mine Adam sent.

XIX.

' And I shall feel your unseen looks
    Innumerous, constant, deep,
And soft as haunted Adam once,
    Though sadder, round me creep;
As slumbering men have mystic ken
    Of watchers on their sleep.

XX.

' And ever, when I lift my brow
    At evening to the sun,
No voice of woman or of child
    Recording ' Day is done,'
Your silences shall a love express,
    More deep than such an one! '

f

PART THE SECOND.

SHOWING TO WHOM THE VOW WAS DECLARED.

I.

THE poet's vow was inly sworn—
   The poet's vow was told :
He shared among his crowding friends
   The silver and the gold ;
They clasping bland his gift,—his hand
   In a somewhat slacker hold.

II.

They wended forth, the crowding friends,
   With farewells smooth and kind—
They wended forth, the solaced friends,
   And left but twain behind :
One loved him true as brothers do,
   And one was Rosalind.

III.

He said—' My friends have wended forth
   With farewells smooth and kind.
Mine oldest friend, my plighted bride,
   Ye need not stay behind.
Friend, wed my fair bride for my sake,
And let my lands ancestral make
   A dower for Rosalind.

IV.

'And when beside your wassail board
 Ye bless your social lot,
I charge you that the giver be
 In all his gifts forgot!
Or alone of all his words recall
 The last,—Lament me not.'

V.

She looked upon him silently,
 With her large, doubting eyes,
Like a child that never knew but love,
 Whom words of wrath surprise;
Till the rose did break from either cheek,
 And the sudden tears did rise.

VI.

She looked upon him mournfully,
 While her large eyes were grown
Yet larger with the steady tears;
 Till, all his purpose known,
She turnéd slow, as she would go—
 The tears were shaken down.

VII.

She turnéd slow, as she would go,
 Then quickly turned again;
And gazing in his face to seek
 Some little touch of pain—
'I thought.' she said,—but shook her head,--
 She tried that speech in vain.

VIII.

' I thought—but I am half a child,
    And very sage art thou—
The teachings of the heaven and earth
    Did keep us soft and low.
They have drawn *my* tears in early years,
    Or ere I wept—as now.

IX.

' But now that in thy face I read
    Their cruel homily,
Before their beauty I would fain
    Untouched, unsoftened be,—
If *I* indeed could look on even
The senseless, loveless earth and heaven
    As *thou* canst look on *me*.

X.

' And couldest thou as calmly view
    Thy childhood's far abode,
Where little feet kept time with thine
    Along the dewy sod?
And thy mother's look from holy book
    Rose, like a thought of God?

XI.

' O brother,—called so, ere her last
    Betrothing words were said!
O fellow-watcher in her room,
    With hushëd voice and tread!
Rememberest thou how, hand in hand,
O friend, O lover, we did stand,
    And knew that she was dead?
7

XII.

' I will not live Sir Roland's bride,—.
   That dower I will not hold!
I tread below my feet that go,
   These parchments bought and sold.
The tears I weep, are mine to keep,
   And worthier than thy gold. '

XIII.

The poet and Sir Roland stood
   Alone, each turned to each ;
Till Roland brake the silence left
   By that soft-throbbing speech—
' Poor heart !" he cried, " it vainly tried
   The distant heart to reach !

XIV.

' And thou, O distant, sinful heart,
   That climbest up so high,
To wrap and blind thee with the snows
   That cause to dream and die—
What blessing can, from lips of man,
   Approach thee with his sigh ?

XV.

' Ay ! what, from earth—create for man,
   And moaning in his moan ?
Ay ! what from stars—revealed to man,
   And man-named, one by one ?
Ay, more ! what blessing can be given,
Where the Spirits seven do show in heaven,
   A MAN upon the throne ?—

XVI.

' A man on earth HE wandered once,
  All meek and undefiled :
And those who loved Him, said 'He wept'—-
  None ever said He smiled ;
Yet there might have been a smile unseen,
When He bowed his blessed face, I ween,
  To bless that happy child.

XVII.

' And now HE pleadeth up in heaven
  For our humanities,
Till the ruddy light on seraphs' wings
  In pale emotion dies.
They can better bear his Godhead's glare,
  Than the pathos of his eyes.

XVIII.

' I will go pray our God to-day
  To teach thee how to scan
His work divine, for human use
  Since earth on axle ran!
To teach thee to discern as plain
His grief divine—the blood-drop's stain
  He left there, MAN for man.

XIX.

' So, for the blood's sake, shed by Him,
  Whom angels God declare,
Tears, like it, moist and warm with love,
  Thy reverent eyes shall wear,
To see i' the face of Adam's race
  The nature God doth share. '

XX.

' I heard,' the poet said, ' thy voice
    As dimly as thy breath!
The sound was like the noise of life
    To one anear his death;
Or of waves that fail to stir the pale
    Sere leaf they roll beneath.

XXI.

' And still between the sound and me
    White creatures like a mist
Did interfloat confusedly,—
    Mysterious shapes unwist!
Across my heart and across my brow
I felt them droop like wreaths of snow
    To still the pulse they kist.

XXII.

' The castle and its lands are thine—
    The poor's—it shall be done:
Go, *man;* to love! I go to live
    In Courland hall, alone.
The bats along the ceilings cling,
The lizards in the floors do run,
And storms and years have worn and reft
The stain by human builders left
    In working at the stone!'

PART THE THIRD.

SHOWING HOW THE VOW WAS KEPT.

I.

He dwelt alone, and, sun and moon,
    Were witness that he made
Rejection of his humanness
    Until they seemed to fade.
His face did so; for he did grow
    Of his own soul afraid.

II.

The self-poised God may dwell alone
    With inward glorying;
But God's chief angel waiteth for
    A brother's voice, to sing.
And a lonely creature of sinful nature—
    It is an awful thing.

III.

An awful thing that feared itself
    While many years did roll,
A lonely man, a feeble man,
    A part beneath the whole—
He bore by day, he bore by night
That pressure of God's infinite
    Upon his finite soul.

7*

IV.

The poet at his lattice sate,
　And downward looked he :
Three Christians wended by to prayers,
　With mute ones in their ee.
Each turned above a face of love,
　And called him to the far chapèlle
With voice more tuneful than its bell—
　But still they wended three.

V.

There journeyed by a bridal pomp,
　A bridegroom and his dame :
She speaketh low for happiness,
　She blusheth red for shame,
But never a tone of benison
　From out the lattice came.

VI.

A little child with inward song,
　No louder noise to dare,
Stood near the wall to see at play
　The lizards green and rare—
Unblessed the while for his childish smile
　Which cometh unaware.

PART THE FOURTH.

I.

In death-sheets lieth Rosalind,
    As white and still as they;
And the old nurse that watched her bed.
    Rose up with ' Well-a-day!'
And oped the casement to let in
The sun, and that sweet doubtful din
Which droppeth from the grass and bough
Sans wind and bird—none knoweth how—
    To cheer her as she lay.

II.

The old nurse started when she saw
    Her sudden look of woe!
But the quick wan tremblings round her mouth
    In a meek smile did go;
And calm she said, " When I am dead,
    Dear nurse, it shall be so.

III.

' Till then, shut out those sights and sounds,
    And pray God pardon me,
That I without this pain, no more
    His blessed works can see!

And lean beside me, loving nurse,
That thou mayst hear, ere I am worse,
What thy last love should be.'

IV.

The loving nurse leant over her,
As white she lay beneath;
The old eyes searching, dim with life,
The young ones dim with death,
To read their look if sound forsook
The trying, trembling breath.—

V.

' When all this feeble breath is done,
And I on bier am laid,
My tresses smoothed for never a feast,
My body in shroud arrayed;
Uplift each palm in a saintly calm,
As if that still I prayed.

VI.

' And heap beneath mine head the flowers
You stoop so low to pull;
The little white flowers from the wood,
Which grow there in the cool;
Which *he* and I, in childhood's games,
Went plucking, knowing not their names,
And filled thine apron full.

VII.

' Weep not! *I* weep not.   Death is strong ;
   The eyes of Death are dry ;
But lay this scroll upon my breast
   When hushed its heavings lie ;
And wait awhile for the corpse's smile
   Which shineth presently.

VIII.

' And when it shineth, straightway call
   Thy youngest children dear,
And bid them gently carry me
   All barefaced on the bier—
But bid them pass my kirkyard grass
   That waveth long anear.

IX.

' And up the bank where I used to sit
   And dream what life would be,
Along the brook, with its sunny look
   Akin to living glee ;
O'er the windy hill, through the forest still,
   Let them gently carry me.

X.

' And through the piney forest still,
   And down the open moorland—
Round where the sea beats mistily
   And blindly on the foreland—
And let them chant that hymn I know,
Bearing me soft, bearing me slow,
   To the old hall of Courland.

F

XI.

'And when withal they near the hall,
  In silence let them lay
My bier before the bolted door,
  And leave it for a day : ·
For I have vowed, though I am proud,
To go there as a guest in shroud,
  And not be turned away.'

XII.

The old nurse looked within her eyes,
  Whose mutual look was gone :
The old nurse stooped upon her mouth,
  Whose answering voice was done ;
And nought she heard, till a little bird
  Upon the casement's woodbine swinging,
Broke out into a loud sweet singing
  For joy o' the summer sun.
"Alack ! alack !"—she watched no more—
  With head on knee she wailéd sore ;
And the little bird sang o'er and o'er
  For joy o' the summer sun.

PART THE FIFTH.

SHOWING HOW THE VOW WAS BROKEN

I.

THE poet oped his bolted door,
  The midnight sky to view.
A spirit-feel was in the air
Which seemed to touch his spirit bare
  Whenever his breath he drew;
And the stars a liquid softness had,
As alone their holiness forbade
  Their falling with the dew.

II.

They shine upon the steadfast hills,
  Upon the swinging tide;
Upon the narrow track of beach,
  And the murmuring pebbles pied;
They shine on every lovely place—
They shine upon the corpse's face,
  As *it* were fair beside.

III.

It lay before him, humanlike,
  Yet so unlike a thing!
More awful in its shrouded pomp
  Than any crownëd king:
All calm and cold, as it did hold
  Some secret, glorying.

IV.

A heavier weight than of its clay
    Clung to his heart and knee:
As if those folded palms could strike,
    He staggered groaningly,
And then o'erhung, without a groan,
The meek close mouth that smiled alone,
    Whose speech the scroll must be.

THE WORDS OF ROSALIND'S SCROLL.

' I LEFT thee last, a child at heart,
    A woman scarce in years:
I come to thee, a solemn corpse,
    Which neither feels nor fears.
I have no breath to use in sighs;
They laid the death-weights on mine eyes,
    To seal them safe from tears.

' Look on me with thine own calm look—-
    I meet it calm as thou!
No look of thine can change *this* smile,
    Or break thy sinful vow.
I tell thee that my poor scorned heart
Is of thine earth . . thine earth —a part—
    It cannot vex thee now.

' But out, alas! these words are writ
    By a living, loving one,
Adown whose cheeks, the proofs of life
    The warm quick tears do run.
Ah, let the unloving corpse control
Thy scorn back from the loving soul
    Whose place of rest is won.

' I have prayed for thee with bursting sobs,
    When passion's course was free:
I have prayed for thee with silent lips,
    In the anguish none could see!
They whispered oft, 'She sleepeth soft'—·
    But I only prayed for thee.

· Go to! I pray for thee no more—
    The corpse's tongue is still:
Its folded fingers point to heaven,
    But point there stiff and chill:
No farther wrong, no farther woe
Hath license from the sin below
    Its tranquil heart to thrill.

' I charge thee, by the living's prayer,
    And the dead's silentness,
To wring from out thy soul a cry
    Which God shall hear and bless!
Lest Heaven's own palm droop in my hand,
And pale among the saints I stand,
    A saint companionless.'

8

v.

Bow lower down before the throne,
  Triumphant Rosalind!
He boweth on thy corpse his face,
  And weepeth as the blind.
'Twas a dread sight to see them so—
For the senseless corpse rocked to and fro
  With the living wail of his mind.

vi.

But dreader sight, could such be seen,
  His inward mind did lie;
Whose long-subjected humanness
  Gave out its lion cry,
And fiercely rent its tenement
  In a mortal agony.

vii.

I tell you, friends, had you heard his wail,
  'Twould haunt you in court and mart,
And in merry feast, until you set
  Your cup down to depart—
That weeping wild of a reckless child
  From a proud man's broken heart.

viii.

O broken heart! O broken vow,
  That wore so proud a feature!
God, grasping as a thunderbolt
  The man's rejected nature,
Smote him therewith—i' the presence high
Of his so worshipped earth and sky

That looked on all indifferently—
　　A wailing human creature.

IX.

A human creature found too weak
　　To bear his human pain—
(May Heaven's dear grace have spoken peace
　　To his dying heart and brain !)
For when they came at dawn of day
To lift the lady's corpse away,
　　Her bier was holding twain.

X.

They dug beneath the kirkyard grass,
　　For both, one dwelling deep :
To which, when years had mossed the stone,
Sir Roland brought his little son
　　To watch the funeral heap.
　　And when the happy boy would rather
Turn upward his blithe eyes to see
The wood-doves nodding from the tree—
　　'Nay, boy, look downward,' said his father,
' Upon this human dust asleep :
And hold it in thy constant ken
That God's own unity compresses
　　One into one, the human many.
And that His everlastingness is
　　The bond which is not loosed by any.
　　For thou and I this law must keep,
If not in love, in sorrow then ;
Though smiling not like other men,
　　Still, like them, we must weep.'

THE ROMAUNT OF MARGRET.

Can my affections find out nothing best,
But still and still remove?—
                                    QUARLES.

I.

I PLANT a tree whose leaf
   The yew-tree leaf will suit;
But when its shade is o'er you laid,
   Turn round and pluck the fruit!
Now reach my harp from off the wall
   Where shines the sun aslant:
The sun may shine and we be cold—
O hearken, loving hearts and bold,
   Unto my wild romaunt,
             Margret, Margret

II.

Sitteth the fair ladye
   Close to the river side,
Which runneth on with a merry tone,
   Her merry thoughts to guide.

It runneth through the trees,
 It runneth by the hill,
Nathless the lady's thoughts have found
 A way more pleasant still.
     Margret, Margret.

III.

The night is in her hair
 And giveth shade to shade,
And the pale moonlight on her forehead white
 Like a spirit's hand is laid:
Her lips part with a smile
 Instead of speakings done—
I ween, she thinketh of a voice,
 Albeit uttering none.
     Margret, Margret.

IV.

All little birds do sit
 With heads beneath their wings:
Nature doth seem in a mystic dream,
 Absorbed from her living things.
That dream by that ladye
 Is certes unpartook,
For she looketh to the high cold stars
 With a tender human look.
     Margret, Margret.

V.

The lady's shadow lies
 Upon the running river:
It lieth no less in its quietness,
 For that which resteth never:

8*

Most like a trusting heart
  Upon a passing faith,—
Or as, upon the course of life,
  The steadfast doom of death.
               Margret, Margret.

VI.

The lady doth not move,
  The lady doth not dream,
Yet she seeth her shade no longer laid
  In rest upon the stream!
It shaketh without wind;
  It parteth from the tide;
It standeth upright in the cleft moonlight—
  It sitteth at her side.
               Margret, Margret.

VII.

Look in its face, ladye,
  And keep thee from thy swound!
With a spirit bold, thy pulses hold,
  And hear its voice's sound!
For so will sound thy voice,
  When thy face is to the wall;
And such will be thy face, ladye,
  When the maidens work thy pall—
               Margret, Margret.

VIII.

' Am I not like to thee? '—
  The voice was calm and low—

And between each word you might have heard
    The silent forests grow.
   ' *The like may sway the like!*
    By which mysterious law
Mine eyes from thine and my lips from thine
    The light and breath may draw.
             Margret, Margret.

IX.

 ' My lips do need thy breath,
    My lips do need thy smile,
And my pallid eyne, that light in thine
    Which met the stars erewhile;
   Yet go with light and life,
    If that thou lovest one
In all the earth, who loveth thee
    As truly as the sun,
            Margret, Margret. '

X.

 Her cheek had waxëd white
    Like cloud at fall of snow;
Then like to one at set of sun,
    It waxëd red also:
   For love's name maketh bold,
    As if the loved were near.
And then she sighed the deep long sigh
    Which cometh after fear.
            Margret, Margret.

XI.

'Now, sooth, I fear thee not—
    Shall never fear thee now!'
(And a noble sight was the sudden light
    Which lit her lifted brow.)
'Can earth be dry of streams.
    Or hearts, of love?' she said—
'Who doubteth love, can know not love:
    He is already dead.'
                    Margret, Margret.

XII.

'I have'... and here her lips
    Some word in pause did keep,
And gave the while a quiet smile,
    As if they paused in sleep;—
'I have ... a brother dear,
    A knight of knightly fame!
I broidered him a knightly scarf
    With letters of my name.
                    Margret, Margret.

XIII.

'I fed his grey goss hawk,
    I kissed his fierce bloodhound;
I sate at home when he might come,
    And caught his horn's far sound:
I sang him hunter's songs,
    I poured him the red wine—
He looked across the cup and said,
    I love thee, sister mine.'
                    Margret, Margret.

XIV.

IT trembled on the grass,
  With a low, shadowy laughter:
The sounding river which rolled for ever,
  Stood dumb and stagnant after.
  "Brave knight thy brother is;
    But better loveth he
Thy chaliced wine than thy chanted song,
  And better both, than thee,
                  Margret, Margret."

XV.

The lady did not heed
  The river's silence while
Her own thoughts still ran at their will,
  And calm was still her smile.
  ' My little sister wears
    The look our mother wore:
I smooth her locks with a golden comb—
  I bless her evermore. '
                  Margret, Margret.

XVI.

' I gave her my first bird,
  When first my voice it knew;
I made her share my posies rare,
  And told her where they grew:
  I taught her God's dear name
    With prayer and praise, to tell—
She looked from heaven into my face,
  And said, *I love thee well.* '
                  Margret, Margret.

XVII.

IT trembled on the grass
  With a low, shadowy laughter:
You could see each bird as it woke and stared
  Through the shrivelled foliage after.
  'Fair child thy sister is;
    But better loveth she
Thy golden comb than thy gathered flowers,
    And better both, than thee,
                    Margret, Margret. '

XVIII.

The lady did not heed
  The withering on the bough:
Still calm her smile albeit the while
  A little pale her brow.
  ' I have a father old,
    The lord of ancient halls:
An hundred friends are in his court,
    Yet only me he calls.
                    Margret, Margret.

XIX.

  'An hundred knights are in his court,
    Yet read I by his knee;
And when forth they go to the tourney show,
    I rise not up to see.
  'Tis a weary book to read—
    My tryst's at set of sun !
But loving and dear beneath the stars
    Is his blessing when I've done. '
                    Margret, Margret.

XX.

IT trembled on the grass
　　With a low, shadowy laughter :
And moon and star though bright and far
　　Did shrink and darken after.
　'High lord thy father is ;
　　But better loveth he
His ancient halls than his hundred friends,
　　His ancient halls, than thee,
　　　　　　　　Margret, Margret.'

XXI.

The lady did not heed
　　That the far stars did fail :
Still calm her smile, albeit the while . . .
　　Nay, but she is not pale !
　'I have a more than friend
　　Across the mountains dim :
No other's voice is soft to me,
　　Unless it nameth *him*. '
　　　　　　　　Margret, Margret.

XXII.

　'Though louder beats mine heart
　　I know his tread again—
And his far plume aye, unless turned away,
　　For the tears do blind me then.
　We brake no gold, a sign
　　Of stronger faith to be ;
But I wear his last look in my soul,
　　Which said, *I love but thee !* '
　　　　　　　　Margret, Margret.

XXIII.

IT trembled on the grass,
  With a low, shadowy laughter;
And the wind did toll, as a passing soul
  Were sped by church-bell after:
And shadows, 'stead of light,
  Fell from the stars above,
In flakes of darkness on her face
  Still bright with trusting love.
                    Margret, Margret

XXIV.

' He *loved* but only thee!
  That love is transient too.
The wild hawk's bill doth dabble still
  I' the mouth that vowed thee true.
Will he open his dull eyes,
  When tears fall on his brow?
Behold, the death-worm to his heart
  Is a nearer thing than *thou*,
                    Margret, Margret.

XXV.

Her face was on the ground—
  None saw the agony!
But the men at sea did that night agree
  They heard a drowning cry.
And when the morning brake,
  Fast rolled the river's tide,
With the green trees waving overhead.
  And a white corse laid beside.
                    Margret, Margret

A knight's bloodhound and he
    The funeral watch did keep :
With a thought o' the chase he stroked its face
    As it howled to see him weep.
A fair child kissed the dead,
    But shrank before the cold :
And alone yet proudly in his hall,
    Did stand a baron old.
                Margret, Margret

XXVII.

Hang up my harp again——
    I have no voice for song.
Not song but wail, and mourners pale
    Not bards, to love belong.
O failing human love !
    O light by darkness known !
O false, the while thou treadest earth !
    O deaf beneath the stone !
                Margret, Margret.

G

ISOBEL'S CHILD.

—— so find we profit,
By losing of our prayers.
SHAKSPEARE.

I.

To rest the weary nurse has gone ;
  An eight-day watch had watchëd she,
Rocking beneath the sun and moon
  The baby on her knee :
Till Isobel its mother said
'The fever waneth—wend to bed—
  For now the watch comes round to me. '

II.

Then wearily the nurse did throw
Her pallet in the darkest place
  Of that sick room, and slept and dreamed
  And as the gusty wind did blow
  The night-lamp's flare across her face,
She saw or seemed to see, but dreamed.
  That the poplars tall on the opposite hill,
  The seven tall poplars on the hill,

Did clasp the setting sun until
His rays dropped from him, pined and still
  As blossoms in frost:
Till he waned and paled, so weirdly crossed,
 To the colour of moonlight which doth pass
 Over the dank ridged churchyard grass.
  The poplars held the sun, and he
 The eyes of the nurse that they should not see,
 Not for a moment, the babe on her knee,
 Though she shuddered to feel that it grew to be
  Too chill, and lay too heavily.

III.

She only dreamed : for all the while
'Twas Lady Isobel that kept
The little baby ; and it slept
Fast, warm, as if its mother's smile,
Laden with love's dewey weight,
And red as rose of Harpocrate
Dropt upon its eyelids, pressed
Lashes to cheek in a sealèd rest.

IV.

And more and more smiled Isobel
To see the baby sleep so well—
 She knew not that she smiled.
Against the lattice, dull and wild
Drive the heavy droning drops,
Drop by drop, the sound being one—
As momently time's segments fall
On the ear of God who hears through all

Eternity's unbroken monotone.
And more and more smiled Isobel
To see the baby sleep so well—
   She knew not that she smiled.
The wind in intermission stops
Down in the beechen forest,
   Then cries aloud
   As one at the sorest,
   Self-stung, self-driven
And rises up to its very tops,
Stiffening erect the branches bowed ;
Dilating with a tempest-soul
The trees that with their dark hands break
Through their own outline and heavily roll
   Shadows as massive as clouds in heaven,
   Across the castle lake.
And more and more smiled Isobel
To see the baby sleep so well ;
She knew not that she smiled—
She knew not that the storm was wild.
Through the uproar drear she could not hear
The castle clock which struck anear—
She heard the low, light breathing of her child.

v.

O sight for wondering look !
While the external nature broke
Into such abandonment ;
While the very mist heart-rent
By the lightning, seemed to eddy
Against nature, with a din—-

A sense of silence and of steady
Natural calm appeared to come
From things without, and enter in
   The human creature's room.

VI.

  So motionless she sate,
The babe asleep upon her knees,
You might have dreamed their souls had gone
Away to things inanimate,
In such to live, in such to moan ;
And that their bodies had ta'en back,
In mystic change, all silences
That cross the sky in cloudy rack,
Or dwell beneath the reedy ground
In waters safe from their own sound.
       Only she wore
The deepening smile I named before,
And *that* a deepening love expressed—
And who at once can love and rest ?

VII.

In sooth the smile that then was keeping
Watch upon the baby sleeping,
Floated with its tender light
Downward, from the drooping eyes,
Upward, from the lips apart,
Over cheeks which had grown white
  With an eight-day weeping.
All smiles come in such a wise,
Where tears shall fall or have of old—

9*

Like northern lights that fill the heart
  Of heaven in sign of cold.

VIII.

  Motionless she sate:
Her hair had fallen by its weight
On each side of her smile, and lay
Very blackly on the arm
Where the baby nestled warm;
Pale as baby carved in stone
Seen by glimpses of the moon
  Up a dark cathedral aisle:
But, through the storm, no moonbeam fell
Upon the child of Isobel—
Perhaps you saw it by the ray
  Alone of her still smile.

IX.

A solemn thing it is to me
To look upon a babe that sleeps—
Wearing in its spirit-deeps
The undeveloped mystery
Of its Adam's taint and woe,
Which, when they developed be,
Will not let it slumber so:
Lying new in life beneath
The shadow of the coming death,
With that soft, low, quiet breath,
  As if it felt the sun!
Knowing all things by their blooms,
Not their roots; yea,—sun and sky,

Only by the warmth that comes
Out of each; earth, only by
The pleasant hues that o'er it run;
And human love, by drops of sweet
White nourishment still hanging round
The little mouth so slumber-bound.
All which broken sentiency
And conclusion incomplete,
Will gather and unite and climb
To an immortality
Good or evil, each sublime,
Through life and death to life again!
O little lids, now folded fast,
Must ye learn to drop at last
Our large and burning tears?
O warm quick body, must thou lie,
When the time comes round to die,
Still from all the whirl of years,
Bare of all the joy and pain?   .
O small frail being, wilt thou stand
      At God's right hand,
Lifting up those sleeping eyes
Dilated by great destinies,
To an endless waking? Thrones and seraphim,
Through the long ranks of their solemnities,
Sunning thee with calm looks of Heaven's sur-
            But thine alone on *Him?*—   [prise—
Or else, self-willed, to tread the godless place,
(God keep thy will!) feel thine own energies
Cold, strong, objectless, like a dead man's clasp,
The sleepless deathless life within thee, grasp;

While myriad faces, like one changeless face,
With woe *not love's*, shall glass thee everywhere,
And overcome thee with thine own despair?

x.

More soft, less solemn images
Drifted o'er the lady's heart,
  Silently as snow:
She had seen eight days depart
Hour by hour, on bended knees,
With pale-wrung hands and prayings low
And broken—through which came the sound
Of tears that fell against the ground,
Making sad stops ;—' Dear Lord, dear Lord!'
She still had prayed—(the heavenly word,
Broken by an earthly sigh)
' Thou, who didst not erst deny
The mother-joy to Mary mild,
Blessed in the blessed child,
Which hearkened in meek babyhood
Her cradle-hymn, albeit used
To all that music interfused
In breasts of angels high and good!
Oh, take not, Lord, my babe away—
Oh, take not to thy songful heaven,
The pretty baby thou hast given,
Or ere that I have seen him play
Around his father's knees and known
That *he* knew how my love hath gone
  From all the world to him.
Think, God among the cherubim,

How I shall shiver every day
In thy June sunshine, knowing where
The grave-grass keeps it from his fair
Still cheeks! and feel at every tread
His little body which is dead
And hidden in the turfy fold,
Doth make thy whole warm earth a-cold!
O God, I am so young, so young—
I am not used to tears at nights
Instead of slumber—nor to prayer
With sobbing lips and hands out-wrung:
Thou knowest all my prayings were
' I bless thee, God, for past delights—
Thank God!'   I am not used to bear
Hard thoughts of death.   The earth doth cover
No face from me of friend or lover:
And must the first who teacheth me
The form of shrouds and funerals, be
Mine own first-born beloved? he
Who taught me first this mother-love?
Dear Lord, who spreadest out above   ·
Thy loving, transpierced hands to meet
All lifted hearts with blessing sweet,—
Pierce not my heart, my tender heart,
Thou madest tender!   Thou who art
So happy in thy heaven alway,
Take not mine only bliss away!'

XI.

She so had prayed: and God, who hears
Through seraph-songs the sound of tears,

From that beloved babe had ta'en
The fever and the beating pain.
And more and more smiled Isobel
To see the baby sleep so well—
    (She knew not that she smiled, I wis,)
Until the pleasant gradual thought
Which near her heart the smile enwrought,
(Soon strong enough her lips to reach,)
Now soft and slow, itself, did seem
To float along a happy dream,
    Beyond it into speech like this.

                XII.

'I prayed for thee. my little child,
And God hath heard my prayer!
And when thy babyhood is gone,
We two together, undefiled
By men's repinings, will kneel down
Upon His earth which will be fair
(Not covering thee, sweet!) to us twain,
And give Him thankful praise.

                XIII.

Dully and wildly drives the rain:
Against the lattices drives the rain.

                XIV.

' I thank Him now, that I can think
    Of those same future days,
Nor from the harmless image shrink
    Of what I there might see—

Strange babies on their mothers' knee,
Whose innocent soft faces might
From off mine eyelids strike the light,
  With looks not meant for me!'

XV.

Gustily blows the wind through the rain,
As against the lattices drives the rain.

XVI.

' But now, O baby mine, together,
We turn this hope of ours again
To many an hour of summer weather
When we shall sit and intertwine
Our spirits, and instruct each other
In the pure loves of child and mother!
Two human loves make one divine. '

XVII.

The thunder tears through the wind and the rain,
As full on the lattices drives the rain.

XVIII.

' My little child, what wilt thou choose?
Let me look at thee and ponder.
What gladness, from the gladnesses
Futurity is spreading under
Thy gladsome sight?   Beneath the trees
Wilt thou lean all day and lose
Thy spirit with the river seen
Intermittently between

The winding beechen alleys,—
Half in labour, half repose,
Like a shepherd keeping sheep,
Thou, with only thoughts to keep
Which never a bound will overpass,
And which are innocent as those
That feed among Arcadian valleys
    Upon the dewy grass?'

XIX.

The large white owl that with age is blind,
That hath sate for years in the old tree hollow,
Is carried away in a gust of wind!
His wings could bear him not as fast
As he goeth now the lattice past—
He is borne by the winds; the rains do follow:
His white wings to the blast out-flowing,
    He hooteth in going,
And still in the lightnings, coldly glitter
    His round unblinking eyes.

XX.

' Or, baby, wilt thou think it fitter
To be eloquent and wise?
One upon whose lips the air
Turns to solemn verities,
For men to breathe anew, and win
A deeper-seated life within?
Wilt be a philosopher,
By whose voice the earth and skies
Shall speak to the unborn?

Or a poet, broadly spreading
The golden immortalities
Of thy soul on natures lorn
And poor of such, them all to guard
From their decay? beneath thy treading,
Earth's flowers recovering hues of Eden;
And stars, drawn downward by thy looks
To shine ascendant in thy books?'

XXI.

The tame hawk in the castle-yard,
How it screams to the lightning, with its we:
Jagged plumes overhanging the parapet!
And at the lady's door the hound
    Scratches with a crying sound!

XXII.

' But, O my babe, thy lids are laid
    Close, fast upon thy cheek!
And not a dream of power and sheen
Can make a passage up between:
Thy heart is of thy mother's made,
    Thy looks are very meek!
And it will be their chosen place
To rest on some beloved face,
As these on thine—and let the noise
Of the whole world go on, nor drown
The tender silence of thy joys;
Or when that silence shall have grown
Too tender for itself, the same
Yearning for sound,—to look above
    10

And utter its one meaning, LOVE,
   That *He* may hear His name!'

XXIII.

No wind—no rain—no thunder!
The waters had trickled not slowly,
The thunder was not spent,
Nor the wind near finishing.   [ishing?
Who would have said that the storm was dimin-
No wind—no rain—no thunder!
Their noises dropped asunder
From the earth and the firmament,
From the towers and the lattices,
Abrupt and echoless
As ripe fruits on the ground unshaken wholly—
      As life in death;
  And sudden and solemn the silence fell,
   Startling the heart of Isobel
         As the tempest could not!
   Against the door went panting the breath
   Of the lady's hound whose cry was still—
   And *she*, constrained howe'er she would not,
   Did lift her eyes, and saw the moon
   Looking out of heaven alone
      Upon the poplared hill,—
      A calm of God, made visible
      That men might bless it at their will.

XXIV.

The moonshine on the baby's face
   Falleth clear and cold.

The mother's looks have fallen back
　To the same place :
Because no moon with silver rack,
Nor broad sunrise in jasper skies
　　Have power to hold
　　Our loving eyes,
　　Which still revert, as ever must
　　Wonder and Hope, to gaze on the dust

XXV.

The moonshine on the baby's face
　Cold and clear remaineth !
The mother's looks do shrink away,
The mother's looks return to stay,
　　As charmëd by what paineth.
Is any glamour in the case ?
Is it dream or is it sight ?
Hath the change upon the wild
Elements, that signs the night,
　　Passed upon the child ?
It is not dream, but sight !—

XXVI.

The babe hath awakened from sleep,
And unto the gaze of its mother
Bent over it, lifted another !
Not the baby-looks that go
Unaimingly to and fro ;
But an earnest gazing deep,
Such as soul gives soul at length,
　　When, by work and wail of years,

It winneth a solemn strength,
  And mourneth as it wears!
A strong man could not brook
With pulse unhurried by fears,
To meet that baby's look
O'erglazed by manhood's tears—
The tears of the man full grown,
With the power to wring our own,
In the eyes all undefiled
Of a little three-months' child!
To see that babe-brow wrought
By the witnessing of thought,
To judgment's prodigy;
And the small soft mouth unweaned,
By mother's kiss o'erleaned
(Putting the sound of loving
Where no sound else was moving,
  Except the speechless cry)
  Quickened to mind's expression,
  Shaped to articulation—
Yea, uttering words—yea, naming woe
In tones that with it strangely went,
Because so baby-innocent,
As the child spake out to the mother so!—

XXVII.

' O mother, mother, loose thy prayer!
  Christ's name hath made it strong!
It bindeth me, it holdeth me
With its most loving cruelty,
From floating my new soul along

The happy heavenly air!
It bindeth me, it holdeth me
In all this dark, upon this dull
Low earth, by only weepers trod!—
It bindeth me, it holdeth me!—
Mine angel looketh sorrowful
   Upon the face of God.*

XXVIII.

' Mother, mother! can I dream
Beneath your earthly trees?
I had a vision and a gleam—
I heard a sound more sweet than these
   When rippled by the wind.
Did you see the Dove with wings
Bathed in golden glisterings
From a sunless light behind,
Dropping on me from the sky
Soft as mother's kiss until
I seemed to leap, and yet was still?
Saw you how his love-large eye
Looked upon me mystic calms,
Till the power of his divine
Vision was indrawn to mine?

XXIX.

' Oh, the dream within the dream!
I saw celestial places even.
Oh, the vistas of high palms,
Making finites of delight

* For I say unto you, that in Heaven their angels do always behold
the face of my Father which is in Heaven.—Matt. ch. xviii. ver. 10.

Through the heavenly infinite—
Lifting up their green still tops
   To the heaven of Heaven!
Oh, the sweet life-tree that drops
Shade like light across the river
Glorified in its for ever
   Flowing from the Throne!
Oh, the shining holinesses
Of the thousand, thousand faces
God-sunned by the thronëd ONE!
And made intense with such a love,
That though I saw them turned above,
Each loving seemed for also me!
And, oh, the Unspeakable! the HE,
The manifest in secrecies,
Yet of mine own heart partaker!
With the overcoming look
Of one who hath been once forsook,
   And blesseth the forsaker.
Mother, mother, let me go
Toward the face that looketh so.
Through the mystic, wingëd Four
Whose are inward, outward eyes
Dark with light of mysteries,
And the restless evermore
' Holy, holy, holy,' —through
The sevenfold Lamps that burn in view
Of cherubim and seraphim;
Through the four-and-twenty crowned
Stately elders, white around,
Suffer me to go to Him!

XXX.

' Is your wisdom very wise,
Mother, on the narrow earth?
Very happy, very worth
That I should stay to learn?
Are these air-corrupting sighs
Fashioned by unlearned breath?
Do the students' lamps that burn
All night, illumine death?
Mother, albeit this be so,
Loose thy prayer and let me go
Where that bright chief angel stands
Apart from all his brother bands,
Too glad for smiling; having bent
In angelic wilderment
O'er the depths of God, and brought
Reeling thence, one only thought
To fill his whole eternity.
He the teacher is for me!—
He can teach what I would know—
Mother, mother, let me go!

XXXI.

' Can your poet make an Eden
    No winter will undo?
And light a starry fire while heeding
    His hearth's is burning too?
Drown in music the earth's din?
And keep his own wild soul within
The law of his own harmony?—
    Mother! albeit this be so,

Let me to my Heaven go!
A little harp me waits thereby—
A harp whose strings are golden all,
And tuned to music spherical,
Hanging on the green life-tree
Where no willows ever be.
Shall I miss that harp of mine?
Mother, no!—the Eye divine
Turned upon it, makes it shine—
And when I touch it, poems sweet
Like separate souls shall fly from it,
Each to an immortal fytte.
We shall all be poets there,
Gazing on the chiefest Fair!

XXXII.

' And love! earth's love! and *can* we love
Fixedly where all things move?
Can the sinning love each other?
        Mother, mother,
I tremble in thy close embrace—
I feel thy tears adown my face—
Thy prayers do keep me out of bliss—
        O dreary earthly love!
Loose thy prayer and let me go
To the place which loving is
Yet not sad! and when is given
Escape to *thee* from this below,
Thou shalt behold me that I wait
For thee beside the happy gate;

And silence shall be up in heaven
　　To hear our greeting kiss."

XXXIII.

The nurse awakes in the morning sun,
And starts to see beside her bed
The lady　with a grandeur spread
Like pathos　o'er her face ; as one
God-satisfied and earth-undone :
　　The babe upon her arm was dead !
And the nurse could utter forth no cry,—
She was awed by the calm in the mother's eye.

XXXIV.

' Wake nurse ! ' the lady said :
' *We* are waking—he and I—
I, on earth, and he, in sky !
And thou must help me to o'erlay
With garment white, this little clay
Which needs no more our lullaby.

XXXV.

' I changed the cruel prayer I made,
And bowed my meekened face, and prayed
That God would do His will ! and thus
He did it, nurse : He parted *us.*
And His sun shows victorious
The dead calm face :—and *I* am calm :
And Heaven is hearkening a new psalm.

XXXVI.

' This earthly noise is too anear,
Too loud, and will not let me near

The little harp.   My death will soon
Make silence. '

           And a sense of tune.
A satisfïed love meanwhile
Which nothing earthly could despoil,
Sang on within her soul.

XXXVII.

         Oh you,
Earth's tender and impassioned few,
Take courage to entrust your love
To Him so Named, who guards above
  Its ends and shall fulfil;
Breaking the narrow prayers that may
Befit your narrow hearts, away
  In His broad, loving will.

A ROMANCE OF THE GANGES.

I.

SEVEN maidens 'neath the midnight
    Stand near the river-sea,
Whose water sweepeth white around
    The shadow of the tree.
The moon and earth are face to face,
    And earth is slumbering deep;
The wave-voice seems the voice of dreams
    That wander through her sleep.
               The river floweth on.

II.

What bring they 'neath the midnight,
    Beside the river-sea?
They bring that human heart wherein
    No nightly calm can be,—
That droppeth never with the wind,
    Nor drieth with the dew:

Oh, calm it God!   *Thy* calm is broad
 To cover spirits, too.
      The river floweth on

III.

The maidens lean them over
 The waters, side by side,
And shun each other's deepening eyes,
 And gaze adown the tide:
For each within a little boat
 A little lamp hath put,
And heaped for freight some lily's weight
 Or scarlet rose half shut.
      The river floweth on.

IV.

Of a shell of cocoa carven,
 Each little boat is made:
Each carries a lamp, and carries a flower,
 And carries a hope unsaid.
And when the boat hath carried the lamp
 Unquenched, till out of sight,
The maidens are sure that love will endure,
 But love will fail with light.
      The river floweth on

V.

Why, all the stars are ready
 To symbolize the soul,
The stars untroubled by the wind,
 Unwearied as they roll:

And yet the soul by instinct sad
  Reverts to symbols low—
To that small flame, whose very name
  Breathed o'er it, shakes it so.
                    The river floweth on

VI.

Six boats are on the river,
  Seven maidens on the shore;
While still above them steadfastly
  The stars shine evermore.
Go, little boats, go soft and safe,
  And guard the symbol spark!—
The boats aright go safe and bright
  Across the waters dark.
                    The river floweth on

VII.

The maiden Luti watcheth
  Where onwardly they float.
That look in her dilating eyes
  Might seem to drive her boat;
Her eyes still mark the constant fire,
  And kindling unawares
That hopeful while, she lets a smile
  Creep silent through her prayers.
                    The river floweth on.

VIII.

The smile—where hath it wandered?
  She riseth from her knee,
  11

She holds her dark, wet locks away—
    There is no light to see!
She cries a quick and bitter cry—
    ' Nuleeni, launch me thine!
We must have light abroad to-night,
    For all the wreck of mine.'

                        The river floweth on.

IX.

' I do remember watching
    Beside this river-bed,
When on my childish knee was laid
    My dying father's head.
I turned mine own, to keep the tears
    From falling on his face—
What doth it prove when Death and Love
    Choose out the self-same place?'

                        The river floweth on.

X.

' They say the dead are joyful
    The death-change here receiving.
Who say—ah, me!—who dare to say
    Where joy comes to the living!
Thy boat, Nuleeni! look not sad—
    Light up the waters rather!
I weep no faithless lover where
    I wept a loving father.'

                        The river floweth on.

XI.

' My heart foretold his falsehood
    Ere my little boat grew dim :

And though I closed mine eyes to dream
    That one last dream of *him*,
They shall not now be wet to see
    The shining vision go:
From earth's cold love I look above
    To the holy house of snow.' *

                The river floweth on.

XII.

' Come *thou*—thou never knewest
    A grief, that thou shouldst fear one;
Thou wearest still the happy look
    That shines beneath a dear one!
Thy humming-bird is in the sun.†
    Thy cuckoo in the grove;
And all the three broad worlds, for thee
    Are full of wandering love. '

                The river floweth on

XIII.

' Why, maiden, dost thou loiter?
    What secret wouldst thou cover?
That peepul cannot hide thy boat,
    And I can guess thy lover:
I heard thee sob his name in sleep . . .
    It was a name I knew—

---

* The Hindoo heaven is localized on the summit of Mount Meru—
one of the mountains of Himalaya or Himmeleh, which signifies, I believe, in Sanscrit, the abode of snow, winter, or coldness.

† Hamadeva, the Indian god of love, is imagined to wander through
the three worlds, accompanied by the humming-bird, cuckoo, and
gentle breezes.

Come, little maid, be not afraid—
　　But let us prove him true!'
　　　　　　　　　　The river floweth on.

XIV.

The little maiden cometh—
　　She cometh shy and slow:
I ween she seeth through her lids,
　　They drop adown so low:
Her tresses meet her small bare feet—
　　She stands and speaketh nought,
Yet blusheth red, as if she said
　　The name she only thought.
　　　　　　　　　　The river floweth on.

XV.

She knelt beside the water,
　　She lighted up the flame,
And o'er her youthful forehead's calm
　　The fitful radiance came :—
' Go, little boat; go, soft and safe,
　　And guard the symbol spark!'
Soft, safe, doth float the little boat
　　Across the waters dark.
　　　　　　　　　　The river floweth on.

XVI.

Glad tears her eyes have blinded;
　　The light they cannot reach:
She turneth with that sudden smile
　　She learnt before her speech—

' I do not hear his voice! the tears
   Have dimmed my light away!
But the symbol light will last to-night
   The love will last for aye. '
               The river floweth on.

XVII.

Then Luti spake behind her—
   Out-spake she bitterly:
' By the symbol light that lasts to-night,
   Wilt vow a vow to me? '—
Nuleeni gazeth up her face—
   Soft answer maketh she:
' By loves that last when lights are past,
   I vow that vow to thee! '
               The river floweth on.

XVIII.

An earthly look had Luti
   Though her voice was deep as prayer—
' The rice is gathered from the plains
   To cast upon thine hair!*
But when *he* comes, his marriage-band
   Around thy neck to throw,
Thy bride-smile raise to meet his gaze,
And whisper,—*There is one betrays,*
   When Luti suffers woe. '
               The river floweth on.

---

* The casting of rice upon the head, and the fixing of the band or tali about the neck, are parts of the Hindoo marriage ceremonial.

11*

XIX.

' And when in seasons after,
　　Thy little bright-faced son
Shall lean against thy knee and ask
　　What deeds his sire hath done,
Press deeper down thy mother-smile
　　His glossy curls among—
View deep his pretty childish eyes,
And whisper,—*There is none denies*,
　　When Luti speaks of wrong. '
　　　　　　　　The river floweth on.

XX.

Nuleeni looked in wonder,
　　Yet softly answered she—
' By loves that last when lights are past,
　　I vowed that vow to thee;
But why glads it thee that a bride-day be
　　By a word of *woe* defiled ?
That a word of *wrong* take the cradle-song
　　From the ear of a sinless child ! '—
' *Why !* ' Luti said, and her laugh was dread,
　　And her eyes dilated wild—
' That the fair new love may her bridegroom
　　　　prove,
And the father shame the child. '
　　　　　　　　The river floweth on.

XXI.

' Thou flowest still, O river,
　　Thou flowest 'neath the moon—

Thy lily hath not changed a leaf,*
    Thy charmëd lute a tune!
He mixed his voice with thine—and *his*
    Was all I heard around;
But now, beside his chosen bride,
    I hear the river's sound.'

                  The river floweth on.

XXII.

' I gaze upon her beauty
    Through the tresses that enwreathe it:
The light above thy wave, is hers—
    My rest, alone beneath it.
Oh, give me back the dying look
    My father gave thy water!
Give back!—and let a little love
    O'erwatch his weary daughter!'

                  The river floweth on.

XXIII.

' Give back!' she hath departed—
    The word is wandering with her;
And the stricken maidens hear afar
    The step and cry together.
Frail symbols?   None are frail enow
    For mortal joys to borrow!—
While bright doth float Nuleeni's boat,
    She weepeth, dark with sorrow.

                  The river floweth on.

---

* The Ganges is represented as a white woman, with a water lily
in her right hand, and in her left a lute.

AN ISLAND.

All goeth but Goddis will.
OLD POET.

I.

My dream is of an island place
  Which distant seas keep lonely ;
A little island, on whose face
  The stars are watchers only.
Those bright still stars ! they need not seem
Brighter or stiller in my dream.

II.

An island full of hills and dells,
  All rumpled and uneven
With green recesses, sudden swells,
  And odorous valleys driven
So deep and straight, that always there
The wind is cradled to soft air.

III.

Hills running up to heaven for light
  Through woods that half-way ran !
As if the wild earth mimicked right
  The wilder heart of man :
Only it shall be greener far
  And gladder than hearts ever are.

IV.

More like, perhaps, that mountain piece
   Of Dante's paradise,
Disrupt to an hundred hills like these,
   In falling from the skies—
Bringing within it, all the roots
Of heavenly trees and flowers and fruits.

V.

For saving where the grey rocks strike
   Their javelins up the azure,
Or where deep fissures, miser-like,
   Hoard up some fountain treasure,
(And e'en in them—stoop down and hear—
Leaf sounds with water in your ear!)

VI.

The place is all awave with trees—
   Limes, myrtles purple-beaded;
Acacias having drunk the lees
   Of the night-dew, faint-headed;
And wan, grey olive-woods, which seem
The fittest foliage for a dream.

VII.

Trees, trees on all sides! they combine
   Their plumy shades to throw;
Through whose clear fruit and blossom fine
   Whene'er the sun may go,
The ground beneath he deeply stains,
As passing through cathedral panes.

ı

VIII.

But little needs this earth of ours
　　That shining from above her,
When many Pleiades of flowers
　　(Not one lost) star her over;
The rays of their unnumbered hues
Being all refracted by the dews.

IX.

Wide-petalled plants, that boldly drink
　`The Amreeta of the sky;
Shut bells, that dull with rapture sink,
　　And lolling buds, half shy;
I cannot count them; but between,
Is room for grass and mosses green,

X.

And brooks, that glass in different strengths
　　All colours in disorder,
Or gathering up their silver lengths
　　Beside their winding border
Sleep, haunted through the slumber hidden,
By lilies white as dreams in Eden.

XI.

Nor think each arched tree with each
　　Too closely interlaces,
To admit of vistas out of reach,
　　And broad moon-lighted places,
Upon whose sward the antlered deer
May view their double image clear.

XII.

For all this island's creature-full,
  Kept happy not by halves;
Mild cows, that at the vine-wreaths pull,
  Then low back at their calves
With tender lowings, to approve
The warm mouths milking them for love.

XIII.

Free gamesome horses, antelopes,
  And harmless leaping leopards,
And buffaloes upon the slopes,
  And sheep unruled by shepherds:
Hares, lizards, hedgehogs, badgers, mice,
Snakes, squirrels, frogs, and butterflies.

XIV.

And birds that live there in a crowd—
  Horned owls, rapt nightingales,
Larks bold with heaven, and peacocks proud,
  Self-sphered in those grand tails;
All creatures glad and safe, I deem:
No guns nor springes in my dream!

XV.

The island's edges are a-wing
  With trees that overbranch
The sea with song-birds, welcoming
  The curlews to green change.
And doves from half-closed lids espy
The red and purple fish go by.

XVI.

One dove is answering in trust
   The water every minute,
Thinking so soft a murmur must
   Have her mate's cooing in it :
So softly doth earth's beauty round
Infuse itself in ocean's sound.

XVII.

My sanguine soul bounds forwarder
   To meet the bounding waves !
Beside them straightway I repair,
   To live within the caves ;
And near me two or three may dwell
Whom dreams fantastic please as well.

XVIII.

Long winding caverns ! glittering far
   Into a crystal distance ;
Through clefts of which, shall many a star
   Shine clear without resistance,
And carry down its rays the smell
Of flowers above invisible.

XIX.

I said that two or three might choose
   Their dwelling near mine own :
Those who would change man's voice and use
   For Nature's way and tone—
Man's veering heart and careless eyes,
For Nature's steadfast sympathies.

XX.

Ourselves to meet her faithfulness,
　　Shall play a faithful part:
Her beautiful shall ne'er address
　　The monstrous at our heart;
Her musical shall ever touch
Something within us also such.

XXI.

Yet shall she not our mistress live,
　　As doth the moon of ocean;
Though gently as the moon she give
　　Our thoughts a light and motion.
More like a harp of many lays,
Moving its master while he plays.

XXII.

No sod in all that island doth
　　Yawn open for the dead:
No wind hath borne a traitor's oath;
　　No earth, a mourner's tread:
We cannot say by stream or shade,
' I suffered *here*,—was *here* betrayed.'

XXIII.

Our only ' farewell ' we shall laugh
　　To shifting cloud or hour;
And use our only epitaph
　　To some bud turned a flower.
Our only tears shall serve to prove
Excess in pleasure or in love.

12

XXIV.

Our fancies shall their plumage catch
   From fairest island birds,
Whose eggs let young ones out at hatch,
   Born singing! then our words
Unconsciously shall take the dyes
Of these prodigious fantasies.

XXV.

Yea, soon, no consonant unsmooth
   Our smile-turned lips shall reach:
Sounds sweet as Hellas spake in youth
   Shall glide into our speech—
(What music certes can you find
As soft as voices which are kind?)

XXVI.

And often by the joy without
   And in us, overcome,
We, through our musing, shall let float
   Such poems,—sitting dumb,—
As Pindar might have writ, if he
Had tended sheep in Arcady;

XXVII.

Or Æschylus—the pleasant fields
   He died in, longer knowing:
Or Homer, had men's sins and shields
   Been lost in Meles flowing;
Or poet Plato, had the undim
Unsetting Godlight broke on him.

XXVIII.

Choose me the cave most worthy choice,
 To make a place for prayer;
And I will choose a praying voice
 To poor our spirits there.
How silverly the echoes run—
Thy will be done,—thy will be done.

XXIX.

Gently yet strangely uttered words !—
 They lift me from my dream.
The island fadeth with its swards
 That did no more than seem!
The streams are dry, no sun could find—
The fruits are fallen, without wind

XXX.

So oft the doing of God's will
 Our foolish wills undoeth!
And yet what idle dream breaks ill,
 Which morning-light subdueth;
And who would murmur and misdoubt,
When God's great sunrise finds him out?

·

THE DESERTED GARDEN.

I MIND me in the days departed,
How often underneath the sun
With childish bounds I used to run
  To a garden long deserted.

The beds and walks were vanished quite;
And wheresoe'er had struck the spade,
The greenest grasses Nature laid,
  To sanctify her right.

I called the place my wilderness,
For no one entered there but I.
The sheep looked in, the grass to espy,
  And passed it ne'ertheless.

The trees were interwoven wild,
And spread their boughs enough about
To keep both sheep and shepherd out,
  But not a happy child.

Adventurous joy it was for me!
I crept beneath the boughs, and found
A circle smooth of mossy ground
  Beneath a poplar tree.

Old garden rose-trees hedged it in,
Bedropt with roses waxen-white
Well satisfied with dew and light
   And careless to be seen.

Long years ago it might befall,
When all the garden flowers were trim,
The grave old gardener prided him
   On these the most of all.

Some Lady, stately overmuch,
Here moving with a silken noise,
Has blushed beside them at the voice
   That likened her to such.

Or these, to make a diadem,
She often may have plucked and twined ;
Half-smiling as it came to mind
   That few would look at *them*.

Oh, little thought that Lady proud,
A child would watch her fair white rose,
When buried lay her whiter brows,
   And silk was changed for shroud !—

Nor thought that gardener, (full of scorns
For men unlearned and simple phrase,)
A child would bring it all its praise,
   By creeping through the thorns !

12*

To me upon my low moss seat,
Though never a dream the roses sent
Of science or love's compliment,
    I ween they smelt as sweet.

It did not move my grief to see
The trace of human step departed.
Because the garden was deserted,
    The blither place for me!

Friends, blame me not! a narrow ken,
Hath childhood twixt the sun and sward:
We draw the moral afterward—
    We feel the gladness then.

And gladdest hours for me did glide
In silence at the rose-tree wall:
A thrush made gladness musical
    Upon the other side.

Nor he nor I did e'er incline
To peck or pluck the blossoms white—
How should I know but roses might
    Lead lives as glad as mine?

To make my hermit-home complete,
I brought clear water from the spring
Praised in its own low murmuring—
    And cresses glossy wet.

And so, I thought my likeness grew
(Without the melancholy tale)
To ' gentle hermit of the dale,'
   And Angelina too.

For oft I read within my nook
Such minstrel stories! till the breeze
Made sounds poetic in the trees,—
   And then I shut the book.

If I shut this wherein I write
I hear no more the wind athwart
Those trees,—nor feel that childish heart
   Delighting in delight.

My childhood from my life is parted,
My footstep from the moss which drew
Its fairy circle round : anew
   The garden is deserted.

Another thrush may there rehearse
The madrigals which sweetest are :
No more for me!—myself afar
   Do sing a sadder verse.

Ah me, ah me! when erst I lay
In that child's-nest so greenly wrought.
I laughed unto myself and thought
   ' The time will pass away.'

And still I laughed and did not fear
But that, whene'er was past away
The childish time, some happier play
   My womanhood would cheer.

I knew the time would pass away ;
And yet, beside the rose-tree wall,
Dear God, how seldom, if at all,
   Did I look up to pray !

The time *is* past :—and now that grows
The cypress high among the trees,
And I behold white sepulchres
   As well as the white rose,—

When graver, meeker thoughts are given.
And I have learnt to lift my face,
Reminded how earth's greenest place
   The colour draws from heaven,—

It something saith for earthly pain,
But more for Heavenly promise free,
That I who was, would shrink to be
   That happy child again.

THE SOUL'S TRAVELLING.

Ἤδη νοερους
Πτεραοι ταρσους.
                    SYNESIUS.

I.

I DWELL amid the city ever.
The great humanity which beats
Its life along the stony streets,
Like a strong and unsunned river
In a self-made course,
I sit and hearken while it rolls.
  Very sad and very hoarse
  Certes is the flow of souls :
  Infinitest tendencies
  By the finite prest and pent,
  In the finite, turbulent
  How we tremble in surprise,
  When sometimes, with an awful sound,
  God's great plummet strikes the ground!

II.

The champ of the steeds on the silver bit,
As they whirl the rich man's carriage by :

The beggar's whine as he looks at it,—
But it goes too fast for charity.
The trail on the street of the poor man's broom,
That the lady who walks to her palace-home,
On her silken skirt may catch no dust:
The tread of the business-men who must
Count their per cents. by the paces they take:
The cry of the babe unheard of its mother
Though it lie on her breast, while she thinks of the
        other
Laid yesterday where it will not wake.
The flower-girl's prayer to buy roses and pinks,
Held out in the smoke, like stars by day:
The gin-door's oath that hollowly chinks
Guilt upon grief and wrong upon hate:
The cabman's cry to get out of the way;
The dustman's call down the area-grate:
The young maid's jest, and the old wife's scold,
The haggling talk of the boys at a stall;
The fight in the street which is backed for gold,
The plea of the lawyers in Westminster Hall:
The drop on the stones of the blind man's staff
As he trades in his own grief's sacredness;
The brothel shriek, and the Newgate laugh,
The hum upon 'Change, and the organ's grinding.
The grinder's face being nevertheless
Dry and vacant of even woe,
While the children's hearts are leaping so
At the merry music's winding!
The black-plumed funeral's creeping train
Long and slow (and yet they will go

As fast as Life though it hurry and strain!)
Creeping the populous houses through
And nodding their plumes at either side,—
At many a house where an infant, new
To the sunshiny world, has just struggled and
    cried :
At many a house, where sitteth a bride
Trying the morrow's coronals
With a scarlet blush to-day.
    Slowly creep the funerals,
As none should hear the noise and say,
The living, the living, must go away
        To multiply the dead !
    Hark! an upward shout is sent!
In grave strong joy from tower to steeple
        The bells ring out—
The trumpets sound, the people shout,
The young Queen goes to her parliament.
She turneth round her large blue eyes
More bright with childish memories
Than royal hopes, upon the people :
On either side she bows her head
    Lowly, with a Queenly grace,
And smile most trusting-innocent,
As if she smiled upon her mother !
The thousands press before each other
    To bless her to her face :
And booms the deep majestic voice
Through trump and drum,— ' May the Queen
    rejoice
    In the people's liberties ! '—

III.

I dwell amid the city,
    And hear the flow of souls in act and speech,
For pomp or trade, for merrymake or folly:
I hear the confluence and sum of each,
    And that is melancholy!—
Thy voice is a complaint, O crownèd city,
The blue sky covering thee like God's great pity.

IV.

O blue sky! it mindeth me
Of places where I used to see
Its vast unbroken circle thrown
From the far pale-peakèd hill
Out to the last verge of ocean—
As by God's arm it were done
Then for the first time, with the emotion
Of that first impulse on it still.
Oh, we spirits fly at will,
Faster than the winged steed
Whereof in old book we read,
With the sunlight foaming back
From his flanks to a misty wrack,
And his nostril reddening proud
As he breasteth the steep thundercloud!
Smoother than Sabrina's chair
Gliding up from wave to air,
Which she smileth debonair
Yet holy, coldly and yet brightly,
Like her own mooned waters nightly,
    Through her dripping hair.

V.

Very fast and smooth we fly,
Spirits, though the flesh be by.
All looks feed not from the eye,
Nor all hearings from the ear;
We can hearken and espy
Without either; we can journey,
Bold and gay as knight to tourney;
And though we wear no visor down
To dark our countenance, the foe
Shall never chafe us as we go.

VI.

I am gone from peopled town!
It passeth its street-thunder round
My body which yet hears no sound:
For now another sound, another
Vision, my soul's senses have.
O'er a hundred valleys deep,
Where the hills' green shadows sleep,
Scarce known, because the valley trees
Cross those upland images—
O'er a hundred hills, each other
Watching to the western wave—
I have travelled,—I have found
The silent, lone, remembered ground.

VII.

I have found a grassy niche
Hollowed in a seaside hill,
As if the ocean-grandeur which

Is aspectable from the place
Had struck the hill as with a mace
Sudden and cleaving.   You might fill
That little nook with the little cloud
Which sometimes lieth by the moon
To beautify a night of June:
A cavelike nook, which, opening all
To the wide sea, is disallowed
From its own earth's sweet pastoral;
Cavelike, but roofless overhead,
And made of verdant banks instead
Of any rocks, with flowerets spread,
Instead of spar and stalactite . . .
Cowslips and daisies, gold and white.
Such pretty flowers on such green sward,
You think the sea they look toward
Doth serve them for another sky
As warm and blue as that on high.

VIII.

And in this hollow is a seat,
And when you shall have crept to it,
Slipping down the banks too steep
To be o'erbrowzed by the sheep,
Do not think—though at your feet
The cliff's disrupt—you shall behold
The line where earth and ocean meet:
You sit too much above to view
The solemn confluence of the two:
You can hear them as they greet;
You can hear that evermore

Distance-softened noise, more old
Than Nereid's singing,—the tide spent
Joining soft issues with the shore
In harmony of discontent,—
And when you hearken to the grave
Lamenting of the underwave,
You must believe in earth's communion,
Albeit you witness not the union.

IX.

Except that sound, the place is full
Of silences, which when you cull
By any word, it thrills you so
That presently you let them grow
To meditations fullest length
Across your soul with a soul's strength :
And as they touch your soul, they borrow
Both of its grandeur and its sorrow,
That deathly odour which the clay
Leaves on its deathlessness alway.

X.

Alway ! alway ! must this be?
Rapid Soul from city gone,
Dost thou carry inwardly
What doth make the city's moan?
Must this deep sigh of thine own
Haunt thee with humanity ?
Green-visioned banks that are too steep
To be o'erbrowzed by the sheep,
May all sad thoughts adown you creep

Without a shepherd?—Mighty sea,
Can we dwarf thy magnitude,
And fit it to our straitest mood?—
O fair, fair Nature! are we thus
Impotent and querulous
Among thy workings glorious,
Wealth and sanctities,—that still
Leave us vacant and defiled,
And wailing like a soft-kissed child,
Kissed soft against his will?

XI.

God, God!
With a child's voice I cry,
Weak, sad, confidingly—
God, God!
Thou knowest eyelids raised not always up
Unto Thy love, (as none of ours are,) droop
As ours, o'er many a tear!
Thou knowest, though thy universe is broad,
Two little tears suffice to cover all.
Thou knowest,—Thou, who art so prodigal
Of beauty,—we are oft but stricken deer
Expiring in the woods—that care for none
Of those delightsome flowers they die upon.

XII.

O blissful Mouth, which breathed the mournful
    breath
We name our souls,—self spoilt!—by that strong
    passion

Which paled thee once with sighs,—by that strong
    death
Which made thee once unbreathing—from the
    wrack
Themselves have called around them, call them back
Back to thee in continuous aspiration !
    For here, O Lord,
For here they travel vainly,—vainly pass
From city pavement to untrodden sward,
Where the lark finds her deep nest in the grass
Cold with the earth's last dew.   Yea, very vain
The greatest speed of all these souls of men,
Unless they travel upward to the throne
Where sittest Thou the satisfying One,
With help for sins and holy perfectings
For all requirements—while the archangel, raising
Unto Thy face his full ecstatic gazing,
Forgets the rush and rapture of his wings.
    13*

SOUNDS.

Πκουσας η ουκ ηκουσας ; . . . .

ÆSCHYLUS.

I.

HEARKEN, hearken!
The rapid river carrieth
Many noises underneath
  The hoary ocean:
Teaching his solemnity
Sounds of inland life and glee,
Learnt beside the waving tree,
When the winds in summer prank
Toss the shades from bank to bank,
And the quick rains, in emotion
Which rather gladdens earth than grieves,
Count and visibly rehearse
The pulses of the universe
Upon the summer leaves—
Learnt among the lilies straight,
When they bow them to the weight
Of many bees whose hidden hum
Seemeth from themselves to come —

Learnt among the grasses green,
Where the rustling mice are seen
By the gleaming, as they run,
Of their quick eyes in the sun;
And lazy sheep are browzing through,
With their noses trailed in dew;
And the squirrel leaps adown,
Holding fast the filbert brown;
And the lark, with more of mirth
In his song that suits the earth,
Droppeth some in soaring high,
To pour the rest out in the sky:
While the woodland doves, apart
In the copse's leafy heart,
Solitary, not ascetic,
Hidden and yet vocal, seem
Joining, in a lovely psalm,
Man's despondence, nature's calm,
Half mystical and half pathetic,
Like a sighing in a dream.*
All these sounds the river telleth,
Softened to an undertone

* "While floating up bright forms ideal,
    Mistress, or friend, around me stream;
    Half sense-supplied, and half unreal,
    Like music mingling with a dream."
                                    John Kenyon.

I do not doubt that the "music" of the two concluding lines mingled, though very unconsciously, with my own "dream," and gave their form and pressure to the above distich. The ideas, however, being sufficiently distinct, I am satisfied with sending this note to the press after my verses, and with acknowledging another obligation to the valued friend to whom I already owe so many.

Which ever and anon he swelleth
By a burden of his own,
   In the ocean's ear.
Ay! and ocean seems to hear
With an inward gentle scorn,
Smiling to his caverns worn.

II.

   Hearken, hearken!
The child is shouting at his play
Just in the tramping funeral's way:
The widow moans as she turns aside
To shun the face of the blushing bride,
While, shaking the tower of the ancient church,
The marriage bells do swing:
And in the shadow of the porch
An idiot sits, with his lean hands full
Of hedgerow flowers and a poet's skull,
Laughing loud and gibbering,
Because it is so brown a thing,
While he sticketh the gaudy poppies red
In and out the senseless head
Where all sweet fancies grew instead.
And you may hear, at the self-same time,
Another poet who reads his rhyme,
Low as a brook in the summer air,—
Save when he droppeth his voice adown,
To dream of the amaranthine crown
His mortal brows shall wear.
And a baby cries with a feeble sound
'Neath the weary weight of the life new-found·

And an old man groans,—with his testament
Only half signed,—for the life that's spent:
And lovers twain do softly say,
As they sit on a grave, ' for aye, for aye!'
And foeman twain, while Earth their mother
Looks greenly upward, curse each other.
A school-boy drones his task, with looks
Cast over the page to the elm-tree rooks:
A lonely student cries aloud
Eureka! clasping at his shroud;
A beldame's age-cracked voice doth sing
To a little infant slumbering:
A maid forgotten weeps alone,
Muffling her sobs on the trysting stone;
A sick man wakes at his own mouth's wail;
A gossip coughs in her thrice told tale;
A muttering gamester shakes the dice:
A reaper foretells goodluck from the skies;
A monarch vows as he lifts his hand to them;
A patriot leaving his native land to them,
Cries to the world against perjured state;
A priest disserts upon linen skirts;
A sinner screams for one hope more;
A dancer's feet do palpitate
A piper's music out on the floor;
And nigh to the awful Dead, the living
Low speech and stealthy steps are giving,
Because he cannot hear;
And *he* who on that narrow bier
Has room enow, is closely wound
In a silence piercing more than sound.

III.

Hearken, hearken!
God speaketh to thy soul;
Using the supreme voice which doth confound
All life with consciousness of Deity,
All senses into one;
As the seer-saint of Patmos, loving John.
For whom did backward roll
The cloud-gate of the future, turned to *see*
The Voice which spake. It speaketh now—
Through the regular breath of the calm creation,
Through the moan of the creature's desolation
Striking, and in its stroke, resembling
The memory of a solemn vow,
Which pierceth the din of a festival
To one in the midst,—and he letteth fall
The cup, with a sudden trembling.

IV.

Hearken, hearken!
God speaketh in thy soul;
Saying, 'O thou that movest
With feeble steps across this earth of mine,
To break beside the fount thy golden bowl
And spill its purple wine,—
Look up to heaven and see how like a scroll,
My right hand hath thine immortality
In an eternal grasping! Thou, that lovest
The songful birds and grasses underfoot,
And also what change mars and tombs pollute—
I am the end of love!—give love to *me!*

O thou that sinnest, grace doth more abound
Than all thy sin! sit still beneath my rood,
And count the droppings of my victim-blood,
    And seek none other sound!'

v.

    Hearken, hearken!
Shall we hear the lapsing river
And our brother's sighing ever,
    And not the voice of God?

NIGHT.

'Neath my moon what doest thou,
With a somewhat paler brow
Than she giveth to the ocean?
He, without a pulse or motion,
Muttering low before her stands,
Lifting his invoking hands,
Like a seer before a sprite,
To catch her oracles of light.
But thy soul out-trembles now
Many pulses on thy brow!
Where be all thy laughters clear,
Others laughed alone to hear?
Where, thy quaint jests, said for fame?
Where, thy dances, mixed with game?
Where, thy festive companies,
Moonèd o'er with ladies' eyes,
All more bright for thee, I trow?
'Neath my moon, what doest thou?

THE MERRY MAN.

I am digging my warm heart,
Till I find its coldest part:
I am digging wide and low,
Further than a spade will go;
Till that, when the pit is deep
And large enough, I there may heap
All my present pain and past
Joy, dead things that look aghast
By the daylight.—Now 'tis done!
Throw them in, by one and one!
I must laugh, at rising sun.

Memories—of fancy's golden
Treasures which my hands have holden,
Till the chillness made them ache:
Of childhood's hopes, that used to wake
If birds were in a singing strain,
And for less cause, sleep again:
Of the moss seat in the wood,
Where I trysted solitude!
Of the hill-top, where the wind
Used to follow me behind,
Then in sudden rush to blind
Both my glad eyes with my hair,
Taken gladly in the snare!
Of the climbing up the rocks,—
Of the playing 'neath the oaks,
Which retain beneath them now
14

Only shadow of the bough :
Of the lying on the grass
While the clouds did overpass,
Only they, so lightly driven,
Seeming betwixt me and Heaven !
Of the little prayers serene,
Murmuring of earth and sin :
Of large-leaved philosophy
Leaning from my childish knee :
Of poetic book sublime,
Soul-kissed for the first dear time,—
Greek or English,—ere I knew
Life was not a poem too !
Throw them in, by one and one !
I must laugh, at rising sun.

Of the glorious ambitions,
Yet unquenched by their fruitions ;
Of the reading out the nights ;
Of the straining of mad heights ;
Of achievements, less descried
By a dear few, than magnified ;
Of praises, from the many earned,
When praise from love was undiscerned ,
Of the sweet reflecting gladness,
Softened by itself to sadness.—
Throw them in, by one and one !
I must laugh, at rising sun.

What are these? more, more than these !
Throw in, dearer memories !—

Of voices—whereof but to speak,
Maketh mine all sunk and weak;
Of smiles, the thought of which is sweeping
All my soul to floods of weeping;
Of looks, whose absence fain would weigh
My looks to the ground for aye;
Of clasping hands—ah me!   I wring
Mine, and in a tremble fling
Downward, downward, all this paining!
Partings, with the sting remaining;
Meetings, with a deeper throe,
Since the joy is ruined so;
Changes, with a fiery burning—
(Shadows upon all the turning.)
Thoughts of—with a storm they came—
Them, I have not breath to name!
Downward, downward be they cast,
In the pit! and now at last
My work beneath the moon is done,
And I shall laugh, at rising sun.

But let me pause or ere I cover
All my treasures darkly over.
I will speak not in thine ears,
Only tell my beaded tears
Silently, most silently!
When the last is calmly told,
Let that same moist rosary,
With the rest sepùlchred be.
Finished now.   The darksome mould
Sealeth up the darksome pit.

I will lay no stone on it:
Grasses I will sow instead,
Fit for Queen Titania's tread;
Flowers, encoloured with the sun,
And ai ai written upon none.
Thus, whenever saileth by
The Lady World of dainty eye,
Not a grief shall here remain,
Silken shoon to damp or stain :
And while she lisps, 'I have not seen
Any place more smooth and clean ' . .
Here she cometh!—Ha, ha !—who
Laughs as loud as I can do ?

EARTH AND HER PRAISERS.

I.

THE Earth is old ;
Six thousand winters make her heart a-cold.
The sceptre slanteth from her palsied hold.
She saith, ' 'Las me !—God's word that I was 'good'
     Is taken back to heaven,
From whence when any sound comes, I am riven
By some sharp bolt.   And now no angel would
Descend with sweet dew-silence on my mountains,
To glorify the lovely river-fountains
     That gush along their side.
I see, O weary change ! I see instead
     This human wrath and pride,
These thrones, and tombs, judicial wrong, and blood :
And bitter words are poured upon mine head—
' O Earth ! thou art a stage for tricks unholy,
A church for most remorseful melancholy !
Thou art so spoilt, we should forget we had
An Eden in thee,—wert thou not so sad.'
Sweet children, I am old ! ye, every one,
Do keep me from a portion of my sun :
     Give praise in change for brightness !
That I may shake my hills in infiniteness

Of breezy laughter, as in youthful mirth,
To hear Earth's sons and daughters praising Earth.'

II.

Whereupon a child began,
With spirit running up to man,
As by angel's shining ladder,
(May he find no cloud above!)
Seeming he had ne'er been sadder
    All his days than now—
Sitting in the chestnut grove,
With that joyous overflow
Of smiling from his mouth, o'er brow
And cheek and chin, as if the breeze
Leaning tricksy from the trees
To part his golden hairs, had blown
Into an hundred smiles that one.

III.

' O rare, rare Earth!' he saith,
    ' I will praise thee presently;
Not to-day; I have no breath!
    I have hunted squirrels three—
Two ran down in the furzy hollow,
Where I could not see nor follow;
One sits at the top of the filbert tree,
With a yellow nut, and a mock at me.
        Presently it shall be done.
When I see which way those two have run;
When the mocking one at the filbert-top
Shall leap a-down, and beside me stop;

Then, rare Earth, rare Earth,
Will I pause, having known thy worth,
  To say all good of thee!'

IV.

Next a lover, with a dream
'Neath his waking eyelids hidden,
And a frequent sigh unbidden,
And an idlesse all the day
Beside a wandering stream ;
And a silence that is made
Of a word he dares not say,—
Shakes slow his pensive head.
  ' Earth, Earth!' saith he.
' If spirits, like thy roses, grew
On one stalk, and winds austere
Could but only blow them near,
  To share each other's dew ;
If, when summer rains agree
To beautify thy hills, I knew
Looking off them I might see
  Some one very beauteous too,—
    Then Earth,' saith he,
' I would praise . . . nay, nay—*not thee!* '

V.

Will the pedant name her next?
Crabbed with a crabbed text,
Sits he in his study nook,
With his elbow on a book,
And with stately crossed knees,

And a wrinkle deeply thrid
Through his lowering brow,
Caused by making proofs enow
That Plato in 'Parmenides'
Meant the same Spinosa did;
Or, that an hundred of the groping
Like himself, had made one Homer,
Homeros being a misnomer.
What hath *he* to do with praise
Of Earth, or aught? whene'er the sloping
Sunbeams through his window daze
His eyes off from the learned phrase,
Straightway he draws close the curtain.
May abstraction keep him dumb!
Were his lips to ope, 'tis certain
" Derivatum est" would come.

VI.

Then a mourner moveth pale
In a silence full of wail,
Raising not his sunken head,
Because he wandered last that way
With that one beneath the clay:
Weeping not, because that one,
The only one who would have said,
' Cease to weep, beloved!' has gone
Whence returneth comfort none.
The silence breaketh suddenly,—
' Earth, I praise thee!' crieth he:
' Thou hast a grave for also *me*. '

VII.

Ha, a poet ! know him by
The ecstasy-dilated eye,
Not uncharged with tears that ran
Upward from his heart of man ;
By the cheek, from hour to hour,
Kindled bright or sunken wan
With a sense of lonely power ;
By the brow, uplifted higher
Than others, for more low declining ;
By the lip which words of fire
Overboiling have burned white,
While they gave the nations light !
Ay, in every time and place
Ye may know the poet's face
   By the shade, or shining.

VIII.

'Neath a golden cloud he stands,
Spreading his impassioned hands.
' O God's Earth ! ' he saith, ' the sign
From the Father-soul to mine
Of all beauteous mysteries,
Of all perfect images,
Which, divine in His divine.
In my human only are
Very excellent and fair ;—
Think not, Earth, that I would raise
Weary forehead in thy praise,
(Weary, that I cannot go
Farther from thy region low,)

If were struck no richer meanings
From thee than thyself.   The leanings
Of the close trees o'er the brim
Of a sunshine-haunted stream,
Have a sound beneath their leaves,
   Not of wind, not of wind,
Which the poet's voice achieves.
The faint mountains heaped behind,
Have a falling on their tops,
   Not of dew, not of dew,
Which the poet's fancy drops.
Viewless things his eyes can view:
Driftings of his dream do light
All the skies by day and night:
And the seas that deepest roll,
Carry murmurs of his soul.
Earth, I praise thee! praise thou *me!*
God perfecteth his creation
With this recipient poet-passion,
And makes the beautiful to be.
I praise thee, O beloved sign,
From the God-soul unto mine!
Praise me, that I cast on thee
The cunning sweet interpretation,
The help and glory and dilation
   Of mine immortality!'

IX.

There was silence.   None did dare
To use again the spoken air
Of that far-charming voice, until

A Christian resting on the hill,
With a thoughtful smile subdued
(Seeming learnt in solitude)
Which a weeper might have viewed
Without new tears, did softly say,
And looked up unto heaven alway
While he praised the Earth—
                    ' O Earth,
I count the praises thou art worth,
By thy waves that move aloud,
By thy hills against the cloud,
By thy valleys warm and green,
By the copses' elms between ;
By their birds which, like a sprite
Scattered by a strong delight
Into fragments musical,
Stir and sing in every bush ;
By thy silver founts that fall,
As if to entice the stars at night
To thine heart ; by grass and rush,
And little weeds the children pull,
Mistook for flowers !
                    —Oh, beautiful
Art thou, Earth, albeit worse
Than in heaven is called good !
Good to us, that we may know
Meekly from thy good to go ;
While the holy, crying Blood
Puts its music kind and low,
'Twixt such ears as are not dull,
    And thine ancient curse !

X.

' Praised be the mosses soft
In thy forest pathways oft,
And the thorns, which make us think
Of the thornless river-brink,
  Where the ransomed tread!
Praised be thy sunny gleams,
And the storm, that worketh dreams
  Of calm unfinished!
Praised be thine active days,
And thy night-time's solemn need,
When in God's dear book we read
  No night shall be therein.
Praised be thy dwellings warm,
By household faggot's cheerful blaze,
Where, to hear of pardoned sin,
Pauseth oft the merry din,
Save the babe's upon the arm,
Who croweth to the crackling wood.
Yea,—and better understood,
Praised be thy dwellings cold,
Hid beneath the churchyard mould,
Where the bodies of the saints,
Separate from earthly taints,
Lie asleep, in blessing bound,
Waiting for the trumpet's sound
To free them into blessing ;—none
Weeping more beneath the sun,
Though dangerous words of human love
Be graven very near, above.

XI.

' Earth, we Christians praise thee thus,
Even for the change that comes,
With a grief, from thee to us !
For thy cradles and thy tombs ;
For the pleasant corn and wine,
And summer-heat ; and also for
The frost upon the sycamore,
   And hail upon the vine ! '
15

THE VIRGIN MARY TO THE CHILD JESUS.

But see, the Virgin blest
Hath laid her babe to rest.
MILTON'S *Hymn on the Nativity.*

I.

SLEEP, sleep, mine Holy One!
My flesh, my Lord!—what name? I do not know
A name that seemeth not too high or low,
    Too far from me or Heaven.
My Jesus, *that* is best! that word being given
By the majestic angel whose command
Was softly as a man's beseeching said,
When I and all the earth appeared to stand
    In the great overflow
Of light celestial from his wings and head.
    Sleep, sleep, my saving One!

II.

And art Thou come for saving, baby-browed
And speechless Being—art Thou come for saving?
The palm that grows beside our door is bowed

By treadings of the low wind from the south,
A restless shadow through the chamber waving :
Upon its bough a bird sings in the sun ;
But Thou, with that close slumber on thy mouth,
Dost seem of wind and sun already weary.
Art come for saving, O my weary One ?

III.

Perchance this sleep that shutteth out the dreary
Earth-sounds and motions, opens on Thy soul
    High dreams on fire with God ;
High songs that make the pathways where they
    roll
More bright than stars do theirs ; and visions new
Of Thine eternal Nature's old abode.
    Suffer this mother's kiss,
    Best thing that earthly is,
To glide the music and the glory through,
Nor narrow in Thy dream the broad upliftings
    Of any seraph wing !
Thus, noiseless, thus.   Sleep, sleep, my dreaming
    One !

IV.

The slumber of His lips meseems to run
Through *my* lips to mine heart ; to all its shiftings
Of sensual life, bringing contrariousness
In a great calm.   I feel, I could lie down
As Moses did, and die,*—and then live most.

* It is a Jewish tradition that Moses died of the kisses of God's lips.

I am 'ware of you, heavenly Presences,
That stand with your peculiar light unlost,
Each forehead with a high thought for a crown,
Unsunned i' the sunshine! I am 'ware. Yet throw
No shade against the wall! How motionless
Ye round me with your living statuary,
While through your whiteness, in and outwardly,
Continual thoughts of God appear to go,
Like light's soul in itself! I bear, I bear,
To look upon the dropt lids of your eyes,
Though their external shining testifies
To that beatitude within, which were
Enough to blast an eagle at his sun.
I fall not on my sad clay face before ye;
   I look on His. I know
My spirit which dilateth with the woe
  Of His mortality,
  May well contain your glory.
  Yea, drop your lids more low.
Ye are but fellow-worshippers with me!
  Sleep, sleep, my worshipped One!

     v.

We sate among the stalls at Bethlehem.
The dumb kine from their fodder turning them,
  Softened their horned faces
  To almost human gazes
  Toward the newly Born.
The simple shepherds from the star-lit brooks
  Brought visionary looks,
As yet in their astonied hearing rung

The strange, sweet angel-tongue.
The magi of the East, in sandals worn,
  Knelt reverent, sweeping round,
With long pale beards, their gifts upon the
 ground,
  The incense, myrrh and gold,
These baby hands were impotent to hold.
So, let all earthlies and celestials wait
  Upon thy royal state!
  Sleep, sleep, my kingly One!

VI.

I am not proud—meek angels, ye invest
New meeknesses to hear such utterance rest
On mortal lips,—' I am not proud '—*not proud!*
Albeit in my flesh God sent His Son,
Albeit over Him my head is bowed
As others bow before Him, still mine heart
Bows lower than their knees. O centuries
That roll, in vision, your futurities
  My future grave athwart,—
Whose murmurs seem to reach me while I keep
  Watch o'er this sleep,—
Say of me as the Heavenly said— ' Thou art
The blessedest of women ! '—blessedest,
Not holiest, not noblest—no high name,
Whose height misplaced may pierce me like a
 shame,
When I sit meek in heaven!
 15*

VII.

                    For me—for me—
God knows that I am feeble like the rest!—
I often wandered forth, more child than maiden,
Among the midnight hills of Galilee,
          Whose summits looked heaven-laden;
Listening to silence as it seemed to be
God's voice, so soft yet strong—so fain to press
Upon my heart as Heaven did on the height,
And waken up its shadows by a light,
And show its vileness by a holiness.
Then I knelt down most silent like the night,
          Too self-renounced for fears,
Raising my small face to the boundless blue
Whose stars did mix and tremble in my tears.
God heard *them* falling after—with his dew.

VIII.

So, seeing my corruption, can I see
This Incorruptible now born of me—
This fair new Innocence no sun did chance
To shine on, (for even Adam was no child,)
Created from my nature all defiled,
This mystery, from out mine ignorance,—
Nor feel the blindness, stain, corruption, more
Than others do, or *I* did heretofore?—
Can hands wherein such burden pure has been,
Not open with the cry 'unclean, unclean!'
More oft than any else beneath the skies?
          Ah King, ah Christ, ah son!
The kine, the shepherds, the abased wise,

Must all less lowly wait
Than I, upon thy state!—
Sleep, sleep, my kingly One!

IX.

Art Thou a King, then?   Come, His universe,
    Come, crown me Him a king!
Pluck rays from all such stars as never fling
    Their light where fell a curse,
And make a crowning for this kingly brow!—
What is my word?—Each empyreal star
        Sits in a sphere afar
        In shining ambuscade:
        The child-brow, crowned by none,
        Keeps its unchildlike shade.
        Sleep, sleep, my crownless One!

X.

Unchildlike shade!—no other babe doth wear
An aspect very sorrowful, as Thou.—
No small babe-smiles, my watching heart has seen,
To float like speech the speechless lips between;
No dovelike cooing in the golden air,
No quick short joys of leaping babyhood.
        Alas, our earthly good
In heaven thought evil, seems too good for Thee:
        Yet, sleep, my weary One!

XI.

And then the drear sharp tongue of prophecy,
With the dread sense of things which shall be done,

Doth smite me inly, like a sword—a sword :—
(*That* 'smites the Shepherd!') then, I think aloud
The words ' despised, '—' rejected,' —every word
Recoiling into darkness as I view
      The DARLING on my knee.
Bright angels,—move not !—lest ye stir the cloud
Betwixt my soul and His futurity !
I must not die, with mother's work to do,
      And could not live—and see.

XII.

It is enough to bear
This image still and fair—
This holier in sleep,
Than a saint at prayer :
This aspect of a child
Who never sinned or smiled—
This presence in an infant's face :
This sadness most like love,
This love than love more deep,
This weakness like omnipotence,
It is so strong to move !
Awful is this watching place,
Awful what I see from hence—
A king, without regalia,
A God, without the thunder,
A child, without the heart for play ;
Ay, a Creator rent asunder
From his first glory and cast away
On His own world, for me alone
To hold in hands created, crying—SON !

XIII.

That tear fell not on Thee
Beloved, yet Thou stirrest in thy slumber!
Thou, stirring not for glad sounds out of number
Which through the vibratory palm trees run
From summer wind and bird,
So quickly hast Thou heard
A tear fall silently?—
Wak'st Thou, O loving One?—

M

.

TO BETTINE,

THE CHILD-FRIEND OF GOETHE.

"I have the second sight, Goethe!"—*Letters of a child.*

I.

BETTINE, friend of Goethe,
Hadst thou the second sight—
Upturning worship and delight
   With such a loving duty
To his grand face, as women will,
The childhood 'neath thine eyelids still?

II.

Before his shrine to doom thee
Using the same child's smile
That heaven and earth, beheld erewhile
   For the first time, won from thee,
Ere star and flower grew dim and dead,
Save at his feet and o'er his head.

III.

Digging thine heart and throwing
Away its childhood's gold,
That so its woman-depth might hold
   His spirit's overflowing.
For surging souls, no worlds can bound,
Their channel in the heart have found.

IV.

O child, to change appointed,
Thou hadst not second sight!
What eyes the future view aright,
   Unless by tears anointed?
Yea, only tears themselves can show
The burning ones that have to flow.

V.

O woman, deeply loving,
Thou hadst not second sight!
The star is very high and bright,
   And none can see it moving.
Love looks around, below, above,
Yet all his prophecy is—love.

VI.

The bird thy childhood's playing
Sent onward o'er the sea,
Thy dove of hope came back to thee
   Without a leaf.   Art laying
Its wet cold wing no sun can dry,
Still in thy bosom secretly?

VII.

Our Goethe's friend, Bettine,
I have the second sight!
The stone upon his grave is white,
    The funeral stone between ye;
And in thy mirror thou hast viewed
Some change as hardly understood.

VIII.

Where's childhood? where is Goethe?
The tears are in thine eyes.
Nay, thou shalt yet reorganise
    Thy maidenhood of beauty
In his own glory, which is smooth
Of wrinkles and sublime in youth.

IX.

The poet's arms have wound thee,
He breathes upon thy brow,
He lifts thee upward in the glow
    Of his great genius round thee,—
The childlike poet undefiled
Preserving evermore THE CHILD.

FELICIA HEMANS.

To L. E. L., REFERRING TO HER MONODY ON THAT POETESS.

I.

Thou bay-crowned living One that o'er the bay-
    crowned Dead art bowing,

And o'er the shadeless moveless brow the vital
    shadow throwing;

And o'er the sighless songless lips the wail and
    music wedding;

And dropping o'er the tranquil eyes, the tears not of
    their shedding!—

II.

Take music from the silent Dead, whose meaning
    is completer;

Reserve thy tears for living brows, where all such
    tears are meeter;

And leave the violets in the grass to brighten where
    thou treadest!

No flowers for her! no need of flowers—albeit
    " bring flowers," thou saidest.

III.

Yes, flowers, to crown the "cup and lute!" since
    both may come to breaking:
Or flowers, to greet the 'bride!' the heart's own
    beating works its aching:
Or flowers, to soothe the 'captive's' sight, from
    earth's free bosom gathered,
Reminding of his earthly hope, then withering as it
    withered!

IV.

But bring not near the solemn corse, a type of
    human seeming!
Lay only dust's stern verity upon the dust undream-
    ing.
And while the calm perpetual stars shall look upon
    it solely,
Her spherëd soul shall look on *them*, with eyes more
    bright and holy.

V.

Nor mourn, O living One, because her part in life
    was mourning.
Would she have lost the poet's fire for anguish of
    the burning?—
The minstrel harp, for the strained string? the
    tripod, for the afflated
Woe? or the vision, for those tears in which it
    shone dilated?

VI.

Perhaps she shuddered while the world's cold hand
    her brow was wreathing,
But never wronged that mystic breath which
    breathed in all her breathing;
Which drew from rocky earth and man, abstrac-
    tions high and moving—
Beauty, if not the beautiful, and love, if not the
    loving.

VII.

Such visionings have paled in sight: the Saviour
    she descrieth,
And little recks *who* wreathed the brow which on
    His bosom lieth.
The whiteness of His innocence o'er all her garments
    flowing,
There, learneth she the sweet 'new song,' she will
    not mourn in knowing.

VIII.

Be happy, crowned and living One! and, as thy
    dust decayeth,
May thine own England say for thee, what now for
    Her it sayeth—
' Albeit softly in our ears her silver song was ring-
    ing,
The foot-fall of her parting soul is softer than her
    singing!'

MEMORY AND HOPE.

I.

BACK-LOOKING Memory
And prophet Hope both sprang from out the ground :
One, where the flashing of Cherubic sword
    Fell sad, in Eden's ward ;
And one, from Eden earth, within the sound
Of the four rivers lapsing pleasantly,
What time the promise after curse was said—
    ' Thy seed shall bruise his head. '

II.

    Poor Memory's brain is wild,
As moonstruck by that flaming atmosphere
When she was born. Her deep eyes shine and shone
    With light that conquereth sun
And stars to wanner paleness year by year :
With odorous gums, she mixeth things defiled :
She trampleth down earth's grasses green and sweet,
    With her far-wandering feet.

III.

She plucketh many flowers,
Their beauty on her bosom's coldness killing :
She teacheth every melancholy sound
            To winds and waters round :
She droppeth tears with seed where man is tilling
The rugged soil in his exhausted hours :
She smileth—ah me! in her smile doth go
            A mood of deeper woe !

IV.

Hope tripped on out of sight
Crowned with an Eden wreath she saw not wither,
And went a-nodding through the wilderness
            With brow that shone no less
Than a sea-gull's wing, brought nearer by rough
                  weather ;
Searching the treeless rock for fruits of light ;
Her fair quick feet being armed from stones and
            By slippers of pure gold.   [cold,

V.

Memory did Hope much wrong
And, while she dreamed, her slippers stole away ;
But still she wended on with mirth unheeding,
            Although her feet were bleeding ;
Till Memory tracked her on a certain day,
And with most evil eyes did search her long
And cruelly, whereat she sank to ground
            In a stark deadly swound.

16*

VI.

And so my Hope were slain,
Had it not been that THOU wert standing near,
Oh Thou, who saidest 'live' to creatures lying
     In their own blood and dying!
For Thou her forehead to thine heart didst rear
And make its silent pulses sing again,—
Pouring a new light o'er her darkened eyne,
     With tender tears from Thine!

VII.

Therefore my Hope arose
From out her swound, and gazed upon Thy face;
And, meeting there that soft subduing look
     Which Peter's spirit shook,
Sank downward in a rapture to embrace
Thy piercèd hands and feet with kisses close,
And prayed Thee to assist her evermore
     To 'reach the things before.'

VIII.

Then gavest Thou the smile
Whence angel-wings thrill quick like summer light-
          ning,
Vouchsafing rest beside Thee, where she never
     From Love and Faith may sever;
Whereat the Eden crown she saw not whitening
A time ago, though whitening all the while,
Reddened with life, to hear the Voice which talked
     To Adam as he walked.

THE SLEEP.

He giveth His beloved sleep.—*Psalm* cxxvii. 2.

I.

Of all the thoughts of God that are
Borne inward unto souls afar,
Along the Psalmist's music deep,
Now tell me if that any is,
For gift or grace, surpassing this—
' He giveth His beloved, sleep ? '

II.

What would we give to our beloved ?
The hero's heart, to be unmoved,
The poet's star-tuned harp, to sweep,
The patriot's voice, to teach and rouse,
The monarch's crown, to light the brows ?—
' He giveth *His* beloved, sleep. '

III.

What do we give to our beloved?
A little faith all undisproved,
A little dust to overweep,
And bitter memories to make
The whole earth blasted for our sake.
' He giveth *His* beloved, sleep. '

IV.

' Sleep soft, beloved ! ' we sometimes say
But have no tune to charm away
Sad dreams that through the eyelids creep
But never doleful dream again
Shall break the happy slumber when
' He giveth *His* beloved, sleep. '

V.

O earth, so full of dreary noises !
O men, with wailing in your voices !
O delvëd gold, the wailers heap !
O strife, O curse, that o'er it fall !
God strikes a silence through you all,
And 'giveth His beloved, sleep. '

VI.

His dews drop mutely on the hill,
His cloud above it saileth still,
Though on its slope men sow and reap.
More softly than the dew is shed.
Or cloud is floated overhead,
' He giveth His beloved, sleep.

VII.

Ay, men may wonder while they scan
A living, thinking, feeling man,
Confirmed in such a rest to keep ;
But angels say—and through the word
I think their happy smile is *heard*—
' He giveth His beloved, sleep. '

VIII.

For me, my heart that erst did go
Most like a tired child at a show,
That sees through tears the mummers leap,
Would now its wearied vision close,
Would childlike on *His* love repose,
Who ' giveth His beloved, sleep ! '

IX.

And, friends, dear friends,—when it shall be
That this low breath is gone from me,
And round my bier ye come to weep,
Let one, most loving of you all,
Say, ' Not a tear must o'er her fall—
He giveth His beloved, sleep. '

MAN AND NATURE.

A sad man on a summer day
Did look upon the earth and say—

' Purple cloud the hill-top binding;
Folded hills, the valleys wind in;
Valleys, with fresh streams among you;
Streams, with bosky trees along you;
Trees, with many birds and blossoms;
Birds, with music-trembling bosoms;
Blossoms, dropping dews that wreathe you
To your fellow flowers beneath you;
Flowers, that constellate on earth;
Earth, that shakest to the mirth
Of the merry Titan ocean,
All his shining hair in motion!
Why am I thus the only one
Who can be dark beneath the sun?'

But when the summer day was past,
He looked to heaven and smiled at last.

Self answered so—

              ' Because, O cloud,
Pressing with thy crumpled shroud
Heavily on mountain top;
Hills that almost seem to drop,
Stricken with a misty death,
To the valleys underneath;
Valleys, sighing with the torrent;
Waters, streaked with branches horrent;
Branchless trees, that shake your head
Wildly o'er your blossoms spread
Where the common flowers are found;
Flowers, with foreheads to the ground;
Ground, that shriekest while the sea
With his iron smiteth thee—
I am, besides, the only one
Who can be bright *without* the sun.'

A SEA-SIDE WALK.

I.

We walked beside the sea
After a day which perished silently
Of its own glory—like the Princess weird
Who, combating the Genius, scorched and seared,
Uttered with burning breath, "Ho! victory!"
And sank adown an heap of ashes pale.
  So runs the Arab tale.

II.

The sky above us showed
An universal and unmoving cloud,
On which the cliffs permitted us to see
Only the outline of their majesty,
As master-minds, when gazed at by the crowd!
And, shining with a gloom, the water grey
  Swang in its moon-taught way.

III.

Nor moon, nor stars were out.
They did not dare to tread so soon about,

Though trembling, in the footsteps of the sun.
The light was neither night's nor day's, but one
Which, life-like, had a beauty in its doubt:
And Silence's impassioned breathings round
    Seemed wandering into sound.

IV.

    O solemn-beating heart
Of nature! I have knowledge that thou art
Bound unto man's by cords he cannot sever—
And, what time they are slackened by him ever,
So to attest his own supernal part,
Still runneth thy vibration fast and strong,
    The slackened cord along.

V.

    For though we never spoke
Of the grey water and the shaded rock,
Dark wave and stone unconsciously were fused
Into the plaintive speaking that we used
Of absent friends and memories unforsook;
And, had we seen each other's face, we had
    Seen haply, each was sad.

17   N

THE SEA-MEW.

AFFECTIONATELY INSCRIBED TO M. E. H.

I.

How joyously the young sea-mew
Lay dreaming on the waters blue,
Whereon our little bark had thrown
A forward shade, the only one,
But shadows ever man pursue.

II.

Familiar with the waves and free
As if their own white foam were he,
His heart upon the heart of ocean
Lay learning all its mystic motion,
And throbbing to the throbbing sea.

III.

And such a brightness in his eye,
As if the ocean and the sky
Within him had lit up and nurst
A soul God gave him not at first,
To comprehend their majesty.

IV.

We were not cruel, yet did sunder
His white wing from the blue waves under,
And bound it, while his fearless eyes
Shone up to ours in calm surprise,
As deeming us some ocean wonder!

V.

We bore our ocean bird unto
A grassy place, where he might view
The flowers that curtsey to the bees,
The waving of the tall green trees,
The falling of the silver dew.

VI.

But flowers of earth were pale to him
Who had seen the rainbow fishes swim;
And when earth's dew around him lay
He thought of ocean's winged spray,
And his eye waxëd sad and dim.

VII.

The green trees round him only made
A prison with their darksome shade:
And drooped his wing, and mournëd he
For his own boundless glittering sea—
Albeit he knew not they could fade.

VIII.

Then One her gladsome face did bring,
Her gentle voice's murmuring,
In ocean's stead his heart to move
And teach him what was human love—
He thought it a strange, mournful thing.

IX.

He lay down in his grief to die,
(First looking to the sea-like sky
That hath no waves!) because, alas!
Our human touch did on him pass,
And with our touch, our agony.

MY DOVES.

O Weisheit! Du red'st wie eine Taube!
GOETHE.

My little doves have left a nest
   Upon an Indian tree,
Whose leaves fantastic take their rest
   Or motion from the sea:
For, ever there, the sea-winds go
With sun-lit paces to and fro.

The tropic flowers looked up to it,
   The tropic stars looked down,
And there my little doves did sit,
   With feathers softly brown,
And glittering eyes that showed their right
To general Nature's deep delight.

And God them taught, at every close
   Of murmuring waves beyond,
And green leaves round, to interpose
   Their choral voices fond;
Interpreting that love must be
The meaning of the earth and sea.

Fit ministers!   Of living loves,
   Theirs hath the calmest fashion;
Their living voice the likest moves
   To lifeless intonation,
Their lovely monotone of springs
And winds and such insensate things.

My little doves were ta'en away
   From that glad nest of theirs,
Across an ocean rolling grey,
   And tempest-clouded airs.
My little doves!—who lately knew
The sky and wave by warmth and blue!

And now, within the city prison,
   In mist and chillness pent,
With sudden upward look they listen
   For sounds of past content—
For lapse of water, swell of breeze,
Or nut-fruit falling from the trees.

The stir without the glow of passion—
   The triumph of the mart—
The gold and silver as they clash on
   Man's cold metallic heart—
The roar of wheels, the cry for bread,—
These only sounds are heard instead.

Yet still, as on my human hand
   Their fearless heads they lean,
And almost seem to understand

What human musings mean—
(Their eyes, with such a plaintive shine,
Are fastened upwardly to mine!)

Soft falls their chant as on the nest,
   Beneath the sunny zone;
For love that stirred it in their breast
   Has not aweary grown,
And 'neath the city's shade can keep
The well of music clear and deep.

And love that keeps the music, fills
   With pastoral memories:
All echoings from out the hills,
   All droppings from the skies,
All flowings from the wave and wind,
Remembered in their chant, I find.

So teach ye me the wisest part,
   My little doves! to move
Along the city-ways with heart
   Assured by holy love,
And vocal with such songs as own
A fountain to the world unknown.

'Twas hard to sing by Babel's stream—
   More hard, in Babel's street!
But if the soulless creatures deem
   Their music not unmeet
For sunless walls—let *us* begin,
Who wear immortal wings within!

To me, fair memories belong
   Of scenes that used to bless;
For no regret, but present song,
   And lasting thankfulness;
And very soon to break away,
Like types, in purer things than they.

I will have hopes that cannot fade,
   For flowers the valley yields:
I will have humble thoughts instead
Of silent, dewy fields:
My spirit and my God shall be
My sea-ward hill, my boundless sea!

TO MARY RUSSELL MITFORD,

IN HER GARDEN.

WHAT time I lay these rhymes anear thy feet,
Benignant friend ! I will not proudly say
As better poets use, ' These *flowers* I lay,'
Because I would not wrong thy roses sweet,
Blaspheming so their name. And yet, repeat
Thou, overleaning them this springtime day,
With heart as open to love as theirs to May,
' Low-rooted verse may reach some heavenly heat,
Even like my blossoms, if as nature-true,
Though not as precious. ' Thou art unperplext,
Dear friend, in whose dear writings drops the dew
And blow the natural airs ; thou, who art next
To nature's self in cheering the world's view,
To preach a sermon on so known a text !

THE EXILE'S RETURN.

I

WHEN from thee, weeping I removed,
   And from my land for years,
I thought not to return, Beloved,
   With those same parting tears.
I come again to hill and lea,
   Weeping for thee.

II.

I clasped thine hand when standing last
   Upon the shore in sight.
The land is green, the ship is fast,
   I shall be there to-night!
I shall be there—no longer *we*—
   No more with thee.

III.

Had I beheld thee dead and still,
   I might more clearly know,
How heart of thine could turn as chill
   As hearts by nature so;
How change could touch the falsehood-free
   And changeless *thee!*

IV.

But now thy fervid looks last-seen
   Within my soul remain,
'Tis hard to think that *they* have been,
   To be no more again—
That I shall vainly wait—ah me!
   A word from thee.

V.

I could not bear to look upon
   That mound of funeral clay,
Where one sweet voice is silence,—one
   Æthereal brow decay:
Where all thy mortal I may see,
   But never thee.

VI.

For thou art where all friends are gone
   Whose parting pain is o'er :
And I who love and weep alone,
   Where thou wilt weep no more,
Weep bitterly and selfishly,
   For *me*, not *thee*.

VII.

I know, Beloved, thou canst not know
   That I endure this pain !
For saints in Heaven, the Scriptures show
   Can never grieve again—
And grief known mine, even there, would be
   Still shared by thee !

A SONG AGAINST SINGING.

TO E. J. H.

I.

They bid me sing to thee,
Thou golden-haired and silver-voicèd child,
With lips by no worse sigh than sleep's defiled;
With eyes unknowing how tears dim the sight;
With feet all trembling at the new delight
    Treaders of earth to be!

II.

Ah no! the lark may bring
A song to thee from out the morning cloud;
The merry river from its lilies bowed;
The brisk rain from the trees; the lucky wind,
That half doth make its music, half doth find:
    But *I*—I may not sing.

III.

How could I think it right,
New-comer on our earth as, Sweet, thou art.
To bring a verse from out an human heart
Made heavy with accumulated tears,
And cross with such amount of weary years
    Thy day-sum of delight!

IV.

E'en if the verse were said,
Thou, who wouldst clap thy tiny hands to hear
The wind or rain, gay bird or river clear,
Wouldst, at that sound of sad humanities,
Upturn thy bright uncomprehending eyes
    And bid me play instead.

V.

    Therefore no song of mine!
But prayer in place of singing! prayer that would
Commend thee to the new-creating God,
Whose gift is childhood's heart without its stain
Of weakness, ignorance, and changing vain—
    That gift of God be thine!

VI.

    So wilt thou aye be young,
In lovelier childhood than thy shining brow
And pretty winning accents make thee now!
Yea, sweeter than this scarce articulate sound
(How sweet!) of ' father,' ' mother,' shall be
        found
    The ABBA on thy tongue.

VII.

    And so, as years shall chase
Each other's shadows, thou wilt less resemble
Thy fellows of the earth who toil and tremble,
Than him thou seest not, thine angel bold
Yet meek, whose ever-lifted eyes behold
    The Ever-loving's face.

18

THE MEASURE.

"He comprehended the dust of the earth in a measure (שָׁלִישׁ)."
                                                        Isaiah xl.

"Thou givest them tears to drink in a measure (שָׁלִישׁ)."*
                                                        Psalm lxxx.

God, the Creator, with a pulseless hand
Of unoriginated power, hath weighed
The dust of earth and tears of man in one
      Measure and by one weight:
      So saith His holy book.

Shall *we*, then, who have issued from the dust,
And there return,—shall *we*, who toil for dust,
And wrap our winnings in this dusty life,
      Say, ' No more tears, Lord God !
      The measure runneth o'er ? '

Oh, holder of the balance, laughest Thou ?
Nay, Lord ! be gentler to our foolishness,
For His sake who assumed our dust and turns
      On thee pathetic eyes
      Still moistened with our tears !

And teach us, O our Father, while we weep,
To look in patience upon earth and learn—
Waiting in that meek gesture, till at last
      These tearful eyes be filled
      With the dry dust of death !

* I believe that the word occurs in no other part of the Hebrew Scriptures.

COWPER'S GRAVE.

I.

It is a place where poets crowned may feel the
  heart's decaying.
It is a place where happy saints may weep amid
  their praying:
Yet let the grief and humbleness, as low as silence,
  languish!
Earth surely now may give her calm to whom she
  gave her anguish.

II.

O poets! from a maniac's tongue was poured the
  deathless singing!
O Christians! at your cross of hope, a hopeless hand
  was clinging!
O men! this man in brotherhood your weary paths
  beguiling,
Groaned inly while he taught you peace, and died
  while ye were smiling!

III.

And now, what time ye all may read through dim-
    ming tears his story,
How discord on the music fell, and darkness on the
    glory,
And how when one by one, sweet sounds and wan-
    dering lights departed,
He wore no less a loving face because so broken-
    hearted ;

IV.

He shall be strong to sanctify the poet's high voca-
    tion,
And bow the meekest Christian down in meeker
    adoration :
Nor ever shall he be, in praise, by wise or good
    forsaken ;
Named softly as the household name of one whom
    God hath taken.

V.

With quiet sadness and no gloom I learn to think
    upon him,
With meekness that is gratefulness to God whose
    heaven hath won him—
Who suffered once the madness-cloud to His own
    love to blind him ;
But gently led the blind along where breath and
    bird could find him ;

VI.

And wrought within his shattered brain such quick
    poetic senses
As hills have language for, and stars, harmonious
    influences!
The pulse of dew upon the grass, kept his within its
    number;
And silent shadows from the trees refreshed him
    like a slumber.

VII.

Wild timid hares were drawn from woods to share
    his home-caresses,
Uplooking to his human eyes with sylvan tender-
    nesses :
The very world, by God's constraint, from false-
    hood's ways removing,
Its women and its men became beside him, true and
    loving.

VIII.

But though in blindness he remained unconscious of
    that guiding,
And things provided came without the sweet sense
    of providing,
He testified this solemn truth, while phrenzy deso-
    lated—
Nor man nor nature satisfy whom only God
    created!

IX.

Like a sick child that knoweth not his mother while
    she blesses
And drops upon his burning brow the coolness of
    her kisses ;
That turns his fevered eyes around— ' My mother !
    where's my mother ? '—
As if such tender words and deeds could come from
    any other !—

X.

The fever gone, with leaps of heart he sees her
    bending o'er him ;
Her face all pale from watchful love, the unweary
    love she bore him !—
Thus, woke the poet from the dream his life's long
    fever gave him,
Beneath those deep pathetic Eyes, which closed in
    death to save him !

XI.

Thus ? oh, not *thus !* no type of earth an image
    that awaking,
Wherein he scarcely heard the chant of seraphs,
    round him breaking,
Or felt the new immortal throb of soul from body
    parted ;
But felt *those eyes alone*, and knew ' *My* Saviour !
    not deserted ! '

XII.

Deserted! who hath dreamt that when the cross in
    darkness rested,
Upon the Victim's hidden face, no love was mani-
    fested?
What frantic hands outstretched have e'er the ato
    ning drops averted,
What tears have washed them from the soul, that
    one should be deserted?

XIII.

Deserted! God could separate from His own essence
    rather:
And Adam's sins *have* swept between the righteous
    Son and Father;
Yea, once, Immanuel's orphaned cry his universe
    hath shaken—
It went up single, echoless, 'My God, I am for-
    saken!'

XIV.

It went up from the Holy's lips amid his lost crea-
    tion,
That, of the lost, no son should use those words of
    desolation;
That earth's worst phrenzies, marring hope, should
    mar not hope's fruition,
And I, on Cowper's grave, should see his rapture
    in a vision!

THE WEAKEST THING.

I.

Which is the weakest thing of all
  Mine heart can ponder?
The sun, a little cloud can pall
  With darkness yonder?
The cloud, a little wind can move
  Where'er it listeth?
The wind, a little leaf above,
  Though sere, resisteth?

II.

What time that yellow leaf was green,
  My days were gladder;
But now, whatever Spring may mean,
  I must grow sadder.
Ah me! a *leaf* with sighs can wring
  My lips asunder—
Then is mine heart the weakest thing
  Itself can ponder.

III.

Yet, Heart, when sun and cloud are pined
  And drop together,
And at a blast which is not wind,
  The forests wither,
Thou, from the darkening deathly curse,
  To glory breakest,—
The Strongest of the universe
  Guarding the weakest!

THE PET-NAME.

—— the name
Which from THEIR lips seemed a caress.
MISS MITFORD'S *Dramatic Scenes.*

I.

I HAVE a name, a little name,
  Uncadenced for the ear,
Unhonoured by ancestral claim,
Unsanctified by prayer and psalm
  The solemn font anear.

II.

It never did, to pages wove
  For gay romance, belong.
It never dedicate did move
As 'Sacharissa,' unto love—
  'Orinda,' unto song.

III.

Though I write books, it will be read
  Upon the leaves of none,
And afterward, when I am dead,

Will ne'er be graved for sight or tread,
　Across my funeral stone.

IV.

This name, whoever chance to call,
　Perhaps your smile may win.
Nay, do not smile! mine eyelids fall
Over mine eyes, and feel withal
　The sudden tears within.

V.

Is there a leaf that greenly grows
　Where summer meadows bloom
But gathereth the winter snows,
And changeth to the hue of those,
　If lasting till they come?

VI.

Is there a word, or jest, or game,
　But time encrusteth round
With sad associate thoughts the same?
And so to me my very name
　Assumes a mournful sound.

VII.

My brother gave that name to me
　When we were children twain;
When names acquired baptismally
'Were hard to utter, as to see
　That life had any pain.

VIII.

No shade was on us then, save one
   Of chesnuts from the hill—
And through the word our laugh did run
As part thereof.   The mirth being done,
   He calls me by it still.

IX.

Nay, do not smile! I hear in it
   What none of you can hear!
The talk upon the willow seat,
The bird and wind that did repeat
   Around, our human cheer.

X.

I hear the birthday's noisy bliss,
   My sisters' woodland glee,—
My father's praise, I did not miss,
When stooping down he cared to kiss
   The poet at his knee;—

XI.

And voices, which to name me, aye
   Their tenderest tones were keeping!—
· To some I never more can say
An answer, till God wipes away
   In heaven these drops of weeping.

XII.

My name to me a sadness wears;
   No murmurs cross my mind:
Now God be thanked for these thick tears,

Which show, of those departed years,
   Sweet memories left behind!

XIII.

Now God be thanked for years enwrought
   With love which softens yet!
Now God be thanked for every thought
Which is so tender it has caught
   Earth's guerdon of regret!

XIV.

Earth saddens, never shall remove,
   Affections purely given;
And e'en that mortal grief shall prove
The immortality of love,
   And brighten it with Heaven.
   19

TO FLUSH, MY DOG.

Loving friend, the gift of one
Who her own true faith hath run,
   Through thy lower nature ;*
Be my benediction said
With my hand upon thy head,
   Gentle fellow-creature !

Like a lady's ringlets brown,
Flow thy silken ears adown
   Either side demurely
Of thy silver-suited breast
Shining out from all the rest
   Of thy body purely.

Darkly brown thy body is,
Till the sunshine striking this
   Alchemise its dulness ;
When the sleek curls manifold
Flash all over into gold,
   With a burnished fulness

---

* This dog was the gift of my dear and admired friend, Miss Mitford,
and belongs to the beautiful race she has rendered celebrated among
English and American readers. The Flushes have their laurels as wel.
as the Cæsars.—the chief difference (at least the very head and front
of it) consisting. perhaps, in the bald head of the latter under the
crown.

Underneath my stroking hand,
Startled eyes of hazel bland
  Kindling, growing larger,
Up thou leapest with a spring,
Full of prank and curveting,
  Leaping like a charger.

Leap! thy broad tail waves a light;
Leap! thy slender feet are bright,
  Canopied in fringes.
Leap—those tasselled ears of thine
Flicker strangely, fair and fine,
  Down their golden inches.

Yet, my pretty, sportive friend,
Little is 't to such an end
  That I praise thy rareness!
Other dogs may be thy peers
Haply in these drooping ears,
  And this glossy fairness.

But of *thee* it shall be said,
This dog watched beside a bed
  Day and night unweary,—
Watched within a curtained room,
Where no sunbeam brake the gloom
  Round the sick and dreary.

Roses, gathered for a vase,
In that chamber died apace,
  Beam and breeze resigning—

This dog only, waited on,
Knowing that when light is gone,
   Love remains for shining.

Other dogs in thymy dew
Tracked the hares and followed through
   Sunny moor or meadow—
This dog only, crept and crept
Next a languid cheek that slept,
   Sharing in the shadow.

Other dogs of loyal cheer
Bounded at the whistle clear,
   Up the woodside hieing—
This dog only, watched in reach
Of a faintly uttered speech,
   Or a louder sighing.

And if one or two quick tears
Dropped upon his glossy ears,
   Or a sigh came double,—
Up he sprang in eager haste,
Fawning, fondling, breathing fast,
   In a tender trouble.

And this dog was satisfied
If a pale thin hand would glide
   Down his dewlaps sloping,—
Which he pushed his nose within,
After,—platforming his chin
   On the palm left open

TO FLUSH, MY DOG.

This dog, if a friendly voice
Call him now to blyther choice
   Than such chamber-keeping,
' Come out !' praying from the door,—
Presseth backward as before,
   Up against me leaping.

Therefore to this dog will I,
Tenderly not scornfully,
   Render praise and favor :
With my hand upon his head,
Is my benediction said
   Therefore, and for ever.

And because he loves me so,
Better than his kind will do
   Often, man or woman,
Give I back more love again
Than dogs often take of men,
   Leaning from my Human.

Blessings on thee, dog of mine,
Pretty collars make thee fine,
   Sugared milk make fat thee !
Pleasures wag on in thy tail—
Hands of gentle motion fail
   Nevermore, to pat thee !

Downy pillow take thy head,
Silken coverlid bestead,
   Sunshine help thy sleeping !

No fly's buzzing wake thee up—
No man break thy purple cup,
   Set for drinking deep in.

Whiskered cats arointed flee—
Sturdy stoppers keep from thee
   Cologne distillations ;
Nuts lie in thy path for stones,
And thy feast-day macaroons
   Turn to daily rations !

Mock I thee, in wishing weal ?—
Tears are in my eyes to feel
   Thou art made so straightly,
Blessing needs must straighten too,—
Little canst thou joy or do,
   Thou who lovest *greatly*.

Yet be blessed to the height
Of all good and all delight
   Pervious to thy nature,
Only *loved* beyond that line,
With a love that answers thine,
   Loving fellow-creature !

SONNETS.

BEREAVEMENT.

WHEN some Beloveds, 'neath whose eyelids lay
The sweet lights of my childhood, one by one
Did leave me dark before the natural sun,
And I astonied fell, and could not pray,
A thought within me to myself did say,
'Is God less God that *thou* art left undone?
Rise, worship, bless Him, in this sackcloth spun,
As in that purple!'—But I answered, Nay!
What child his filial heart in words can loose,
If he behold his tender father raise
The hand that chastens sorely? can he choose
But sob in silence with an upward gaze?—
And *my* great Father, thinking fit to bruise,
Discerns in speechless tears, both prayer and praise.

CONSOLATION.

ALL are not taken! there are left behind
Living Beloveds, tender looks to bring,

And make the daylight still a happy thing,
And tender voices, to make soft the wind.
But if it were not so—if I could find
No love in all the world for comforting,
Nor any path but hollowly did ring,
Where 'dust to dust' the love from life disjoined—
And if before those sepulchres unmoving
I stood alone, (as some forsaken lamb
Goes bleating up the moors in weary dearth)
Crying 'Where are ye, O my loved and loving?'...
I know a Voice would sound, 'Daughter, I AM.
Can I suffice for HEAVEN, and not for earth?'

THE SOUL'S EXPRESSION.

WITH stammering lips and insufficient sound
I strive and struggle to deliver right
That music of my nature, day and night
With dream and thought and feeling interwound,
And inly answering all the senses round
With octaves of a mystic depth and height
Which step out grandly to the infinite
From the dark edges of the sensual ground!
This song of soul I struggle to outbear
Through portals of the sense, sublime and whole,
And utter all myself into the air:
But if I did it,—as the thunder-roll
Breaks its own cloud,—my flesh would perish there,
Before that dread apocalypse of soul.

THE SERAPH AND POET.

THE seraph sings before the manifest
God-one, and in the burning of the Seven,
And with the full life of consummate Heaven
Heaving beneath him like a mother's breast
Warm with her first-born's slumber in that nest!
The poet sings upon the earth grave-riven :
Before the naughty world soon self-forgiven
For wronging him ; and in the darkness prest
From his own soul by worldly weights.   Even so,
Sing, seraph with the glory!   Heaven is high—
Sing, poet with the sorrow!   Earth is low.
The universe's inward voices cry
' Amen ' to either song of joy and wo—
Sing seraph,—poet,—sing on equally

ON A PORTRAIT OF WORDSWORTH,

BY R. B. HAYDON.

WORDSWORTH upon Helvellyn!   Let the cloud
Ebb audibly along the mountain-wind,
Then break against the rock, and show behind
The lowland valleys floating up to crowd
The sense with beauty.   *He*, with forehead bowed
And humble-lidded eyes, as one inclined
Before the sovran thought of his own mind,
And very meek with inspirations proud,—
Takes here his rightful place as poet-priest
By the high-altar, singing prayer and prayer

P

To the higher Heavens.   A noble vision free
Our Haydon's hand has flung out from the mist !
No portrait this, with Academic air—
This is the poet and his poetry.

PAST AND FUTURE

My future will not copy fair my past
On any leaf but Heaven's.   Be fully done,
Supernal Will !   I would not fain be one
Who, satisfying thirst and breaking fast
Upon the fulness of the heart, at last
Says no grace after meat.   My wine hath run
Indeed out of my cup, and there is none
To gather up the bread of my repast
Scattered and trampled ;—yet·I find some good
In earth's green herbs, and streams that bubble up
Clear from the darkling ground,—content until
I sit with angels before better food.
Dear Christ ! when thy new vintage fills my cup,
This hand shall shake no more, nor that wine spill

IRREPARABLENESS.

I HAVE been in the meadows all the day
And gathered there the nosegay that you see ;
Singing within myself as bird or bee
When such do field-work on a morn of May :
But now I look upon my flowers,—decay
Has met them in my hands more fatally

Because more warmly clasped; and sobs are free
To come instead of songs.   What do you say,
Sweet counsellors, dear friends? that I should go
Back straightway to the fields, and gather more?
Another, sooth, may do it,—but not I:
My heart is very tired—my strength is low—
My hands are full of blossoms plucked before,
Held dead within them till myself shall die.

TEARS.

THANK God, bless God, all ye who suffer not
More grief than ye can weep for.   That is well—
That is light grieving! lighter, none befell,
Since Adam forfeited the primal lot.
Tears! what are tears?   The babe weeps in its cot,
The mother singing; at her marriage-bell
The bride weeps; and before the oracle
Of high-faned hills, the poet has forgot
Such moisture on his cheeks.   Thank God for grace,
Ye who weep only! If, as some have done,
Ye grope tear-blinded in a desert place,
And touch but tombs,—look up! Those tears will run
Soon in long rivers down the lifted face,
And leave the vision clear for stars and sun.

GRIEF.

I TELL you, hopeless grief is passionless—
That only men incredulous of despair,

Half-taught in anguish, through the midnight air
Beat upward to God's throne in loud access
Of shrieking and reproach.   Full desertness
In souls as countries, lieth silent-bare
Under the blanching, vertical eye-glare
Of the absolute Heavens.   Deep-hearted man, express
Grief for thy Dead in silence like to death ;
Most like a monumental statue set
In everlasting watch and moveless wo,
Till itself crumble to the dust beneath.
Touch it : the marble eyelids are not wet—
If it could weep, it could arise and go.

SUBSTITUTION

WHEN some beloved voice that was to you
Both sound and sweetness, faileth suddenly,
And silence against which you dare not cry,
Aches round you like a strong disease and new—
What hope ? what help ? what music will undo
That silence to your sense ?   Not friendship's sigh—
Not reason's subtle count !   Not melody
Of viols, nor of pipes that Faunus blew—
Not songs of poets, nor of nightingales,
Whose hearts leap upward through the cypress trees
To the clear moon ; nor yet the spheric laws
Self-chanted,—nor the angels' sweet All hails,
Met in the smile of God.   Nay, none of these.
Speak THOU, availing Christ !—and fill this pause.

COMFORT

Speak low to me, my Saviour, low and sweet
From out the hallelujahs, sweet and low,
Lest I should fear and fall, and miss thee so
Who art not missed by any that entreat.
Speak to me as to Mary at thy feet—
And if no precious gums my hands bestow,
Let my tears drop like amber, while I go
In reach of thy divinest voice complete
In humanest affection—thus, in sooth,
To lose the sense of losing! As a child,
Whose song-bird seeks the wood for evermore,
Is sung to in its stead by mother's mouth ;
Till, sinking on her breast, love-reconciled,
He sleeps the faster that he wept before.

PERPLEXED MUSIC.

Experience, like a pale musician, holds
A dulcimer of patience in his hand
Whence harmonies we cannot understand,
Of God's will in His worlds, the strain unfolds
In sad, perplexed minors. Deathly colds
Fall on us while we hear and countermand
Our sanguine heart back from the fancy-land
With nightingales in visionary wolds.
We murmur,—' Where is any certain tune
Or measured music, in such notes as these ?'—

20

But angels, leaning from the golden seat,
Are not so minded : their fine ear hath won
The issue of completed cadences ;
And, smiling down the stars, they whisper—SWEET.

WORK.

What are we set on earth for ?   Say, to toil—
Nor seek to leave thy tending of the vines,
For all the heat o' the day, till it declines,
And Death's mild curfew shall from work assoil.
God did anoint thee with his odorous oil,
To wrestle, not to reign ; and He assigns
All thy tears over, like pure crystallines,
For younger fellow-workers of the soil
To wear for amulets.   So others shall
Take patience, labor, to their heart and hand,
From thy hand, and thy heart, and thy brave cheer,
And God's grace fructify through thee to all.
The least flower, with a brimming cup, may stand
And share its dew-drop with another near.

FUTURITY.

AND, O beloved voices, upon which
Ours passionately call, because erelong
Ye brake off in the middle of that song
We sang together softly, to enrich
The poor world with the sense of love, and witch
The heart out of things evil,—I am stron ,

Knowing ye are not lost for aye among
The hills, with last year's thrush.   God keeps a niche
In Heaven to hold our idols : and albeit
He brake them to our faces, and denied
That our close kisses should impair their white,—
I know we shall behold them raised, complete,
The dust swept from their beauty,—glorified
New Memnons singing in the great God-light

THE TWO SAYINGS.

Two sayings of the Holy Scriptures beat
Like pulses in the church's brow and breast ;
And by them, we find rest in our unrest,
And heart-deep in salt tears, do yet entreat
God's fellowship, as if on Heavenly seat.
The first is JESUS WEPT,—whereon is prest
Full many a sobbing face that drops its best
And sweetest waters on the record sweet :
And one is, where the Christ denied and scorned
LOOKED UPON PETER.   Oh, to render plain,
By help of having loved a little and mourned,
That look of sovran love and sovran pain
Which He who could not sin yet suffered, turned
On him who could reject but not sustain !

THE LOOK.

THE Saviour looked on Peter.   Ay, no word—
No gesture of reproach !   The Heavens serene

Though heavy with armed justice, did not lean
Their thunders that way.   The forsaken Lord
Looked only, on the traitor.   None record
What that look was ; none guess : for those who have
      seen
Wronged lovers loving through a death-pang keen,
Or pale-cheeked martyrs smiling to a sword,
Have missed Jehovah at the judgment-call.
And Peter, from the height of blasphemy—
' I never knew this man '—did quail and fall,
As knowing straight THAT GOD,—and turned free
And went out speechless from the face of all,
And filled the silence, weeping bitterly.

THE MEANING OF THE LOOK.

I THINK that look of Christ might seem to say—
' Thou Peter ! art thou then a common stone
Which I at last must break my heart upon,
For all God's charge to His high angels may
Guard my foot better ?   Did I yesterday
Wash *thy* feet, my beloved, that they should run
Quick to deny me 'neath the morning-sun,
And do thy kisses, like the rest, betray ?
The cock crows coldly.—Go, and manifest
A late contrition, but no bootless fear !
For when thy final need is dreariest,
Thou shalt not be denied, as I am here
My voice, to God and angels, shall attest,
Because I KNOW *this man, let him be clear* '

A THOUGHT FOR A LONELY DEATH-BED.

INSCRIBED TO MY FRIEND E. C.

IF God compel thee to this destiny,
To die alone,—with none beside thy bed
To ruffle round with sobs thy last word said,
And mark with tears the pulses ebb from thee,—
Pray then alone— ' O Christ, come tenderly!
By thy forsaken Sonship in the red
Drear wine-press,—by the wilderness outspread,—
And the lone garden where Thine agony
Fell bloody from thy brow,—by all of those
Permitted desolations, comfort mine!
No earthly friend being near me, interpose
No deathly angel 'twixt my face and Thine,
But stoop Thyself to gather my life's rose,
And smile away my mortal to Divine. '

WORK AND CONTEMPLATION

THE woman singeth at her spinning-wheel
A pleasant chant, ballad or barcarolle;
She thinketh of her song, upon the whole,
Far more than of her flax; and yet the reel
Is full, and artfully her fingers feel
With quick adjustment, provident controul,
The lines, too subtly twisted to unroll,
Out to a perfect thread. I hence appeal
To the dear Christian church—that we may do
Our Father's business in these temples mirk,

20*

Thus, swift and steadfast ; thus, intent and strong ;
While, thus, apart from toil, our souls pursue
Some high, calm, spheric tune, and prove our work
The better for the sweetness of our song.

PAIN IN PLEASURE.

A Thought lay like a flower upon mine heart,
And drew around it other thoughts like bees
For multitude and thirst of sweetnesses ;
Whereat rejoicing, I desired the art
Of the Greek whistler, who to wharf and mart
Could lure those insect swarms from orange-trees,
That I might hive with me such thoughts, and please
My soul so, always.   Foolish counterpart
Of a weak man's vain wishes !   While I spoke,
The thought I called a flower, grew nettle-rough—
The thoughts, called bees, stung me to festering.
Oh, entertain (cried Reason, as she woke,)
Your best and gladdest thoughts but long enough
And they will all prove sad enough to sting.

AN APPREHENSION.

If all the gentlest-hearted friends I know
Concentred in one heart their gentleness,
That still grew gentler, till its pulse was less
For life than pity,—I should yet be slow
To bring my own heart nakedly below
The palm of such a friend, that he should press

Motive, condition, means, appliances,
My false ideal joy and fickle wo,
Out full to light and knowledge.   I should fear
Some plait between the brows—some rougher chime
In the free voice . , . . O angels, let the flood
Of bitter scorn dash on me !   Do ye hear
What *I* say, who bear calmly all the time
This everlasting face to face with GOD ? .

DISCONTENT.

LIGHT human nature is too lightly tost
And ruffled without cause ; complaining on—
Restless with rest—until, being overthrown,
It learneth to lie quiet.   Let a frost
Or a small wasp have crept to the innermost
Of our ripe peach ; or let the wilful sun
Shine westward of our window—straight we run
A furlong's sigh as if the world were lost.
But what time through the heart and through the brain
God hath transfixed us,—we, so moved before,
Attain to a calm.   Ay, shouldering weights of pain,
We anchor in deep waters, safe from shore ;
And hear, submissive, o'er the stormy main,
God's chartered judgments walk for evermore.

PATIENCE TAUGHT BY NATURE.

' O DREARY life !   we cry, ' O dreary life ! '
And still the generations of the birds

Sing through our sighing, and the flocks and herds
Serenely live while we are keeping strife
With Heaven's true purpose in us, as a knife
Against which we may struggle.   Ocean girds
Unslackened the dry land : savannah-swards
Unweary sweep : hills watch, unworn ; and rife
Meek leaves drop yearly from the forest-trees,
To show above the unwasted stars that pass
In their old glory.   O thou God of old !
Grant me some smaller grace than comes to *these;*—
But so much patience, as a blade of grass
Grows by contented through the heat and cold.

CHEERFULNESS TAUGHT BY REASON

I THINK we are too ready with complaint
In this fair world of God's.   Had we no hope
Indeed beyond the zenith and the slope
Of yon gray blank of sky, we might be faint
To muse upon eternity's constraint
Round our aspirant souls.   But since the scope
Must widen early, is it well to droop
For a few days consumed in loss and taint ?
O pusillanimous Heart, be comforted,—
And, like a cheerful traveller, take the road,
Singing beside the hedge.   What if the bread
Be bitter in thine inn, and thou unshod
To meet the flints ?—At least it may be said,
' Because the way is *short*, I thank thee. God ! '

EXAGGERATION.

WE overstate the ills of life, and take
Imagination, given us to bring down
The choirs of singing angels overshone
By God's clear glory,—down our earth to rake
The dismal snows instead; flake following flake,
To cover all the corn. We walk upon
The shadow of hills across a level thrown,
And pant like climbers. Near the alderbrake
We sigh so loud, the nightingale within
Refuses to sing loud, as else she would.
O brothers! let us leave the shame and sin
Of taking vainly, in a plaintive mood,
The holy name of GRIEF!—holy herein,
That, by the grief of ONE, came all our good

ADEQUACY.

Now by the verdure on thy thousand hills,
Beloved England,—doth the earth appear
Quite good enough for men to overbear
The will of God in, with rebellious wills!
We cannot say the morning-sun fulfils
Ingloriously its course; nor that the clear
Strong stars without significance insphere
Our habitation. We, meantime, our ills
Heap up against this good; and lift a cry
Against this work-day world, this ill-spread feast,

As if ourselves were better certainly
Than what we come to.   Maker and High Priest,
I ask thee not my joys to multiply,—
Only to make me worthier of the least.

TO GEORGE SAND.

A DESIRE.

Thou large-brained woman and large-hearted man,
Self-called George Sand! whose soul amid the lions
Of thy tumultuous senses, moans defiance,
And answers roar for roar, as spirits can :
I would some mild miraculous thunder ran
Above the applauded circus, in appliance
Of thine own nobler nature's strength and science,
Drawing two pinions, white as wings of swan,
From thy strong shoulders, to amaze the place
With holier light!   That thou to woman's claim,
And man's, might join beside the angel's grace
Of a pure genius sanctified from blame ;
Till child and maiden pressed to thine embrace,
To kiss upon thy lips a stainless fame

TO GEORGE SAND.

A RECOGNITION.

True genius, but true woman! dost deny
Thy woman's nature with a manly scorn,

And break away the gauds and armlets worn
By weaker women in captivity?
Ah, vain denial! that revolted cry
Is sobbed in by a woman's voice forlorn:—
Thy woman's hair, my sister, all unshorn,
Floats back dishevelled strength in agony,
Disproving thy man's name: and while before
The world thou burnest in a poet fire,
We see thy woman-heart beat evermore
Through the large flame. Beat purer, heart, and higher,
Till God unsex thee on the heavenly shore,
Where unincarnate spirits purely aspire.

THE PRISONER.

I count the dismal time by months and years,
Since last I felt the green sward under foot,
And the great breath of all things summer-mute
Met mine upon my lips. Now earth appears .
As strange to me as dreams of distant spheres,
Or thoughts of Heaven we weep at. Nature's lute
Sounds on behind this door so closely shut,
A strange, wild music to the prisoner's ears,
Dilated by the distance, till the brain
Grows dim with fancies which it feels too fine;
While ever, with a visionary pain,
Past the precluded senses, sweep and shine
Streams, forests, glades,—and many a golden train
Of sunlit hills, transfigured to Divine

INSUFFICIENCY.

When I attain to utter forth in verse
Some inward thought, my soul throbs audibly
Along my pulses, yearning to be free
And something farther, fuller, higher, rehearse,
To the individual, true, and the universe,
In consummation of right harmony.
But, like a wind-exposed, distorted tree,
We are blown against for ever by the curse
Which breathes through nature. O, the world is weak-
The effluence of each is false to all;
And what we best conceive, we fail to speak.
Wait, soul, until thine ashen garments fall!
And then resume thy broken strains, and seek
Fit peroration, without let or thrall

FLUSH OR FAUNUS.

You see this dog.   It was but yesterday
I mused forgetful of his presence here,
Till thought on thought drew downward tear on tear;
When from the pillow, where wet-cheeked I lay,
A head as hairy as Faunus, thrust its way
Right sudden against my face,—two golden-clear
Great eyes astonished mine,—a drooping ear
Did flap me on either cheek to dry the spray !
I started first, as some Arcadian,
Amazed by goatly god in twilight grove :
But as my bearded vision closelier ran
My tears off, I knew Flush, and rose above
Surprise and sadness ; thanking the true PAN,
Who, by low creatures, leads to heights of love.

21   Q

FINITE AND INFINITE.

The wind sounds only in opposing straights,
The sea, beside the shore; man's spirit rends
Its quiet only up against the ends
Of wants and oppositions, loves and hates.
Where worked and worn by passionate debates.
And losing by the loss it apprehends,
The flesh rocks round, and every breath it sends,
Is ravelled to a sigh.   All tortured states
Suppose a straightened place.   Jehovah Lord,
Make room for rest, around me!   Out of sight
Now float me, of the vexing land abhorred,
Till, in deep calms of space, my soul may right
Her nature; shoot large sail on lengthening cord,
And rush exultant on the Infinite.

TWO SKETCHES.

I.

The shadow of her face upon the wall
May take your memory to the perfect Greek;
But when you front her, you would call the cheek
Too full, sir, for your models, if withal
That bloom it wears could leave you critical,
And that smile reaching toward the rosy streak:
For one who smiles so, has no need to speak
To lead your thoughts along, as steed to stall!

A smile that turns the sunny side o' the heart
On all the world, as if herself did win
By what she lavished on an open mart:—
Let no man call the liberal sweetness, sin,—
While friends may whisper, as they stand apart,
" Methinks there's still some warmer place within."

II.

Her azure eyes, dark lashes hold in fee:
Her fair superfluous ringlets, without check,
Drop after one another down her neck;
As many to each cheek as you might see
Green leaves to a wild rose. This sign outwardly,
And a like woman-covering seems to deck
Her inner nature. For she will not fleck
World's sunshine with a finger. Sympathy
Must call her in Love's name! and then, I know,
She rises up, and brightens as she should,
And lights her smile for comfort, and is slow
In nothing of high-hearted fortitude.
To smell this flower, come near it: such can grow
In that sole garden where Christ's brow dropped
blood.

MOUNTAINEER AND POET.

THE simple goatherd, between Alp and sky,
Seeing his shadow in that awful tryst,
Dilated to a giant's on the mist,
Esteems not his own stature larger by
The apparent image, but more patiently
Strikes his staff down beneath his cienching fist—
While the snow-mountains lift their amethyst
And sapphire crowns of splendor, far and nigh,
Into the air around him.   Learn from hence
Meek morals, all ye poets that pursue
Your way still onward, up to eminence!
Ye are not great, because creation drew
Large revelations round your earliest sense,
Nor bright, because God's glory shines for you.

THE POET.

THE poet hath the child's sight in his breast,
And sees all *new*.   What oftenest he has viewed,
He views with the first glory.   Fair and good
Pall never on him, at the fairest, best,
But stand before him holy and undressed
In week-day false conventions, such as would
Drag other men down from the altitude
Of primal types, too early dispossessed.

Why, God would tire of all his heavens as soon
As thou, O godlike, childlike poet, didst,
Of daily and nightly sights of sun and moon!
And therefore hath He set thee in the midst,
Where men may hear thy wonder's ceaseless tune,
And praise His world for ever, as thou bidst.

HIRAM POWERS' GREEK SLAVE.

They say Ideal Beauty cannot enter
The house of anguish.   On the threshold stands
An alien Image with enshackled hands,
Called the Greek Slave: as if the artist meant her,
(That passionless perfection which he lent her,
Shadowed not darkened where the sill expands)
To, so, confront man's crimes in different lands
With man's ideal sense.   Pierce to the centre,
Art's fiery finger!—and break up ere long
The serfdom of this world!   Appeal, fair stone,
From God's pure heights of beauty, against man's
          wrong!
Catch up in thy divine face, not alone
East griefs but west,—and strike and shame the
          strong,
By thunders of white silence, overthrown.

21*

LIFE.

EACH creature holds an insular point in space:
Yet what man stirs a finger, breathes a sound,
But all the multitudinous beings round
In all the countless worlds, with time and place
For their conditions, down to the central base,
Thrill, haply, in vibration and rebound,
Life answering life across the vast profound,
In full antiphony, by a common grace!
I think, this sudden joyaunce which illumes
A child's mouth sleeping, unaware may run
From some soul newly loosened from earth's
    tombs:
I think, this passionate sigh, which half-begun
I stifle back, may reach and stir the plumes
Of God's calm angel standing in the sun.

LOVE.

WE cannot live, except thus mutually
We alternate, aware or unaware,
The reflex act of life: and when we bear
Our virtue outward most impulsively,
Most full of invocation, and to be
Most instantly compellant, certes, there
We live most life, whoever breathes most air
And counts his dying years by sun and sea.

But when a soul, by choice and conscience, doth
Throw out her full force on another soul,
The conscience and the concentration both
Make mere life, Love.   For Life in perfect whole
And aim consummated, is Love in sooth,
As nature's magnet-heat rounds pole with pole.

HEAVEN AND EARTH.

'And there was silence in heaven for the space of half-an-hour.'
Revelation.

God, who, with thunders and great voices kept
Beneath thy throne, and stars most silver-paced
Along the inferior gyres, and open-faced
Melodious angels round ;—canst intercept
Music with music ;—yet, at will, hast swept
All back, all back, (said he in Patmos placed,)
To fill the heavens with silence of the waste,
Which lasted half-an-hour !—Lo, I who have wept
All day and night, beseech Thee by my tears,
And by that dread response of curse and groan
Men alternate across these hemispheres,
Vouchsafe us such a half-hour's hush alone,
In compensation for our stormy years !
As heaven has paused from song, let earth, from moan.

THE PROSPECT.

METHINKS we do as fretful children do,
Leaning their faces on the window-pane
To sigh the glass dim with their own breath's stain,
And shut the sky and landscape from their view.
And thus, alas! since God the maker drew
A mystic separation 'twixt those twain,
The life beyond us, and our souls in pain,
We miss the prospect which we're called unto
By grief we're fools to use.   Be still and strong,
O man, my brother! hold thy sobbing breath,
And keep thy soul's large window pure from
          wrong,—
That so, as life's appointment issueth,
Thy vision may be clear to watch along
The sunset consummation-lights of death.

HUGH STUART BOYD.*

HIS BLINDNESS.

GOD would not let the spheric Lights accost
This God-loved man, and bade the earth stand off
With all her beckoning hills, whose golden stuff
Under the feet of the royal sun is crossed.

---

* To whom was inscribed, in grateful affection, my poem of 'Cyprus
Wine.'   There comes a moment in life when even gratitude and affection turn to pain, as they do now with me.   This excellent and learned
man, enthusiastic for the good and the beautiful, and one of the most

Yet such things were to him not wholly lost,—
Permitted, with his wandering eyes light-proof,
To have fair visions rendered full enough
By many a ministrant accomplished ghost:
And seeing, to sounds of softly-turned book-leaves,
Sappho's crown-rose, and Meleager's spring,
And Gregory's starlight on Greek-burnished eves:
Till Sensuous and Unsensuous seemed one thing
Viewed from one level;—earth's reapers at the
        sheaves
Scarce plainer than Heaven's angels on the wing!

HUGH STUART BOYD.

HIS DEATH, 1848.

BELOVED friend, who living many years
With sightless eyes raised vainly to the sun,
Didst learn to keep thy patient soul in tune
To visible nature's elemental cheers!
God has not caught thee to new hemispheres
Because thou wast aweary of this one:—
I think thine angel's patience first was done,
And that he spake out with celestial tears,

simple and upright of human beings. passed out of his long darkness
through death in the summer of 1848; Dr. Adam Clarke's daughter and
biographer, Mrs. Smith, (happier in this than the absent) fulfilling a
double filial duty as she sate by the death-bed of her father's friend
and hers.

' Is it enough, dear God ! then lighten so
This soul that smiles in darkness ! '

                      Stedfast friend,
Who never didst my heart or life misknow,
Nor either's faults too keenly apprehend,—
How can I wonder when I see thee go
To join the Dead found faithful to the end ?

HUGH STUART BOYD.

LEGACIES.

THREE gifts the Dying left me; Æschylus,
And Gregory Nazianzen, and a clock
Chiming the gradual hours out like a flock
Of stars whose motion is melodious.
The books were those I used to read from, thus
Assisting my dear teacher's soul to unlock
The darkness of his eyes : now, mine they mock,
Blinded in turn, by tears : now, murmurous
Sad echoes of my young voice, years agone
Entoning from these leaves the Græcian phrase,
Return and choke my utterance.   Books, lie down
In silence on the shelf there. within gaze !
And thou, clock, striking the hour's pulses on,
Chime in the day which ends these parting days !

LOVED ONCE

I CLASSED, appraising once,
Earth's lamentable sounds : the welladay,
    The jarring yea and nay,
The fall of kisses on unanswering clay,
The sobbed farewell, the welcome mournfuller ;—
    But all did leaven the air
With a less bitter leaven of sure despair,
    Than these words—'I loved ONCE.'

And who saith, 'I loved ONCE ?'
Not angels, whose clear eyes, love, love, foresee,
    Love through eternity,
And by To Love do apprehend To Be.
Not God, called LOVE, his noble crown-name,—casting
    A light too broad for blasting !
The great God changing not from everlasting,
    Saith never, 'I loved ONCE.'

Oh, never is 'Loved ONCE,'
Thy word, thou Victim-Christ, misprized friend
    Thy cross and curse may rend ;
But having loved Thou lovest to the end !
It is man's saying—man's. Too weak to move
    One sphered star above,
Man desecrates the eternal God-word Love
    With his No More, and Once.

How say ye, ' We loved once,'
Blasphemers ?   Is your earth not cold enow,
      Mourners, without that snow ?
Ah, friends ! and would ye wrong each other so ?
And could ye say of some whose love is known,
      Whose prayers have met your own,
Whose tears have fallen for you, whose smiles have
          shone
      So long.—' We loved them ONCE ?'

      Could ye, ' We loved her once,'
Say calm of *me*, sweet friends, when out of sight ?
      When hearts of better right
Stand in between me and your happy light ?
And when, as flowers kept too long in the shade,
      Ye find my colors fade,
And all that is not love in me, decayed ?
      Such words—Ye loved me ONCE !

      Could ye, ' We loved her once,'
Say cold of me when further put away
      In earth's sepulchral clay ?
When mute the lips which deprecate to-day ?
Not so ! not then—*least* then ! When Life is shriven,
      And Death's full joy is given,—
Of those who sit and love you up in Heaven,
      Say not, ' We loved them once.'

      Say never, ye loved ONCE !
God is too near above, the grave, beneath,
      And all our moments breathe
Too quick in mysteries of life and death,

For such a word.   The eternities avenge
   Affections light of range—
There comes no change to justify that change,
   Whatever comes—loved ONCE!

   And yet that same word ONCE
Is humanly acceptive !   Kings have said
   Shaking a discrowned head,
' We ruled once,'—dotards,'We once taught and led'—
Cripples once danced i' the vines—and bards approved
   Were once by scornings, moved :
But love strikes one hour—LOVE.   Those *never* loved,
   Who dream that they loved ONCE.

22

A RHAPSODY OF LIFE'S PROGRESS.

"Fill all the stops of life with tuneful breath."
POEMS ON MAN, BY CORNELIUS MATHEWS.*

WE are borne into life—it is sweet, it is stange !
We lie still on the knee of a mild Mystery,
       Which smiles with a change !
But we doubt not of changes, we know not of spaces ;
The Heavens seem as near as our own mother's face is,
And we think we could touch all the stars that we see ;
And the milk of our mother is white on our mouth !
And, with small childish hands, we are turning around
The apple of Life which another has found :
It is warm with our touch, not with sun of the south,
And we count, as we turn it, the red side for four—
       O Life, O Beyond,
       Thou art sweet, thou art strange evermore.

Then all things look strange in the pure gold·n æther :
We walk through the gardens with hands linked
       together,
       And the lilies look large as the trees ;
And as loud as the birds, sing the bloom-loving bees,
And the birds sing like angels, so mystical fine ;
And the cedars are brushing the archangel's feet ;

* A small volume, by an American poet—as remarkable, in thought
and manner for a vital sinewy vigour, as the right arm of Pathfinder.

And time is eternity,--love is divine,
    And the world is complete.
Now, God bless the child,—father, mother, respond!
    O Life, O Beyond,
    Thou art strange, thou art sweet.

Then we leap on the earth with the armor of youth,
    And the earth rings again :
And we breathe out, ' O beauty,'—we cry out, ' O
    truth,'
And the bloom of our lips drops with wine ;
And our blood runs amazed 'neath the calm hyaline,
The earth cleaves to the foot, the sun burns to the
    brain,—
What is this exultation, and what this despair?—
The strong pleasure is smiting the nerves into pain,
And we drop from the Fair as we climb to the Fair,
    And we lie in a trance at its feet ;
And the breath of an angel cold-piercing the air
    Breathes fresh on our faces in swoon ;
And we think him so near he is this side the sun ;
And we wake to a whisper self-murmured and fond,
    O Life, O Beyond,
    Thou art strange, thou art sweet!

And the winds and the waters in pastoral measures
Go winding around us, with roll upon roll,
Till the soul lies within in a circle of pleasures
    Which hideth the soul :
And we run with the stag, and we leap with the horse,
And we swim with the fish through the broad water-
    course,

And we strike with the falcon, and hunt with the hound,
And the joy which is in us, flies out by a wound,
And we shout so aloud, ' We exult, we rejoice.'
That we lose the low moan of our brothers around.
And we shout so adeep down creation's profound,
   We are deaf to God's voice--
And we bind the rose-garland on forehead and ears,
   Yet we are not ashamed ;
And the dew of the roses that runneth unblamed
   Down our cheeks, is not taken for tears.
Help us, God, trust us, man, love us, woman ! ' I hold
Thy small head in my hands,—with its grapelets of
  gold
Growing bright through my fingers,—like altar for
  oath,
'Neath the vast golden spaces like witnessing faces
That watch the eternity strong in the troth—
   I love thee, I leave thee,
   Live for thee, die for thee !
   I prove thee, deceive thee,
   Undo evermore thee !
Help me, God, slay me, man !—one is mourning for
  both !'
And we stand up though young near the funeral-
  sheet
Which covers the Cæsar and old Pharamond ;
And death is so nigh us, Life cools from its heat—
   O Life, O Beyond,
   Art thou fair,—*art* thou sweet ?

Then we act to a purpose—we spring up erect—

We will tame the wild mouths of the wilderness-
    steeds;
We will plough up the deep in the ships double-
    decked;
We will build the great cities, and do the great
    deeds,
Strike the steel upon steel, strike the soul upon soul.
Strike the dole on the weal, overcoming the dole,
Let the cloud meet the cloud in a grand thunder-roll!
While the eagle of Thought rides the tempest in
    scorn,
Who cares if the lightning is burning the corn?
            Let us sit on the thrones
                In a purple sublimity,
            And grind down men's bones
                To a pale unanimity!
Speed me, God!—serve me, man!—I am god over
    men!
When I speak in my cloud, none shall answer again—
            'Neath the stripe and the bond,
                Lie and mourn at my feet!'—
            O thou Life, O Beyond,
                Thou art strange, thou art sweet!

Then we grow into thought,—and with inward ascen-
    sions,
            Touch the bounds of our Being!
We lie in the dark here, swathed doubly around
With our sensual relations and social conventions,
Yet are 'ware of a sight, yet are 'ware of a sound
        Beyond Hearing and Seeing,—

22*   R

Are aware that a Hades rolls deep on all sides
      With its infinite tides
About and above us,—until the strong arch
Of our life creaks and bends as if ready for falling,
And through the dim rolling, we hear the sweet
    calling
Of spirits that speak in a soft under-tongue
The sense of the mystical march :
And we cry to them softly, ' Come nearer, come
    nearer,
And lift up the lap of this Dark, and speak clearer,
      And teach us the song that ye sung.'
And we smile in our thought if they answer or no,
For to dream of a sweetness is sweet as to know!
      Wonders breathe in our face
        And we ask not their name ;
        Love takes all the blame
      Of the world's prison-place.
And we sing back the songs as we guess them, aloud ;
And we send up the lark of our music that cuts
      Untired through the cloud,
To beat with its wings at the lattice Heaven shuts:
Yet the angels look down and the mortals look up
      As the little wings beat,
And the poet is blessed with their pity or hope
'Twixt the Heavens and the earth *can* a poet despond ?
      O Life, O Beyond,
      Thou art strange, thou art sweet !

Then we wring from our souls their applicative strength,
And bend to the cord the strong bow of our ken .

And bringing our lives to the level of others
Hold the cup we have filled, to their uses at length.
'Help me, God! love me, man! I am man among men,
         And my life is a pledge
         Of the ease of another's!'
From the fire and the water we drive out the steam,
With a rush and a roar and the speed of a dream!
And the car without horses, the car without wings
         Roars onward and flies
         On its grey iron edge,
'Neath the heat of a Thought sitting still in our eyes—
And the hand knots in air, with the bridge that it
    flings,
Two peaks far disrupted by ocean and skies —
And, lifting a fold of the smooth flowing Thames,
Draws under the world with its turmoils and pothers;
While the swans float on softly, untouched in their
    calms
By Humanity's hum at the root of the springs!
And with reachings of Thought we reach down to
    the deeps
         Of the souls of our brothers,
And teach them full words with our slow-moving lips
'God,' 'Liberty,' 'Truth,'—which they hearken and
    think
And work into harmony, link upon link,
Till the silver meets round the earth gelid and dense,
Shedding sparks of electric responderce intense
         On the dark of eclipse!
Then we hear through the silence and glory afar,
         As from shores of a star

In aphelion,—the new generations that cry,
Disenthralled by our voice to harmonious reply,
'God,' ' Liberty,' ' Truth !'
We are glorious forsooth—
And our name has a seat,
Though the shroud should be donned !
O Life, O Beyond,
Thou art strange, thou art sweet !

Help me, God—help me, man ! I am low, I am
weak—
Death loosens my sinews and creeps in my veins ;
My body is cleft by these wedges of pains
From my spirit's serene ;
And I feel the externe and insensate creep in
On my organized clay.
I sob not, nor shriek,
Yet I faint fast away !
I am strong in the spirit,—deep-thoughted, clear-
eyed,—
I could walk, step for step, with an angel beside,
On the Heaven-heights of Truth !
Oh, the soul keeps its youth—
But the body faints sore, it is tired in the race,
It sinks from the chariot ere reaching the goal ;
It is weak, it is cold,
The rein drops from its hold—
It sinks back, with the death in its face.
On, chariot—on, soul,
Ye are all the more fleet—
Be alone at the goal
Of the strange and the sweet '

Love us, God! love us, man! We believe, we
    achieve—
        Let us love, let us live,
        For the acts correspond—
        We are glorious—and DIE!
And again on the knee of a mild Mystery
      That smiles with a change,
        Here we lie!
        O DEATH, O BEYOND,
      Thou art sweet, thou art strange!

THE HOUSE OF CLOUDS.

I WOULD build a cloudy House
    For my thoughts to live in :
When for earth too fancy-loose,
    And too low for Heaven !
Hush ! I talk my dream aloud—
    I build it bright to see,—
I build it on the moonlit cloud
    To which I looked with *thee*.

Cloud-walls of the morning's grey,
    Faced with amber column,
Crowned with crimson cupola
    From a sunset solemn !
May-mists, for the casements, fetch,
    Pale and glimmering ;
With a sunbeam hid in each,
    And a smell of spring.

Build the entrance high and proud,
    Darkening and then brightening,
Of a riven thunder-cloud,
    Veined by the lightning.
Use one with an iris-stain
    For the door within ;
Turning to a sound like rain
    As we enter in.

Build a spacious hall thereby :
  Boldly, never fearing.
Use the blue place of the sky
  Which the wind is clearing ;
Branched with corridors sublime,
  Flecked with winding stairs—
Such as children wish to climb,
  Following their own prayers.

In the mutest of the house,
  I will have my chamber :
Silence at the door shall use
  Evening's light of amber,
Solemnising every mood,
  Softening in degree,
Turning sadness into good
  As I turn the key.

Be my chamber tapestried
  With the showers of summer,
Close, but soundless,—glorified
  When the sunbeams come here ;
Wandering harper, harping on
  Waters stringed for such,
Drawing colour, for a tune,
  With a vibrant touch.

Bring a shadow green and still
  From the chesnut forest,
Bring a purple from the hill,
  When the heat is sorest ;

Spread them out from wall to wall,
   Carpet-wove around,
Whereupon the foot shall fall
   In light instead of sound.

Bring the fantastic cloudlets home
   From the noontide zenith ;
Ranged for sculptures round the room
   Named as Fancy weeneth :
Some be Junos, without eyes ;
   Naiads, without sources ;
Some be birds of paradise,
   Some, Olympian horses.

Bring the dews the birds shake off,
   Waking in the hedges,—
Those too, perfumed for a proof,
   From the lilies' edges :
From our England's field and moor,
   Bring them calm and white in ;
Whence to form a mirror pure
   For Love's self-delighting.

Bring a grey cloud from the east
   Where the lark is singing ;
Something of the song at least,
   Unlost in the bringing :
That shall be a morning chair,
   Poet-dream may sit in,
When it leans out on the air,
   Unrhymed and unwritten.

Bring the red cloud from the sun!
　　While he sinketh, catch it.
That shall be a couch,—with one
　　Sidelong star to watch it,—
Fit for poet's finest thought
　　At the curfew-sounding,
Things unseen being nearer brought
　　Than the seen, around him.

Poet's thought,—not poet's sigh!
　　'Las, they come together!
Cloudy walls divide and fly,
　　As in April weather!
Cupola and column proud,
　　Structure bright to see—
Gone!—except that moonlit cloud,
　　To which I looked with *thee!*

Let them!　Wipe such visionings
　　From the Fancy's cartel—
Love secures some fairer things
　　Dowered with his immortal.
The sun may darken,—heaven be bowed—
　　But still unchanged shall be,—
Here in my soul,—that moonlit cloud,
　　To which I looked with THEE!

23

CATARINA TO CAMOËNS.

DYING IN HIS ABSENCE ABROAD, AND REFERRING TO THE POEM IN
WHICH HE RECORDED THE SWEETNESS OF HER EYES.

On the door you will not enter,
    I have gazed too long—adieu!
Hope withdraws her peradventure—
    Death is near me,—and not *you* !
            Come, O lover !
            Close and cover
    These poor eyes, you called, I ween,
'Sweetest eyes, were ever seen.'

When I heard you sing that burden
    In my vernal days and bowers,
Other praises disregarding,
    I but hearkened that of yours,—
            Only saying
            In heart-playing,
'Blessed eyes mine eyes have been,
If the sweetest, HIS have seen !'

But all changes.   At this vesper,
    Cold the sun shines down the door.
If you stood there, would you whisper
    'Love, I love you,' as before,—

Death pervading
Now, and shading
Eyes you sang of, that yestreen,
As the sweetest ever seen?

Yes! I think, were you beside them,
  Near the bed I die upon,—
Though their beauty you denied them,
  As you stood there looking down,
    You would truly
    Call them duly,
For the love's sake found therein,—
' Sweetest eyes were ever seen.'

And if *you* looked down upon them,
  And if *they* looked up to *you*,
All the light which has forgone them
  Would be gathered back anew!
    They would truly
    Be as duly
Love-transformed to Beauty's sheen,—
' Sweetest eyes, were ever seen.'

But, ah me! you only see me
  In your thoughts of loving man,
Smiling soft perhaps and dreamy
  Through the wavings of my fan,—
    And unweeting
    Go repeating,
In your reverie serene,
· Sweetest eyes, were ever seen.'

While my spirit leans and reaches
   From my body still and pale,
Fain to hear what tender speech is
   In your love to help my bale—
      O my poet
      Come and show it!
Come, of latest love to glean
' Sweetest eyes, were ever seen.'

O my poet, O my prophet,
   When you praised their sweetness so,
Did you think, in singing of it,
   That it might be near to go ?
      Had you fancies
      From their glances,
That the grave would quickly screen
' Sweetest eyes, were ever seen ?'

No reply !   The fountain's warble
   In the court-yard sounds alone :
As the water to the marble
   So my heart falls with a moan,
      From love-sighing
      To this dying!
Death forerunneth Love, to win
' Sweetest eyes, were ever seen.'

Will you come ? when I'm departed
   Where all sweetnesses are hid—
When thy voice, my tender-hearted,
   Will not lift up either lid

Cry, O lover,
Love is over!
Cry beneath the cypress green—
'Sweetest eyes, were ever seen.'

When the angelus is ringing,
    Near the convent will you walk,
And recall the choral singing
    Which brought angels down our talk?
        Spirit-shriven
        I viewed Heaven,
Till you smiled—' Is earth unclean,
'Sweetest eyes, were ever seen?'

When beneath the palace-lattice,
    You ride slow as you have done,
And you see a face there—*that* is
    Not the old familiar one,—
        Will you oftly
        Murmur softly,
'Here, ye watched me morn and e'en,
Sweetest eyes, were ever seen!'

When the palace ladies sitting
    Round your gittern, shall have said,
' Poet, sing those verses written
    For the lady who is dead,'
        Will you tremble,
        Yet dissemble,—
Or sing hoarse, with tears between,
'Sweetest eyes, were ever seen?'

23*

Sweetest eyes!   How sweet in flowings,
   The repeated cadence is !
Though you sang a hundred poems,
   Still the best one would be this.
      I can hear it
      'Twixt my spirit
And the earth-noise intervene—
' Sweetest eyes, were ever seen !'

But the priest waits for the praying,
   And the choir are on their knees,
And the soul must pass away in
   Strains more solemn high than these !
      Miserere
      For the weary—
Oh, no longer for Catrine,
' Sweetest eyes, were ever seen !'

Keep my riband, take and keep it,
   I have loosed it from my hair ;*
Feeling, while you overweep it,
   Not alone in your despair,
      Since with saintly
      Watch, unfaintly,
Out of Heaven shall o'er you lean
' Sweetest eyes, were ever seen.'

But—but *now*—yet unremoved
   Up to Heaven, they glisten fast :
You may cast away, Beloved,
   In your future all my past ;

---

* She left him the riband from her hair.

Such old phrases
May be praises
For some fairer bosom-queen—
' Sweetest eyes, were ever seen !'

Eyes of mine, what are ye doing ?
    Faithless, faithless,—praised amiss
If a tear be of your showing,
    Drop for any hope of HIS !
        Death hath boldness
        Besides coldness,
If unworthy tears demean
' Sweetest eyes, were ever seen.'

I will look out to his future—
    I will bless it till it shine :
Should he ever be a suitor
    Unto sweeter eyes than mine,
        Sunshine gild them,
        Angels shield them,
Whatsoever eyes terrene
Be the sweetest HIS have seen '

WINE OF CYPRUS.

GIVEN TO ME BY H. S. BOYD, ESQ., AUTHOR OF "SELECT PASSAGES FROM THE GREEK FATHERS," ETC., TO WHOM THESE STANZAS ARE ADDRESSED.

IF old Bacchus were the speaker
   He would tell you with a sigh,
Of the Cyprus in this beaker
   I am sipping like a fly,—
Like a fly or gnat on Ida
   At the hour of goblet-pledge,
By queen Juno brushed aside, a
   Full white arm-sweep, from the edge.

Sooth, the drinking should be ampler
   When the drink is so divine ;
And some deep-mouthed Greek exemplar
   Would become your Cyprus wine !
Cyclop's mouth might plunge aright in,
   While his one eye over-leered—
Nor too large were mouth of Titan,
   Drinking rivers down his beard.

Pan might dip his head so deep in,
   That his ears alone pricked out ;
Fauns around him, pressing, leaping,
   Each one pointing to his throat :

While the Naiads like Bacchantes,
　　Wild, with urns thrown out to waste,
Cry—' O earth, that thou wouldst grant us
　　Springs to keep, of such a taste !'

But for me, I am not worthy
　　After gods and Greeks to drink ;
And my lips are pale and earthy
　　To go bathing from this brink !
Since you heard them speak the last time,
　　They have faded from their blooms ;
And the laughter of my pastime
　　Has learnt silence at the tombs.

Ah, my friend ! the antique drinkers
　　Crowned the cup and crowned the brow :
Can I answer the old thinkers
　　In the forms they thought of, now ?
Who will fetch from garden closes
　　Some new garlands while I speak ?
That the forehead, crowned with roses,
　　May strike scarlet down the cheek ?

Do not mock me ! with my mortal,
　　Suits no wreath again, indeed !
I am sad-voiced as the turtle
　　Which Anacreon used to feed :
Yet as that same bird demurely
　　Wet her beak in cup of his,
So, without a garland, surely
　　I may touch the brim of this.

Go !—let others praise the Chian !—
    This is soft as Muses' string—
This is tawny as Rhea's lion,
    This is rapid as its spring,
Bright as Paphia's eyes e'er met us,
    Light as ever trod her feet !
And the brown bees of Hymettus
    Make their honey not so sweet.

Very copious are my praises,
    Though I sip it like a fly !—
Ah—but, sipping—times and places
    Change before me suddenly—
As Ulysses' old libation
    Drew the ghosts from every part,
So your Cyprus wine, dear Græcian,
    Stirs the Hades of my heart.

And I think of those long mornings,
    Which my Thought goes far to seek,
When, betwixt the folio's turnings,
    Solemn flowed the rhythmic Greek.
Past the pane the mountain spreading,
    Swept the sheep-bell's tinkling noise,
While a girlish voice was reading,
    Somewhat low for *ai*'s and *oi*'s.

Then what golden hours were for us !—
    While we sate together there,
How the white vests of the chorus
    Seemed to wave up a live air !

How the cothurns trod majestic
   Down the deep iambic lines :
And the rolling anapæstic
   Curled like vapor over shrines !

Oh, our Æschylus, the thunderous !
   How he drove the bolted breath
Through the cloud, to wedge it ponderous
   In the gnarled oak beneath.
Oh, our Sophocles, the royal,
   Who was born to monarch's place—
And who made the whole world loyal,
   Less by kingly power than grace.

Our Euripides, the human—
   With his droppings of warm tears ;
And his touches of things common,
   Till they rose to touch the spheres !
Our Theocritus, our Bion,
   And our Pindar's shining goals !—
These were cup-bearers undying,
   Of the wine that's meant for souls.

And my Plato,   the divine one,
   If men know the gods aright
By their motions as they shine on
   With a glorious trail of light !
And your noble Christian bishops,
   Who mouthed grandly the last Greek :
Though the sponges on their hyssops
   Were distent with wine—too weak

Yet, your Chrysostom, you praised him
  As a liberal mouth of gold;
And your Basil, you upraised him
  To the height of speakers old:
And we both praised Heliodorus
  For his secret of pure lies :—
Who forged first his linked stories
  In the heat of lady's eyes.

And we both praised your Synesius,
  For the fire shot up his odes :
Though the Church was scarce propitious
  As he whistled dogs and gods.
And we both praised Nazianzen,
  For the fervid heart and speech :
Only I eschewed his glancing
  At the lyre hung out of reach.

Do you mind that deed of Atè,
  Which you bound me to so fast,—
Reading " De Virginitate,"
  From the first line to the last ?
How I said at ending, solemn,
  As I turned and looked at you,
That St. Simeon on the column
  Had had somewhat less to do?

For we sometimes gently wrangled
  Very gently, be it said,
For our thoughts were disentangled
  By no breaking of the thread !

And I charged you with extortions
  On the nobler fames of old—
Ay, and sometimes thought your Porsons
  Stained the purple they would fold.

For the rest——a mystic moaning,
  Kept Cassandra at the gate,
With wild eyes the vision shone in
  And wide nostrils scenting fate.
And Prometheus, bound in passion
  By brute Force to the blind stone,
Showed us looks of invocation
  Turned to ocean and the sun.

And Medea we saw burning
  At her nature's planted stake ;
And proud Œdipus, fate-scorning
  While the cloud came on to break—
While the cloud came on slow—slower,
  Till he stood discrowned, resigned !
But the reader's voice dropped lower
  When the poet called him BLIND !

Ah, my gossip ! you were older,
  And more learned, and a man !
Yet that shadow —the enfolder
  Of your quiet eyelids —ran
Both our spirits to one level ;
  And I turned from hill and lea
And the summer-sun's green revel,
  To your eyes that *could not see.*

24

WINE OF CYPRUS.

Now Christ bless you with the one light
  Which goes shining night and day!
May the flowers which grow in sunlight
  Shed their fragrance in your way!
Is it not right to remember
  All your kindness, friend of mine,
When we two sat in the chamber,
  And the poets poured us wine?

So, to come back to the drinking
  Of this Cyprus!—it is well—
But those memories, to my thinking,
  Make a better œnomel:
And whoever be the speaker,
  None can murmur with a sigh
That, in drinking from *that* beaker,
  I am sipping like a fly.

THE DEAD PAN.

Excited by Schiller's 'Götter Griechenlands,' and partly founded on a well-known tradition mentioned in a treatise of Plutarch, (' De Oraculorum Defectu,') according to which, at the hour of the Saviour's agony, a cry of 'Great Pan is dead!' swept across the waves in the hearing of certain mariners,—and the oracles ceased.

It is in all veneration to the memory of the deathless Schiller, that I oppose a doctrine still more dishonoring to poetry than to Christianity.

As Mr. Kenyon's graceful and harmonious paraphrase of the German poem was the first occasion of the turning of my thoughts in this direction, I take advantage of the pretence to indulge my feelings (which overflow on other grounds) by inscribing my lyric to that dear friend and relative, with the earnestness of appreciating esteem as well as of affectionate gratitude.

GODS of Hellas, gods of Hellas,
Can ye listen in your silence?
Can your mystic voices tell us
Where ye hide? In floating islands,
With a wind that evermore
Keeps you out of sight of shore?
     Pan, Pan is dead.

In what revels are ye sunken,
In old Ethiopia?
Have the Pygmies made you drunken,
Bathing in mandragora
Your divine pale lips that shiver
Like the lotus in the river?
     Pan, Pan is dead.

Do ye sit there still in slumber,
In gigantic Alpine rows?
The black poppies out of number

Nodding, dripping from your brows
To the red lees of your wine,
And so kept alive and fine ?
                        Pan, Pan is dead.

Or lie crushed your stagnant corses
Where the silver spheres roll on,
Stung to life by centric forces
Thrown like rays out from the sun ?—
While the smoke of your old altars
Is the shroud that round you welters ?
                        Great Pan is dead.

Gods of Hellas, gods of Hellas,
Said the old Hellenic tongue !
Said the hero-oaths, as well as
Poets' songs the sweetest sung,
Have ye grown deaf in a day ?
Can ye speak not yea or nay—
                        Since Pan is dead ?

Do ye leave your rivers flowing
All alone, O Naiades,
While your drenched locks dry slow in
This cold feeble sun and breeze ?
Not a word the Naiads say,
Though the rivers run for aye.
                        For Pan is dead.

From the gloaming of the oak wood,
O ye Dryads, could ye flee ?
At the rushing thunderstroke, would
No sob tremble through the tree ? —

Not a word the Dryads say,
Though the forests wave for aye.
> For Pan is dead.

Have ye left the mountain places,
Oreads wild, for other tryst ?
Shall we see no sudden faces
Strike a glory through the mist ?
Not a sound the silence thrills
Of the everlasting hills.
> Pan, Pan is dead.

O twelve gods of Plato's vision,
Crowned to starry wanderings,—
With your chariots in procession,
And your silver clash of wings !
Very pale ye seem to rise,
Ghosts of Grecian deities—
> Now Pan is dead !

Jove, that right hand is unloaded,
Whence the thunder did prevail ;
While in idiocy of godhead
Thou art staring the stars pale !
And thine eagle, blind and old,
Roughs his feathers in the cold.
> Pan, Pan is dead.

Where, O Juno, is the glory
Of thy regal look and tread !
Will they lay, for evermore, thee,
On thy dim, straight golden bed ?
Will thy queendom all lie hid
24*

Meekly under either lid?

> Pan, Pan is dead.

Ha, Apollo! Floats his golden
Hair all mist-like where he stands;
While the Muses hang enfolding
Knee and foot with faint wild hands?
'Neath the clanging of thy bow,
Niobe looked lost as thou!

> Pan, Pan is dead.

Shall the casque with its brown iron,
Pallas' broad blue eyes, eclipse,
And no hero take inspiring
From the God-Greek of her lips?
'Neath her olive dost thou sit,
Mars the mighty, cursing it?

> Pan, Pan is dead.

Bacchus, Bacchus! on the panther
He swoons,—bound with his own vines!
And his Mænads slowly saunter,
Head aside, among the pines,
While they murmur dreamingly,
'Evohe—ah—evohe—!'

> Ah, Pan is dead.

Neptune lies beside the trident,
Dull and senseless as a stone:
And old Pluto deaf and silent
Is cast out into the sun.
Ceres smileth stern thereat,
'We *all* now are desolate—'

> Now Pan is dead.

Aphrodite! dead and driven
As thy native foam, thou art,
With the cestus long done heaving
On the white calm of thy heart!
Ai Adonis!   At that shriek,
Not a tear runs down her cheek—
                    Pan, Pan is dead.

And the Loves we used to know from
One another,—huddled lie,
Frore as taken in a snow-storm,
Close beside her tenderly,—
As if each had weakly tried
Once to kiss her as he died.
                    Pan, Pan is dead.

What, and Hermes!   Time enthralleth
All thy cunning, Hermes, thus,—
And the ivy blindly crawleth
Round thy brave caduceus!
Hast thou no new message for us,
Full of thunder and Jove-glories?
                    Nay, Pan is dead.

Crowned Cybele's great turret
Rocks and crumbles on her head:
Roar the lions of her chariot
Toward the wilderness, unfed:
Scornful children are not mute,—
' Mother, mother, walk a-foot—
                    Since Pan is dead.'

In the fiery-hearted centre
Of the solemn universe,
Ancient Vesta,—who could enter
To consume thee with this curse?
Drop thy gray chin on thy knee,
O thou palsied Mystery!

        For Pan is dead.

Gods! we vainly do adjure you,—
Ye return nor voice nor sign:
Not a votary could secure you
Even a grave for your Divine!
Not a grave, to show thereby,
Here these gray old gods do lie!

        Pan, Pan is dead.

Even that Greece who took your wages,
Calls the obolus outworn;
And the hoarse deep-throated ages
Laugh your godships unto scorn—
And the Poets do disclaim you,
Or grow colder if they name you—

        And Pan is dead.

Gods bereaved, gods belated,
With your purples rent asunder!
Gods discrowned and desecrated,
Disinherited of thunder!
Now, the goats may climb and crop
The soft grass on Ida's top—

        Now Pan is dead.

Calm, of old, the bark went onward,
When a cry more loud than wind,
Rose up, deepened, and swept sunward,
From the pilèd Dark behind :
And the sun shrank and grew pale,
Breathed against by the great wail—
    Pan, Pan is dead.

And the rowers from the benches
Fell,—each shuddering on his face—
While departing Influences
Struck a cold back through the place :
And the shadow of the ship
Reeled along the passive deep—
    Pan, Pan is dead.

And that dismal cry rose slowly,
And sank slowly through the air ;
Full of spirit's melancholy
And eternity's despair !
And they heard the words it said—
PAN IS DEAD—GREAT PAN IS DEAD—
    PAN, PAN IS DEAD.

'T was the hour when One in Sion
Hung for love's sake on a cross—
When His brow was chill with dying,
And His soul was faint with loss ;
When his priestly blood dropped downward,
And his kingly eyes looked throneward—
    Then, Pan was dead.

By the love He stood alone in,
His sole Godhead stood complete:
And the false gods fell down moaning,
Each from off his golden seat—
All the false gods with a cry
Rendered up their deity—
                    Pan, Pan was dead.

Wailing wide across the islands,
They rent, vest-like, their Divine!
And a darkness and a silence
Quenched the light of every shrine:
And Dodona's oak swang lonely
Henceforth, to the tempest only.
                    Pan, Pan was dead.

Pythia staggered,—feeling o'er her,
Her lost god's forsaking look!
Straight her eye-balls filmed with horror,
And her crispy fillets shook—
And her lips gasped through their foam,
For a word that did not come.
                    Pan, Pan was dead.

O ye vain false gods of Hellas,
Ye are silent evermore!
And I dash down this old chalice,
Whence libations ran of yore.
See! the wine crawls in the dust
Wormlike—as your glories must!
                    Since Pan is dead.

Get to dust, as common mortals,
By a common doom and track!
Let no Schiller from the portals
Of that Hades, call you back,
Or instruct us to weep all
At your antique funeral.

            Pan, Pan is dead

By your beauty, which confesses
Some chief Beauty conquering you,—
By our grand heroic guesses,
Through your falsehood, at the True,—
We will weep *not* . . . ! earth shall roll
Heir to each god's aureole--

            And Pan is dead.

Earth outgrows the mythic fancies
Sung beside her in her youth :
And those debonaire romances
Sound but dull beside the truth.
Phœbus' chariot-course is run !
Look up, poets, to the sun !

            Pan, Pan is dead

Christ hath sent us down the angels ;
And the whole earth and the skies
Are illumed by altar-candles
Lit for blessed mysteries :
And a Priest's Hand, through creation,
Waveth calm and consecration—

            And Pan is dead.

Truth is fair : should we forego it ?
Can we sigh right for a wrong ?
God Himself is the best Poet,
And the Real is His song.
Sing his Truth out fair and full,
And secure His beautiful.

　　　　　　　Let Pan be dead.

Truth is large.　Our aspiration
Scarce embraces half we be.
Shame ! to stand in His creation
And doubt Truth's sufficiency !
To think God's song unexcelling
The poor tales of our own telling—

　　　　　　　When Pan is dead

What is true and just and honest,
What is lovely, what is pure—
All of praise that hath admonish'd—
All of virtue, shall endure,—
These are themes for poets' uses,
Stirring nobler than the Muses,

　　　　　　　Ere Pan was dead

O brave poets, keep back nothing ;
Nor mix falsehood with the whole !
Look up Godward ! speak the truth in
Worthy song from earnest soul !
Hold, in high poetic duty,
Truest Truth the fairest Beauty '

　　　　　　　Pan, Pan is dead.

SLEEPING AND WATCHING.

Sleep on, Baby, on the floor,
　Tired of all the playing,
Sleep with smile the sweeter for
　That you dropped away in !
On your curls' full roundness, stand
　Golden lights serenely—
One cheek, pushed out by the hand,
　Folds the dimple inly :
Little head and little foot
　Heavy laid for pleasure,
Underneath the lids half shut,
　Slants the shining azure ;—
Open-soul　in　noonday sun,
　So, you lie and slumber !
Nothing evil　having done,
　Nothing can encumber.

I, who cannot sleep as well,
　Shall I sigh to view you ?
Or sigh further to foretell
　All that may undo you ?
Nay, keep smiling, little child,
　Ere the sorrow neareth.
I will smile too !　Patience mild
　Pleasure's token weareth.

Nay, keep sleeping before loss ;
  I shall sleep though losing !
As by cradle, so by cross,
  Sure is the reposing.

And God knows who sees us twain,
  Child at childish leisure,
I am near as tired of pain
  As you seem of pleasure ;
Very soon too, by His grace
  Gently wrapt around me,
Shall I show as calm a face,
  Shall I sleep as soundly !
Differing in this, that *you*
  Clasp your playthings sleeping,
While my hand shall drop the few
  Given to my keeping ;
Differing in this, that *I*
  Sleeping, shall be colder,
And in waking presently,
  Brighter to beholder !
Differing in this beside
  (Sleeper, have you heard me :
Do you move, and open wide
  Eyes of wonder towards me :)···
That while you, I thus recall
  From your sleep,—I solely,
Me from mine an angel shall,
  With reveille holy !

LESSONS FROM THE GORSE.

"To win the secret of a weed's plain heart."
LOWELL.

MOUNTAIN gorses, ever golden !
Cankered not the whole year long !
Do you teach us to be strong,
Howsoever pricked and holden
Like your thorny blooms, and so
Trodden on by rain and snow
Up the hill-side of this life, as bleak as where ye grow ?

Mountain blossoms, shining blossoms !
Do ye teach us to be glad
When no summer can be had,
Blooming in our inward bosoms ?
Ye, whom God preserveth still,
Set as lights upon a hill
Tokens to the wintry earth that Beauty liveth still !

Mountain gorses, do ye teach us
From that academic chair
Canopied with azure air,
That the wisest word Man reaches
Is the humblest he can speak ?
Ye, who live on mountain peak,
Yet live low along the ground, beside the grasses
meek !

Mountain gorses! since Linnæus
Knelt beside you on the sod,
For your beauty thanking God,—
For your teaching, ye should see us
Bowing in prostration new.
    Whence arisen,—if one or two
Drops be on our cheeks—O world! they are not tears,
        but dew.

THE CLAIM.

I.

GRIEF sate upon a rock and sighed one day:
 (Sighing is all her rest!)
"Wellaway, wellaway, ah, wellaway!"
As ocean beat the stone, did she her breast. . .
"Ah, wellaway!..ah me! alas, ah me!"
 Such sighing uttered she.

II.

A Cloud spake out of heaven, as soft as rain
 That falls on water; "Lo,
The Winds have wandered from me! I remain
Alone in the sky-waste, and cannot go
To lean my whiteness on the mountain blue.
 Till wanted for more dew.

III.

"The Sun has struck my brain to weary peace,
 Whereby, constrained and pale,
I spin for him a larger golden fleece
Than Jason's, yearning for as full a sail!
Sweet Grief, when thou hast sighed to thy mind,
 Give me a sigh for wind,—

25*

IV.

And let it carry me adown the west!'
    But Love, who, prostrated,
Lay at Grief's foot, . . his lifted eyes possessed
Of her full image, . . answered in her stead :
' Now nay, now nay ! she shall not give away
What is my wealth, for any Cloud that flieth.
    Where Grief makes moan,
    Love claims his own !
And therefore do I lie here night and day,
And eke my life out with the breath she sigheth.

A SABBATH MORNING AT SEA.

I.

The ship went on with solemn face:
    To meet the darkness on the deep,
        The solemn ship went onward.
I bowed down weary in the place;
    For parting tears and present sleep
        Had weighed mine eyelids downward.

II.

Thick sleep which shut all dreams from me,
    And kept my inner self apart
        And quiet from emotion,
Then brake away and left me free,
    Made conscious of a human heart
        Betwixt the heaven and ocean.

III.

The new sight, the new wondrous sight!
    The waters round me, turbulent,
        The skies impassive o'er me,
Calm in a moonless, sunless light,
    Half glorified by that intent
        Of holding the day-glory!

IV.

Two pale thin clouds did stand upon
  The meeting line of sea and sky,
    With aspect still and mystic.
I think they did foresee the sun,
  And rested on their prophecy
    In quietude majestic;

V.

Then flushed to radiance where they stood,
  Like statues by the open tomb
    Of shining saints half risen.—
The sun!—he came up to be viewed;
  And sky and sea made mighty room
    To inaugurate the vision!

VI.

I oft had seen the dawnlight run,
  As red wine, through the hills, and break
    Through many a mist's inurning;
But, here, no earth profaned the sun!
  Heaven, ocean, did alone partake
    The sacrament of morning.

VII.

Away with thoughts fantasticaly!
  I would be humble to my worth,
    Self-guarded as self-doubted.
Though here no earthly shadows fall,
  I, joying, grieving without earth,
    May desecrate without it.

VIII.

God's sabbath morning sweeps the waves:
  I would not praise the pageant high,
    Yet miss the dedicature:
I, carried toward the sunless graves
  By force of natural things,—should I
    Exult in only nature?

IX.

And could I bear to sit alone
  'Mid nature's fixed benignities,
    While my warm pulse was moving.
Too dark thou art, O glittering sun,
  Too strait ye are, capacious seas,
    To satisfy the loving.

X.

It seems a better lot than so,
  To sit with friends beneath the beech,
    And call them dear and dearer;
Or follow children as they go
  In pretty pairs, with softened speech
    As the church-bells ring nearer.

XI.

Love me, sweet friends, this sabbath day.
  The sea sings round me while ye roll
    Afar the hymn unaltered,
And kneel, where once I knelt to'pray,
  And bless me deeper in the soul,
    Because the voice has faltered.

XII.

And though this sabbath comes to me
  Without the stolèd minister
    Or chanting congregation,
God's spirit brings communion, HE
  Who brooded soft on waters drear,
    Creator on creation.

XIII.

Himself, I think, shall draw me higher,
  Where keep the saints with harp and song
    An endless sabbath morning,
And on that sea commixed with fire
  Oft drop their eyelids raised too long
    To the full Godhead's burning.

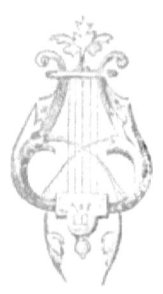

THE MASK.

I.

I HAVE a smiling face, she said,
  I have a jest for all I meet;
I have a garland for my head
  And all its flowers are sweet,—
And so you call me gay, she said.

II.

Grief taught to me this smile, she said,
  And Wrong did teach this jesting bold;
These flowers were plucked from garden-bed
  While a death-chime was tolled—
And what now will you say?—she said.

III.

Behind no prison-grate, she said,
  Which slurs the sunshine half a mile,
Live captives so uncomforted,
  As souls behind a smile.
God's pity let us pray, she said.

IV.

I know my face is bright, she said,—
  Such brightness, dying suns diffuse!

I bear upon my forehead shed
    The sign of what I lose,—
The ending of my day, she said.

v.

If I dared leave this smile, she said,
    And take a moan upon my mouth,
And tie a cypress round my head,
    And let my tears run smooth,—
It were the happier way, she said.

vi.

And since that must not be, she said,
    I fain your bitter world would leave.
How calmly, calmly, smile the Dead,
    Who do not, therefore, grieve!
The yea of Heaven is yea, she said.

vii.

But in your bitter world, she said,
    Face-joy's a costly mask to wear,
'Tis bought with pangs long nourishèd
    And rounded to despair.
Grief's earnest makes life's play, she said.

viii.

Ye weep for those who weep? she said—
    Ah fools! I bid you pass them by;
Go, weep for those whose hearts have bled,
    What time their eyes were dry!
Whom sadder can I say?—she said.

STANZAS.

I MAY sing; but minstrel's singing
Ever ceaseth with his playing.
I may smile; but time is bringing
Thoughts for smiles to wear away in.
I may view thee, mutely loving;
But *shall* view thee so in dying!
I may sigh; but life's removing,
And with breathing endeth sighing!
     Be it so!

When no song of mine comes near thee,
Will its memory fail to soften?
When no smile of mine can cheer thee,
Will thy smile be used as often?
When my looks the darkness boundeth,
Will thine own be lighted after?
When my sigh no longer soundeth,
Wilt thou list another's laughter?
     Be it so!

THE YOUNG QUEEN.

This awful responsibility is imposed upon me so suddenly and at so early a period of my life, that I should feel myself utterly oppressed by the burden, were I not sustained by the hope that Divine Providence, which has called me to this work, will give me strength for the performance of it.   THE QUEEN'S DECLARATION IN COUNCIL.

THE shroud is yet unspread
To wrap our crownèd dead ;
His soul hath scarcely hearkened for the thrilling
        word of doom ;
And Death that makes serene
Ev'n brows where crowns have been,
Hath scarcely time to meeten his, for silence of the
        tomb.

St. Paul's king-dirging note
The city's heart hath smote—
The city's heart is struck with thought more solemn
        than the tone !
A shadow sweeps apace
Before the nation's face,
Confusing in a shapeless blot, the sepulchre and
        throne.

The palace sounds with wail—
The courtly dames are pale—
A widow o'er the purple bows, and weeps its splendor
dim :
And we who hold the boon,
A king for freedom won,
Do feel eternity rise up between our thanks and him.

And while all things express
All glory's nothingness,
A royal maiden treadeth firm where *that* departed
trod !
The deathly scented crown
Weighs her shining ringlets down ;
But calm she lifts her trusting face, and calleth upon
God.

Her thoughts are deep within her :
No outward pageants win her
From memories that in her soul are rolling wave on
wave—
Her palace walls enring
The dust that was a king—
And very cold beneath her feet, she feels her father's
grave.

And One, as fair as she,
Can scarce forgotten be,—
Who clasp'd a little infant dead, for all a kingdom's
worth !

The mournëd, blessëd One,
Who views Jehovah's throne,
Aye smiling to the angels, that she lost a throne on
        earth.

Perhaps our youthful Queen
Remembers what has been—
Her childhood's rest by loving heart, and sport on
        grassy sod—
Alas! can others wear
A mother's heart for her?
But calm she lifts her trusting face, and calleth upon
        God.

Yea! on God, thou maiden
Of spirit nobly laden,
And leave such happy days behind, for happy-making
        years!
A nation looks to thee
For stedfast sympathy:
Make room within thy bright clear eyes, for all its
        gathered tears.

And so the grateful isles
Shall give thee back their smiles,
And as thy mother joys in thee, in them shalt *thou*
        rejoice;
Rejoice to meekly bow
A somewhat paler brow,
While the King of kings shall bless thee by the
        British people's voice!

VICTORIA'S TEARS.

Hark! the reiterated clangor sounds!
Now murmurs, like the sea or like the storm,
Or like the flames on forests, move and mount
From rank to rank, and loud and louder roll,
Till all the people is one vast applause.

LANDOR'S *Gebir*

"O MAIDEN! heir of kings!
A king has left his place!
The majesty of Death has swept
All other from his face!
And thou upon thy mother's breast,
No longer lean adown,
But take the glory for the rest,
And rule the land that loves thee best!"
She heard and wept—
She wept, to wear a crown!

They decked her courtly halls;
They reined her hundred steeds;
They shouted at her palace gate,
"A noble Queen succeeds!"
Her name has stirred the mountain's sleep,
Her praise has filled the town!
And mourners God had stricken deep,
Looked hearkening up, and did not weep.
Alone she wept,
Who wept, to wear a crown!

She saw no purple shine,
    For tears had dimmed her eyes;
She only knew her childhood's flowers
    Were happier pageantries!
And while her heralds played the part,
    For million shouts to drown—
" God save the Queen " from hill to mart.—
She heard through all her beating heart,
        And turned and wept—
        She wept, to wear a crown!

God save thee, weeping Queen!
    Thou shalt be well beloved!
The tyrant's sceptre cannot move,
    As those pure tears have moved!
The nature in thine eyes we see,
    That tyrants cannot own—
The love that guardeth liberties!
Strange blessing on the nation lies,
        Whose Sovereign wept—
        Yea! wept, to wear its crown!

God bless thee, weeping Queen,
    With blessing more divine!
And fill with happier love than earth's,
    That tender heart of thine!
That when the thrones of earth shall be
    As low as graves brought down;
A piercëd hand may give to thee
The crown which angels shout to see!
        Thou wilt not *weep*,
        To wear that heavenly crown!

PROMETHEUS BOUND.

PROMETHEUS BOUND.

PERSONS OF THE DRAMA.

PROMETHEUS.   HEPHÆSTUS.
OCEANUS.   Io, daughter of Inachus.
HERMES.   STRENGTH and FORCE.
          CHORUS of Ocean Nymphs.

SCENE.—STRENGTH *and* FORCE, HEPHÆSTUS *and* PROMETHEUS, *at
the Rocks.*

Strength.

WE reach the utmost limit of the earth,
The Scythian track, the desert without man,
And now, Hephæstus, thou must needs fulfil
The mandate of our father, and with links
Indissoluble of adamantine chains,
Fasten against this beetling precipice
This guilty god!   Because he filched away
Thine own bright flower, the glory of plastic fire,
And gifted mortals with it,—such a sin
It doth behove he expiate to the gods,
Learning to accept the empery of Zeus,
And leave off his old trick of loving man.
    Hephæstus.   O Strength and Force,—for you, o-
        Zeus's will
Presents a deed for doing.—No more!—but *I*,
I lack your daring, up this storm-rent chasm
To fix with violent hands a kindred god,
Howbeit necessity compels me so

That I must dare it,—and our Zeus commands
With a most inevitable word.   Ho, thou!
High-thoughted son of Themis who is sage,
Thee loth, I loth must rivet fast in chains
Against this rocky height unclomb by man,
Where never human voice nor face shall find
Out thee who lov'st them!—and thy beauty's
      flower,
Scorched in the sun's clear heat, shall fade away.
Night shall come up with garniture of stars
To comfort thee with shadow, and the sun
Disperse with retrickt beams the morning frosts;
And through all changes, sense of present woe
Shall vex thee sore, because with none of them
There comes a hand to free.   Such fruit is plucked
From love of man!—for in that thou, a god,
Didst brave the wrath of gods and give away
Undue respect to mortals; for that crime
Thou art adjudged to guard this joyless rock,
Erect, unslumbering, bending not the knee,
And many a cry and unavailing moan
To utter on the air!   For Zeus is stern,
And new-made kings are cruel.
    Strength.   Be it so.
Why loiter in vain pity?   Why not hate
A god the gods hate?—one too who betrayed
Thy glory unto men?
    Hephæstus.   An awful thing
Is kinship joined to friendship.
    Strength.   Grant it be;
Is disobedience to the Father's word
A possible thing?   Dost quail not more for *that?*
    Hephæstus.   *Thou,* at least, art a stern one! ever
      bold!

Strength.   Why, if I wept, it were no remedy.
And do not *thou* spend labor on the air
To bootless uses.

Hephæstus.   Cursed handicraft!
I curse and hate thee, O my craft!

Strength.   Why hate
Thy craft most plainly innocent of all
These pending ills?

Hephæstus.   I would some other hand
Were here to work it!

Strength.   All work hath its pain,
Except to rule the gods.   There is none free
Except King Zeus.

Hephæstus.   I know it very well:
I argue not against it.

Strength.   Why not, then,
Make haste and lock the fetters over HIM,
Lest Zeus behold thee lagging?

Hephæstus.   Here be chains.
Zeus may behold these.

Strength.   Seize him,—strike amain!
Strike with the hammer on each side his hands—
Rivet him to the rock.

Hephæstus.   The work is done,
And thoroughly done.

Strength.   Still faster grapple him,—
Wedge him in deeper,—leave no inch to stir!
He's terrible for finding a way out
From the irremediable.

Hephæstus.   Here's an arm, at least,
Grappled past freeing.

Strength.   Now, then, buckle me
The other securely.   Let this wise one learn
He's duller than our Zeus.

Hephæstus.   Oh, none but he
Accuse me justly!

Strength.   Now, straight through the chest
Take him and bite him with the clenching tooth
Of the adamantine wedge, and rivet him.

Hephæstus.   Alas, Prometheus! what thou suffer-
     est here
I sorrow over.

Strength.   Dost thou flinch again,
And breathe groans for the enemies of Zeus?
Beware lest thine own pity find thee out.

Hephæstus. Thou dost behold a spectacle that turns
The sight o' the eyes to pity.

Strength.   I behold
A sinner suffer his sin's penalty.
But lash the thongs about his sides.

Hephæstus.   So much,
I must do.   Urge no farther than I must.

Strength.   Ay, but I *will* urge!—and, with shout
     on shout,
Will hound thee at this quarry!   Get thee down
And ring amain the iron round his legs!

Hephæstus.   That work was not long doing.

Strength.   Heavily now
Let fall the strokes upon the perforant gyves!
For He who rates the work has a heavy hand.

Hephæstus.   Thy speech is savage as thy shape.

Strength.   Be thou
Gentle and tender! but revile not me
For the firm will and the untruckling hate.

Hephæstus.   Let us go!   He is netted round with
     chains.

Strength.   Here, now, taunt on! and having
     spoiled the gods

Of honors, crown withal thy mortal men
Who live a whole day out!   Why how could *they*
Draw off from thee one single of thy griefs?
Methinks the Demons gave thee a wrong name,
Prometheus, which means Providence,—because
Thou dost thyself need providence to see
Thy roll and ruin from the top of doom.

    Prometheus alone.   O holy Æther, and swift
      winged Winds,
And River-wells, and laughter innumerous
Of yon Sea-waves!   Earth, mother of us all,
And all-viewing cyclic Sun, I cry on you!—
Behold me a god, what I endure from gods!
      Behold, with throe on throe,
      How, wasted by this woe,
    I wrestle down the myriad years of Time!
      Behold, how fast around me,
    The new King of the happy ones sublime
    Has flung the chain he forged, has shamed and
      bound me!
    Woe, woe! to-day's woe and the coming mor-
      row's,
    I cover with one groan! And where is found me
      A limit to these sorrows?
And yet what word do I say? I have foreknown
Clearly all things that should be—nothing done
Comes sudden to my soul—and I must bear
What is ordained with patience, being aware
Necessity doth front the universe
With an invincible gesture.   Yet this curse
Which strikes me now, I find it hard to brave
In silence or in speech.   Because I gave
Honor to mortals, I have yoked my soul
To this compelling fate!   Because I stole

The secret fount of fire, whose bubbles went
Over the ferule's brim, and manward sent
Art's mighty means and perfect rudiment,
That sin I expiate in this agony ;
    Hung here in fetters, 'neath the blanching sky !
        Ah, ah me ! what a sound,
What a fragrance sweeps up from a pinion unseen
Of a god, or a mortal, or nature between,
Sweeping up to this rock where the earth has her
        bound,
To have sight of my pangs,—or some guerdon
        obtain—
Lo ! a god in the anguish, a god in the chain !
        The god, Zeus hateth sore
        And his gods hate again,
As many as tread on his glorified floor,
Because I loved mortals too much evermore !
Alas me ! what a murmur and motion I hear,
        As of birds flying near !
        And the air undersings
        The light stroke of their wings—
And all life that approaches I wait for in fear.

        Chorus of Sea Nymphs, 1st Strophe.
        Fear nothing ! our troop
        Floats lovingly up
        With a quick-oaring stroke
        Of wings steered to the rock ;
Having softened the soul of our father below !
For the gales of swift-bearing have sent me a sound,
And the clank of the iron, the malleted blow,
        Smote down the profound
        Of my caverns of old,
And struck the red light in a blush from my brow,—

Till I sprang up unsandalled, in haste to behold,
And rushed forth on my chariot of wings manifold.

Prometheus. Alas me!—alas me!
Ye offspring of Tethys who bore at her breast
Many children; and eke of Oceanus,—he,
Coiling still around earth with perpetual unrest;
    Behold me and see
    How transfixed with the fang
    Of a fetter I hang
On the high-jutting rocks of this fissure, and keep
An uncoveted watch o'er the world and the deep.

Chorus, 1st Antistrophe.

I behold thee, Prometheus—yet now, yet now,
A terrible cloud whose rain is tears
Sweeps over mine eyes that witness how
    Thy body appears
Hung awaste on the rocks by infrangible chains!
For new is the hand and the rudder that steers
The ship of Olympus through surge and wind—
And of old things passed, no track is behind.

Prometheus. Under earth, under Hades,
    Where the home of the shade is,
  All into the deep, deep Tartarus,
    I would he had hurled me adown!
I would he had plunged me, fastened thus
In the knotted chain-with the savage clang,
All into the dark, where there should be none,
Neither god nor another, to laugh and see!
    But now the winds sing through and shake
    The hurtling chains wherein I hang,—
    And I, in my naked sorrows, make
    Much mirth for my enemy.

Chorus, 2d Strophe.

Nay! who of the gods hath a heart so stern
   As to use thy woe for a mock and mirth?
Who would not turn more mild to learn
   Thy sorrows? who of the heaven and earth,
       Save Zeus! But he
       Right wrathfully
Bears on his sceptral soul unbent,
And rules thereby the heavenly seed;
Nor will he pause till he content
His thirsty heart in a finished deed;
Or till Another shall appear,
To win by fraud, to seize by fear
The hard-to-be-captured government.

Prometheus.   Yet even of *me* he shall have need,
   That monarch of the blessed seed;
   Of me, of me, who now am cursed
     By his fetters dire,—
   To wring my secret out withal
     And learn by whom his sceptre shall
   Be filched from him—as was, at first,
       His heavenly fire!
   But he never shall enchant me
     With his honey-lipped persuasion;
   Never, never shall he daunt me
     With the oath and threat of passion,
   Into speaking as they want me,
   Till he loose this savage chain,
     And accept the expiation
   Of my sorrow, in his pain.

Chorus, 2d Antistrophe.

Thou art, sooth, a brave god,
    And, for all thou hast borne
From the stroke of the rod,
    Nought relaxest from scorn!
But thou speakest unto me
    Too free and unworn—
And a terror strikes through me
    And festers my soul
    And I fear, in the roll
Of the storm, for thy fate
    In the ship far from shore—
Since the son of Saturnius is hard in his hate
    And unmoved in his heart evermore.

Prometheus.   I know that Zeus is stern!
I know he metes his justice by his will!
And yet, his soul shall learn
More softness when once broken by this ill,—
And curbing his unconquerable vaunt
He shall rush on in fear to meet with me
Who rush to meet with him in agony,
To issues of harmonious covenant.
    Chorus. Remove the veil from all things, and
      relate
The story to us!—of what crime accused,
Zeus smites thee with dishonorable pangs.
Speak! if to teach us do not grieve thyself.
    Prometheus. The utterance of these things is
      torture to me,
But so, too, is their silence! each way lies
Woe strong as fate!
                When gods began with wrath,

27*

And war rose up between their starry brows,
Some choosing to cast Chronos from his throne
That Zeus might king it there; and some in haste
With opposite oaths that they would have no Zeus
To rule the gods forever,—I, who brought
The counsel I thought meetest, could not move
The Titans, children of the Heaven and Earth,
What time disdaining in their rugged souls
My subtle machinations, they assumed
It was an easy thing for force to take
The mastery of fate.   My mother, then,
Who is called not only Themis but Earth too,
(Her single beauty joys in many names,)
Did teach me with reiterant prophecy
What future should be,—and how conquering gods
Should not prevail by strength and violence,
But by guile only.   When I told them so,
They would not deign to contemplate the truth
On all sides round;—whereat I deemed it best
To lead my willing mother upwardly,
And set my Themis face to face with Zeus
As willing to receive her!   Tartarus,
With its abysmal cloister of the Dark,
Because I gave that counsel, covers up
The antique Chronos and his siding hosts;
And, by that counsel helped, the king of gods
Hath recompensed me with these bitter pangs!
For kingship wears a cancer at the heart,—
Distrust in friendship.   Do ye also ask,
What crime it is for which he tortures me—
That shall be clear before you.   When at first
He filled his father's throne, he instantly
Made various gifts of glory to the gods,
And dealt the empire out.   Alone of men,

Of miserable men he took no count,
But yearned to sweep their track off from the world,
And plant a newer race there!   Not a god
Resisted such desire except myself!
I dared it!   *I* drew mortals back to light,
From meditated ruin deep as hell,—
For which wrong I am bent down in these pangs
Dreadful to suffer, mournful to behold,—
And I, who pitied man, am thought myself
Unworthy of pity,—while I render out
Deep rhythms of anguish 'neath the harping hand
That strikes me thus!—a sight to shame your
          Zeus!
    Chorus.   Hard as thy chains, and cold as all these
          rocks,
Is he, Prometheus, who withholds his heart
From joining in thy woe.   I yearned before
To fly this sight—and, now I gaze on it,
I sicken inwards.
    Prometheus.   To my friends, indeed,
I must be a sad sight.
    Chorus.   And didst thou sin
No more than so?
    Prometheus.   I did restrain besides
My mortals from premeditating death.
    Chorus.   How didst thou medicine the plague-fear
          of death?
    Prometheus.   I set blind Hopes to inhabit in their
          house.
    Chorus.   By that gift, thou didst help thy mortals
          well.
    Prometheus.   I gave them also,—fire.
    Chorus.   And have they now
Those creatures of a day, the red-eyed fire?

Prometheus. They have! and shall learn by it,
   many arts.
   Chorus. And, truly, for such sins Zeus tortures
      thee,
And will remit no anguish? Is there set
No limit before thee to thine agony?
   Prometheus. No other! only what seems good
      to HIM.
   Chorus. And how will it seem good? what hope
      remains?
Seest thou not that thou hast sinned? But that
      thou hast sinned
It glads me not to speak of, and grieves *thee*—
Then let it pass from both! and seek thyself
Some outlet from distress.
   Prometheus.   It is in truth
An easy thing to stand aloof from pain
And lavish exhortation and advice
On one vexed sorely by it. I have known
All in prevision! By my choice, my choice,
I freely sinned—I will confess my sin—
And helping mortals, found mine own despair!
I did not think indeed that I should pine
Beneath such pangs against such skiey rocks,
Doomed to this drear hill and no neighboring
Of any life!—but mourn not *ye* for griefs
I bear to-day!—hear rather, dropping down
To the plain, how other woes creep on to me,
And learn the consummation of my doom.
Beseech you, nymphs, beseech you!—grieve for me
Who now am grieving!—for grief walks the earth,
And sits down at the foot of each by turns.
   Chorus. We hear the deep clash of thy words.
      Prometheus, and obey!

And I spring with a rapid foot away
From the rushing car and the holy air
      The track of birds—
And I drop to the rugged ground and there
  Await the tale of thy despair.

Enter OCEANUS.

Oceanus. I reach the bourne of my weary road,
  Where I may see and answer thee,
  Prometheus, in thine agony!
On the back of the quick-winged bird I glode,
     And I bridled him in
     With the will of a god,
  Behold thy sorrow aches in me,
    Constrained by the force of kin.
Nay, though that tie were all undone,
For the life of none beneath the sun,
Would I seek a larger benison
  Than I seek for thine!
And thou shalt learn my words are truth,—
That no fair parlance of the mouth
  Grows falsely out of mine!
Now give me a deed to prove my faith,—
For no faster friend is named in breath
  Than I, Oceanus, am thine.

Prometheus. Ha! what has brought thee? Hast
    thou also come
To look upon my woe? How hast thou dared
To leave the depths called after thee, the caves
Self-hewn and self-roofed with spontaneous rock,
To visit Earth, the mother of my chain?
Hast come indeed to view my doom and mourn
That I should sorrow thus? Gaze on, and see

x

         fain
Exhort thee, though already subtle enough,
To a better wisdom. Titan, know thyself,
And take new softness to thy manners, since
A new king rules the gods. If words like these,
Harsh words and trenchant. thou wilt fling abroad,
Zeus haply, though he sit so far and high,
May hear thee do it; and, so, this wrath of his
Which now affects thee fiercely, shall appear
A mere child's sport at vengeance! Wretched god,
Rather dismiss the passion which thou hast,
And seek a change from grief. Perhaps I seem
To address thee with old saws and outworn sense,—
Yet such a curse, Prometheus, surely waits
On lips that speak too proudly!—thou, meantime,
Art none the meeker, nor dost yield a jot
To evil circumstance, preparing still
To swell the account of grief with other griefs
Than what are borne! Beseech thee, use me then
For counsel! Do not spurn against the pricks,—
Seeing that who reigns, reigns by cruelty
Instead of right. And now, I go from hence,
And will endeavor if a power of mine
Can break thy fetters through. For thee,—be calm,
And smooth thy words from passion. Knowest thou
         not
Of perfect knowledge, thou who knowest too much,
That where the tongue wags, ruin never lags?
   Prometheus. I gratulate thee who hast shared
      and dared

All things with me, except their penalty !
Enough so ! leave these thoughts ! It cannot be
That thou shouldst move HIM.   HE may *not* be
          moved !
And *thou*, beware of sorrow on this road.
   Oceanus.   Ay ! ever wiser for another's use
Than thine ! the event, and not the prophecy,
Attests it to me.   Yet where now I rush,
Thy wisdom hath no power to drag me back ;
Because I glory—glory, to go hence
And win for thee deliverance from thy pangs,
As a free gift from Zeus.
   Prometheus.   Why there, again,
I give thee gratulation and applause !
Thou lackest no good-will.   But, as for deeds,
Do nought ! 'twere all done vainly ! helping nought,
Whatever thou wouldst do.   Rather take rest,
And keep thyself from evil.   If I grieve,
I do not therefore wish to multiply
The griefs of others.   Verily, not so !
For still my brother's doom doth vex my soul,—
My brother Atlas, standing in the west,
Shouldering the column of the heaven and earth,
A difficult burden !   I have also seen,
And pitied as I saw, the earth-born one,
The inhabitant of old Cilician caves,
The great war-monster of the hundred heads,
(All taken and bowed beneath the violent Hand,)
Typhon the fierce, who did resist the gods,
And, hissing slaughter from his dreadful jaws,
Flash out ferocious glory from his eyes,
As if to storm the throne of Zeus !   Whereat,
The sleepless arrow of Zeus flew straight at him,—

The headlong bolt of thunder breathing flame,
And struck him downward from his eminence
Of exultation! Through the very soul,
It struck him, and his strength was withered up
To ashes, thunder-blasted. Now, he lies
A helpless trunk supinely, at full length
Beside the strait of ocean, spurred into
By roots of Ætna,—high upon whose tops
Hephæstus sits and strikes the flashing ore.
From thence the rivers of fire shall burst away
Hereafter, and devour with savage jaws
The equal plains of fruitful Sicily!
Such passion he shall boil back in hot darts
Of an insatiate fury and sough of flame,
Fallen Typhon;—howsoever struck and charred
By Zeus's bolted thunder! But for thee,
Thou art not so unlearned as to need
My teaching—let thy knowledge save thyself.
I quaff the full cup of a present doom,
And wait till Zeus hath quenched his will in wrath.

    Oceanus.   Prometheus, art thou ignorant of
        this,—
That words do medicine anger?

    Prometheus.   If the word
With seasonable softness touch the soul,
And, where the parts are ulcerous, scar them not
By any rudeness.

    Oceanus.   With a noble aim
To dare as nobly—is there harm in *that?*
Dost thou discern it? Teach me.

    Prometheus.   I discern
Vain aspiration,—unresultive work.

    Oceanus.   Then suffer me to bear the brunt of
        this!

Since it is profitable that one who is wise
Should seem not wise at all.

   Prometheus.   And such would seem
My very crime.

   Oceanus.   In truth thine argument
Sends me back home.

   Prometheus.   Lest any lament for me
Should cast thee down to hate.

   Oceanus.   The hate of Him,
Who sits a new king on the absolute throne?

   Prometheus. Beware of him,—lest thine heart
      grieve by him.

   Oceanus. Thy doom, Prometheus, be my teacher!

   Prometheus.   Go!
Depart—beware!—and keep the mind thou hast.

   Oceanus. Thy words drive after, as I rush before!
Lo! my four-footed Bird sweeps smooth and wide
The flats of air with balanced pinions, glad
To bend his knee at home in the ocean-stall.

                    [*Exit* OCEANUS.

       Chorus, 1st Strophe.

  I moan thy fate, I moan for thee,
    Prometheus! From my eyes too tender,
Drop after drop incessantly
    The tears of my heart's pity render
My cheeks wet from their fountains free.—
    Because that Zeus, the stern and cold,
    Whose law is taken from his breast,
    Uplifts his sceptre manifest
      Over the gods of old.

       1st Antistrophe.

  All the land is moaning
With a murmured plaint to-day!
28

All the mortal nations,
    Having habitations
Near the holy Asia.
    Are a dirge entoning
For thine honor and thy brother's,
Once majestic beyond others
    In the old belief,—
Now are groaning in the groaning
    Of thy deep-voiced grief.

2d Strophe.

Mourn the maids inhabitant
    Of the Colchian land.
Who with white, calm bosoms, stand
    In the battle's roar—
Mourn the Scythian tribes that haunt
The verge of earth, Mæotis' shore—

2d Antistrophe.

Yea! Arabia's battle crown.
And dwellers in the beetling town
Mount Caucasus sublimely nears,—
An iron squadron, thundering down
    With the sharp-prowed spears.

But one other before, have I seen to remain,
        By invincible pain
Bound and vanquished,—one Titan !—'twas Atlas
            who bears,
In a curse from the gods, by that strength of his own
        Which he evermore wears,
The weight of the heaven on his shoulder alone,
        While he sighs up the stars !
And the tides of the ocean wail bursting their bars,—

Murmurs still the profound,—
And black Hades roars up through the chasm of the
ground,—
And the fountains of pure-running rivers moan low
In a pathos of woe.

Prometheus. Beseech, you, think not I am silent
thus
Through pride or scorn! I only gnaw my heart
With meditation, seeing myself so wronged.
For so—their honours to these new-made gods,
What other gave but I,—and dealt them out
With distribution? Ay—but here I am dumb;
For here, I should repeat your knowledge to you,
If I spake aught. List rather to the deeds
I did for mortals,—how, being fools before,
I made them wise and true in aim of soul.
And let me tell you—not as taunting men,
But teaching you the intention of my gifts;
How, first beholding, they beheld in vain,
And hearing, heard not, but like shapes in dreams,
Mixed all things wildly down the tedious time,
Nor knew to build a house against the sun
With wicketed sides, nor any woodcraft knew,
But lived, like silly ants, beneath the ground
In hollow caves unsunned. There, came to them
No stedfast sign of winter, nor of spring
Flower-perfumed, nor of summer full of fruit,
But blindly and lawlessly they did all things,
Until I taught them how the stars do rise
And set in mystery; and devised for them
Number, the inducer of philosophies,
The synthesis of Letters, and, beside,
The artificer of all things, Memory,

That sweet Muse-mother.   I was first to yoke
The servile beasts in couples, carrying
An heirdom of man's burdens on their backs!
I joined to chariots, steeds, that love the bit
They champ at—the chief pomp of golden ease.
And none but I, originated ships,
The seaman's chariots, wandering on the brine
With linen wings!   And I—oh, miserable!—
Who did devise for mortals all these arts,
Have no device left now to save myself
From the woe I suffer.

    Chorus.   Most unseemly woe
Thou sufferest and dost stagger from the sense,
Bewildered!   Like a bad leech falling sick
Thou art faint at soul, and canst not find the drugs
Required to save thyself.

    Prometheus.   Harken the rest,
And marvel further—what more arts and means
I did invent,—this, greatest!—if a man
Fell sick, there was no cure, nor esculent
Nor chrism nor liquid, but for lack of drugs
Men pined and wasted, till I showed them all
Those mixtures of emollient remedies
Whereby they might be rescued from disease.
I fixed the various rules of mantic art,
Discerned the vision from the common dream,
Instructed them in vocal auguries
Hard to interpret, and defined as plain
The wayside omens,—flights of crook-clawed birds,—
Showed which are, by their nature, fortunate,
And which not so, and what the food of each,
And what the hates, affections, social needs,
Of all to one another,—taught what sign
Of visceral lightness, coloured to a shade,

May charm the genial gods, and what fair spots
Commend the lung and liver. Burning so
The limbs encased in fat, and the long chine,
I led my mortals on to an art abstruse,
And cleared their eyes to the image in the fire,
Erst filmed in dark. Enough said now of this.
For the other helps of man hid underground,
The iron and the brass, silver and gold,
Can any dare affirm he found them out
Before me? None, I know! Unless he choose
To lie in his vaunt. In one word learn the whole,—
That all arts came to mortals from Prometheus.
 Chorus. Give mortals now no inexpedient help,
Neglecting thine own sorrow! I have hope still
To see thee, breaking from the fetter here,
Stand up as strong as Zeus.
 Prometheus.   This ends not thus,
The oracular Fate ordains. I must be bowed
By infinite woes and pangs, to escape this chain.
Necessity is stronger than mine art.
 Chorus. Who holds the helm of that Necessity?
 Prometheus. The threefold Fates and the unfor-
  getting Furies.
 Chorus. Is Zeus less absolute than these are?
 Prometheus.   Yea,
And therefore cannot fly what is ordained.
 Chorus. What is ordained for Zeus, except to be
A king forever?
 Prometheus. 'Tis too early yet
For thee to learn it: ask no more.
 Chorus.   Perhaps
Thy secret may be something holy?
 Prometheus.   Turn
To another matter! this, it is not time

To speak abroad, but utterly to veil
In silence. For by that same secret kept,
I 'scape this chain's dishonor and its woe.

Chorus, 1st Strophe.

Never, oh never,
May Zeus, the all-giver,
Wrestle down from his throne
In that might of his own,
To antagonize mine!
Nor let me delay
As I bend on my way
Toward the gods of the shrine,
Where the altar is full
Of the blood of the bull,
Near the tossing brine
Of Ocean my father.
May no sin be sped in the word that is said,
But my vow be rather
Consummated,
Nor evermore fail, nor evermore pine.

1st Antistrophe.

'Tis sweet to have
Life lengthened out
With hopes proved brave
By the very doubt,
Till the spirit enfold
Those manifest joys which were foretold!
But I thrill to behold
Thee, victim doomed,
By the countless cares
And the drear despairs,
Forever consumed.

And all because thou, who art fearless now
     Of Zeus above,
Didst overflow for mankind below,
     With a free-souled, reverent love.

  Ah friend, behold and see !
What's all the beauty of humanity ?
     Can it be fair ?
What's all the strength ?—is it strong ?
  And what hope can they bear,
These dying livers—living one day long ?
  Ah seest thou not, my friend,
     How feeble and slow,
     And like a dream, doth go
This poor blind manhood, drifted from its end ?
  And how no mortal wranglings can confuse
     The harmony of Zeus ?

Prometheus, I have learnt these things
  From the sorrow in thy face !
  Another song did fold its wings
  Upon my lips in other days,
  When round the bath and round the bed
  The hymeneal chant instead
     I sang for thee, and smiled,—
  And thou didst lead, with gifts and vows,
     Hesione, my father's child,
  To be thy wedded spouse.

Io enters.

  Io. What land is this ? what people is here ?
And who is he that writhes, I see,
     In the rock-hung chain ?
Now what is the crime that hath brought thee to pain ?

And what is the land—make answer free—
Which I wander through, in my wrong and fear?
     Ah! ah! ah me!
The gad-fly stingeth to agony!
O Earth, keep off that phantasm pale
Of earth-born Argus!—ah!—I quail
     When my soul descries
That herdsman with the myriad eyes
Which seem, as he comes, one crafty eye!
Graves hide him not, though he should die,
But he doggeth me in my misery
From the roots of death, on high—on high—
And along the sands of the siding deep,
All famine-worn, he follows me,
And his waxen reed doth undersound
     The waters round,
And giveth a measure that giveth sleep.

     Woe, woe, woe!
Where shall my weary course be done?—
What wouldst thou with me, Saturn's son?
And in what have I sinned, that I should go
Thus yoked to grief by thine hand for ever?
     Ah! ah! dost vex me so.
       That I madden and shiver,
       Stung through with dread?
     Flash the fire down, to burn me!
     Heave the earth up, to cover me!
Or plunge me in the deep, with the salt waves over
     me,
     Where the sea-beasts may be fed!
     O king, do not spurn me
       In my prayer!
For this wandering everlonger, evermore,

Hath overworn me,—
And I know not on what shore
I may rest from my despair.

Chorus.   Hearest thou what the ox-horned maid-
en saith?
Prometheus.   How could I choose but hearken
what she saith,
The frenzied maiden?—Inachus's child?—
Who love-warms Zeus's heart, and now is lashed
By Here's hate, along the unending ways?

Io.   Who taught thee to articulate that name,—
My father's?   Speak to his child,
By grief and shame defiled!
Who art thou, victim, thou—who dost acclaim
Mine anguish in true words, on the wide air?
And callest too by name, the curse that came
From Here unaware,
To waste and pierce me with the maddening goad.
Ah—ah—I leap
With the pang of the hungry—I bound on the
road—
I am driven by my doom—
I am overcome
By the wrath of an enemy strong and deep!
Are any of those who have tasted pain,
Alas!—as wretched as I?
Now tell me plain, doth aught remain
For my soul to endure beneath the sky?
Is there any help to be holpen by?
If knowledge be in thee, let it be said—
Cry aloud—cry
To the wandering, woeful maid.

Prometheus. Whatever thou wouldst learn I will
    declare,—
No riddle upon my lips, but such straight words,
As friends should use to each other when they talk.
Thou seest Prometheus, who gave mortals fire.

Io. O common Help of all men, known of all,
O miserable Prometheus,—for what cause
Dost thou endure thus?

Prometheus. I have done with wail
For my own griefs—but lately—

Io. Wilt thou not
Vouchsafe the boon to me?

Prometheus. Say which thou wilt,
For I vouchsafe all.

Io. Speak then, and reveal
Who shut thee in this chasm.

Prometheus. The will of Zeus,
The hand of his Hephæstus.

Io. And what crime,
Dost expiate so?

Prometheus. I have told enough for thee,
In so much only.

Io. Nay—but show besides
The limit of my wandering, and the time
Which yet is lacking to fulfill my grief.

Prometheus. Why, not to know were better
    than to know,
For such as thou.

Io. Beseech thee, blind me not
To that which I must suffer.

Prometheus. If I do
The reason is not that I grudge the boon.

Io. What reason, then, prevents thy speaking
    out?

Prometheus. No grudging! but a fear to break
    thine heart.

Io.   Less care for me, I pray thee! Certainty,
I count for advantage.

Prometheus.   Thou wilt have it so,
And, therefore, I must speak. Now hear—

  Chorus.   Not yet!
Give half the guerdon my way. Let us learn
First, what the curse is that befell the maid,—
Her own voice telling her own wasting woes!
The sequence of that anguish shall await
The teaching of thy lips.

  Prometheus.   It doth behove
That thou, maid Io, shouldst vouchsafe to these
The grace they pray; the more, because they are
    called
Thy father's sisters; since to open out
And mourn out grief where it is possible
To draw a tear from the audience, is a work
That pays its own price well.

  Io.   I cannot choose
But trust you, nymphs, and tell you all ye ask,
In clear words—though I sob amid my speech
In speaking of the storm-curse sent from Zeus,
And of my beauty, from which height it took
Its swoop on me, poor wretch! left thus deformed,
And monstrous to your eyes. For evermore
Around my virgin chamber, wandering went
The nightly visions which entreated me
With syllabled smooth sweetness.—' Blessed maid,
Why lengthen out thy maiden hours when fate
Permits the noblest spousal in the world?
When Zeus burns with the arrow of thy love,
And fain would touch thy beauty.—Maiden, thou

Despise not Zeus! depart to Lerne's mead
That's green around thy father's flocks and stalls,
Until the passion of the heavenly eye
Be quenched in sight.' Such dreams did all night
        long
Constrain me—me, unhappy!—till I dared
To tell my father how they trod the dark
With visionary steps; whereat he sent
His frequent heralds to the Pythian fane,
And also to Dodona, and inquired
How best, by act or speech, to please the gods,
The same returning, brought back oracles
Of doubtful sense, indefinite response,
Dark to interpret; but at last there came
To Inachus an answer that was clear,—
Thrown straight as any bolt, and spoken out.
This—' he should drive me from my home and
        land,
And bid me wander to the extreme verge
Of all the earth—or, if he willed it not,
Should have a thunder with a fiery eye
Leap straight from Zeus to burn up all his race
To the last root of it.' By which Loxian word
Subdued, he drove me forth, and shut me out,
He loth, me loth,—but Zeus's violent bit
Compelled him to the deed!—when instantly
My body and soul were changed and distraught,
And, hornëd as ye see, and spurred along
By the fanged insect, with a maniac leap
I rushed on to Cerchnea's limpid stream
And Lerne's fountain-water. There, the earth
        born,
The herdsman Argus, most immitigable
Of wrath, did find me out, and track me out

With countless eyes, yet staring at my steps!—
And though an unexpected sudden doom
Drew him from life—I, curse-tormented still,
Am driven from land to land before the scourge
The gods hold o'er me.   So, thou hast heard the
		past,
And if a bitter future thou canst tell,
Speak on!   I charge thee, do not flatter me
Through pity, with false words! for, in my mind,
Deceiving works more shame than torturing doth.

Chorus.

Ah! silence here!
Nevermore, nevermore,
Would I languish for
The stranger's word
To thrill mine ear!—
Nevermore for the wrong and the woe and the fear,
So hard to behold,
So cruel to bear,
Piercing my soul with a double-edged sword
Of a sliding cold!
Ah Fate!—ah me!—
I shudder to see
This wandering maid in her agony.

Prometheus.   Grief is too quick in thee, and fear
	too full!
Be patient till thou hast learnt the rest!
	Chorus.				Speak—teach!
To those who are sad already, it seems sweet,
By clear foreknowledge to make perfect, pain,
	Prometheus. The boon ye asked me first was
		lightly won,—
29						Y

For first ye asked the story of this maid's grief
As her own lips might tell it—now remains
To list what other sorrows she so young
Must bear from Heré!—Inachus's child,
O thou!—drop down thy soul my weighty words,
And measure out the landmarks which are set
To end thy wandering.   Toward the orient sun
First turn thy face from mine, and journey on
Along the desert flats, till thou shalt come
Where Scythia's shepherd peoples dwell aloft,
Perched in wheeled wagons under woven roofs,
And twang the rapid arrow past the bow—
Approach them not; but siding in thy course,
The rugged shore-rocks resonant to the sea,
Depart that country.   On the left hand dwell
The iron-workers, called the Chalybes,
Of whom beware! for certes they are uncouth,
And nowise bland to strangers.   Reaching so
The stream Hybristes, (well the *scorner* called),
Attempt no passage;—it is hard to pass.
Or ere thou come to Caucasus itself,
That highest of mountains,—where the river leaps
The precipice in his strength!—thou must toil up
Those mountain-tops that neighbor with the stars,
And tread the south way, and draw near, at last,
The Amazonian host that hateth man,
Inhabitants of Themiscyra, close
Upon Thermodon, where the sea's rough jaw
Doth gnash at Salmydessa and provide
A cruel host to seamen, and to ships
A stepdame.   They, with unreluctant hand,
Shall lead thee on and on, till thou arrive
Just where the ocean gates show narrowest

On the Cimmerian isthmus.   Leaving which,
Behoves thee swim with fortitude of soul
The strait Mæotis.   Ay! and evermore
That traverse shall be famous on men's lips,
That strait, called Bosphorus, the horned one's road,
So named because of thee, who so wilt pass
From Europe's plain to Asia's continent.
How think ye, nymphs? the king of gods appears
Impartial in ferocious deeds?   Behold
The god desirous of this mortal's love
Hath cursed her with these wanderings.   Ah, fair
      child,
Thou hast met a bitter groom for bridal troth!
For all thou yet hast heard, can only prove
The incompleted prelude of thy doom.

    Io.   Ah, ah!
    Prometheus.   Is't thy turn, now, to shriek and
      moan?
How wilt thou, when thou hast hearkened what re-
      mains?
    Chorus.   Besides the grief thou hast told, can
      aught remain?
    Prometheus.   A sea—of foredoomed evil worked
      to storm.
    Io.   What boots my life, then?   why not cast
      myself
Down headlong from this miserable rock,
That, dashed against the flats, I may redeem
My soul from sorrow?   Better once to die,
Than day by day to suffer.
    Prometheus.   Verily,
It would be hard for thee to bear my woe,
For whom it is appointed not to die.
Death frees from woe: but I before me see

In all my far prevision, not a bound
To all I suffer, ere that Zeus shall fall
From being a king.

  Io.   And can it ever be
That Zeus shall fall from empire?

  Prometheus.   *Thou*, methinks,
Wouldst take some joy to see it.

  Io.   Could I choose;
I, who endure such pangs, now, by that god!

  Prometheus. Learn from me, therefore, that the
    event shall be.

  Io. By whom shall his imperial sceptred hand
Be emptied so?

  Prometheus. Himself shall spoil himself,
Through his idiotic counsels.

  Io.   How? declare;
Unless the word bring evil.

  Prometheus.   He shall wed—
And in the marriage-bond be joined to grief.

  Io. A heavenly bride—or human? Speak it out,
If it be utterable.

  Prometheus. Why should I say which?
It ought not to be uttered, verily.

  Io.   Then,
It is his wife shall tear him from his throne?

  Prometheus. It is his wife shall bear a son to him,
More mighty than the father.

  Io.   From this doom
Hath he no refuge?

  Prometheus. None—or ere that I,
Loosed from these fetters—

  Io.   Yea—but who shall loose
While Zeus is adverse?

  Prometheus. One who is born of *thee*,—

It is ordained so.

Io.   What is this thou sayest—
A son of mine shall liberate thee from woe?

Prometheus.   After ten generations, count three
      more,
And find him in the third.

Io.   The oracle
Remains obscure.

Prometheus.   And search it not, to learn
Thine own griefs from it.

Io.   Point me not to a good.
To leave me straight bereaved.

Prometheus.   I am prepared
To grant thee one of two things.

Io.   But which two?
Set them before me—grant me power to choose.

Prometheus.   I grant it—choose now! shall name
      aloud
What griefs remain to wound thee, or what hand
Shall save me out of mine.

Chorus.   Vouchsafe, O god,
The one grace of the twain to her who prays,
The next to me—and turn back neither prayer
Dishonored by denial. To herself
Recount the future wandering of her feet—
Then point me to the looser of thy chain—
Because I yearn to know it.

Prometheus.   Since ye will,
Of absolute will, this knowledge, I will set
No contrary against it, nor keep back
A word of all ye ask for. Io, first
To thee I must relate thy wandering course
Far winding; as I tell it, write it down
In thy soul's book of memories. When thou hast past
   29*

The refluent bound that parts two continents,
Track on the footsteps of the orient sun
In his own fire—across the roar of seas,
Fly till thou hast reached the Gorgonæan flats
Beside Cisthene—there the Phorcides,
Three ancient maidens, live, with shape of swan,
One tooth between them, and one common eye,
On whom the sun doth never look at all
With all his rays, nor evermore the moon,
When she looks through the night. Anear to whom
Are the Gorgon sisters three, enclothed with wings,
With twisted snakes for ringlets, man-abhorred.
There is no mortal gazes in their face,
And gazing can breathe on. I speak of such
To guard thee from their horror. Ay! and list
Another tale of a dreadful sight! beware
The Griffins, those unbarking dogs of Zeus,
Those sharp-mouthed dogs!—and the Arimaspian
　　　host
Of one-eyed horsemen, habiting beside
The river of Pluto that runs bright with gold.
Approach them not, beseech thee. Presently
Thou'lt come to a distant land, a dusky tribe
Of dwellers at the fountain of the Sun,
Whence flows the river Æthiops!—wind along
Its banks and turn off at the cataracts,
Just as the Nile pours, from the Bybline hills,
His holy and sweet wave! his course shall guide
Thine own to that triangular Nile-ground,
Where, Io, is ordained for thee and thine
A lengthened exile. Have I said, in this,
Aught darkly or incompletely?—now repeat
The question, make the knowledge fuller! Lo,

I have more leisure than I covet, here.

Chorus. If thou canst tell us aught that's left untold
Or loosely told of her most dreary flight,
Declare it straight! but if thou hast uttered all,
Grant us that latter grace for which we prayed,
Remembering how we prayed it.

Prometheus.　　　　　She has heard
The uttermost of her wandering. There it ends.
But that she may be certain not to have heard
All vainly, I will speak what she endured
Ere coming hither, and invoke the past
To prove my prescience true. And so—to leave
A multitude of words, and pass at once
To the subject of thy course!—When thou hadst gone
To those Molossian plains which sweep around
Dodona shouldering Heaven, whereby the fane
Of Zeus Thesprotian keepeth oracle,
And wonder, past belief, where oaks do wave
Articulate adjurations—(ay, the same
Saluted thee in no perplexed phrase,
But clear with glory, noble wife of Zeus
That shouldst be, there,—some sweetness took thy sense!)
Thou didst rush further onward,—stung along
The ocean-shore,—toward Rhea's mighty bay,
And, tost back from it, was tost to it again
In stormy evolution!—and, know well,
In coming time that hollow of the sea
Shall bear the name Ionian, and present
A monument of Io's passage through,
Unto all mortals. Be these words the signs

Of my soul's power to look beyond the veil
Of visible things.   The rest, to you and her,
I will declare in common audience, nymphs,
Returning thither, where my speech brake off.
There is a town Canobus, built upon
The earth's fair margin, at the mouth of Nile,
And on the mound washed up by it !—Io, there
Shall Zeus give back to thee thy perfect mind,
And only by the pressure and the touch
Of a hand not terrible ; and thou to Zeus
Shalt bear a dusky son, who shall be called
Thence, Epaphus, Touched !   That son shall pluck
          the fruit
Of all that land wide-watered by the flow
Of Nile ; but after him, when counting out
As far as the fifth full generation, then
Full fifty maidens, a fair woman-race,
Shall back to Argos turn reluctantly,
To fly the proffered nuptials of their kin,
Their father's brothers.   These being passion-struck,
Like falcons bearing hard on flying doves,
Shall follow, hunting at a quarry of love
They should not hunt—till envious Heaven main
          tain
A curse betwixt that beauty and their desire,
And Greece receive them, to be overcome
In murtherous woman-war, by fierce red hands
Kept savage by the night.   For every wife
Shall slay a husband, dyeing deep in blood
The sword of a double edge !   (I wish indeed
As fair a marriage-joy to all my foes !)
One bride alone shall fail to smite to death
The head upon her pillow, touched with love,

Made impotent of purpose, and impelled
To choose the lesser evil—shame on her cheeks,
The blood-guilt on her hands.   Which bride shall
    bear
A royal race in Argos—tedious speech
Were needed to relate particulars
Of these things—'tis enough that from her seed,
Shall spring the strong He—famous with the bow,
Whose arm shall break my fetters off!   Behold,
My mother Themis, that old Titaness,
Delivered to me such an oracle;
But how and when, I should be long to speak,
And thou, in hearing, wouldst not gain at all.

    Io.   Eleleu, eleleu !
        How the spasm and the pain
        And the fire on the brain
           Strike, burning me through !
How the sting of the curse, all aflame as it flew,
      Pricks me onward again !
How my heart, in its terror, is spurning my
    breast,
And my eyes, like the wheels of a chariot, roll
    round,—
I am whirled from my course, to the east, to the west,
In the whirlwind of frenzy all madly inwound—
And my mouth is unbridled for anguish and hate,
And my words beat in vain, in wild storms of
    unrest,
      On the sea of my desolate fate.

        Chorus.—Strophe.

    Oh! wise was he, oh, wise was he,
    Who first within his spirit knew

And with his tongue declared it true,
That love comes best that comes unto
    The equal of degree !
And that the poor and that the low
Should seek no love from those above
Whose souls are fluttered with the flow
Of airs about their golden height,
Or proud because they see arow
    Ancestral crowns of light !

Antistrophe.

Oh ! never, never, may ye, Fates,
    Behold me with your awful eyes
    Lift mine too fondly up the skies
Where Zeus upon the purple waits !—
    Nor let me step too near—too near—
To any suitor, bright from heaven—
    Because I see—because I fear
This loveless maiden vexed and lader.
By this fell curse of Here,—driven
    On wanderings dread and drear !

Epode.

Nay, grant an equal troth instead
    Of nuptial love to bind me by !—
It will not hurt—I shall not dread
    To meet it in reply.
But let not love from those above
Revert and fix me, as I said,
    With that inevitable Eye !
I have no sword to fight that fight—
I have no strength to tread that path—
I know not if my nature hath
The power to bear,—I cannot see,

Whither, from Zeus's infinite,
I have the power to flee.

Prometheus. Yet Zeus, albeit most absolute of
    will
Shall turn to meekness,—such a marriage-rite
He holds in preparation, which anon
Shall thrust him headlong from his gerent seat
Adown the abysmal void, and so the curse
His father Chronos muttered in his fall,
As he fell from his ancient throne and cursed,
Shall be accomplished wholly—no escape
From all that ruin shall the filial Zeus
Find granted to him from any of his gods,
Unless I teach him. I, the refuge, know,
And I, the means—Now, therefore, let him sit
And brave the imminent doom, and fix his faith
On his supernal noises, hurtling on
With restless hand, the bolt that breathes out fire—
For these things shall not help him—none of them—
Nor hinder his perdition when he falls
To shame, and lower than patience.—Such a foe
He doth himself prepare against himself,
A wonder of unconquerable Hate,
An organiser of sublimer fire
Than glares in lightnings, and of grander sound
Than aught the thunder rolls,—outthundering it,
With power to shatter in Poseidon's fist
The trident spear, which, while it plagues the sea,
Doth shake the shores around it. Ay, and Zeus,
Precipitated thus, shall learn at length
The difference betwixt rule and servitude.

    Chorus. Thou makest threats for Zeus of thy
      desires.

Prometheus.   I tell you, all these things shall be
     fulfilled,
Even so as I desire them.
Chorus.   Must we then
Look out for one shall come to master Zeus !
Prometheus.   These chains weigh lighter than his
     sorrows shall.
Chorus.   How art thou not afraid to utter such
     words ?
Prometheus.   What should *I* fear, who cannot die ?
Chorus.   But *he*
Can visit thee with dreader woe than death's.
Prometheus.   Why let him do it !—I am here,
     prepared
For all things and their pangs.
Chorus.   The wise are they
Who reverence Adrasteia.
Prometheus.   Reverence thou,
Adore thou, flatter thou, whomever reigns,
Whenever reigning—but for me, your Zeus
Is less than nothing !   Let him act and reign
His brief hour out according to his will—
He will not, therefore, rule the gods too long !
But lo ! I see that courier-god of Zeus,
That new-made menial of the new-crowned king—
He doubtless comes to announce to us something new.

                HERMES *enters.*

Hermes.   I speak to thee, the sophist, the talker
     down
Of scorn by scorn,—the sinner against gods,
The reverencer of men,—the thief of fire,—
I speak to and adjure thee !   Zeus requires
Thy declaration of what marriage-rite

Thus moves thy vaunt and shall hereafter cause
His fall from empire.   Do not wrap thy speech
In riddles, but speak clearly!   Never cast
Ambiguous paths, Prometheus, for my feet—
Since Zeus, thou may'st perceive, is scarcely won
To mercy by such means.

Prometheus.   A speech well-mouthed
In the utterance, and full-minded in the sense,
As doth befit a servant of the gods!
New gods, ye newly reign, and think forsooth
Ye dwell in towers too high for any dart
To carry a wound there!—have I not stood by
While two kings fell from thence? and shall I not
Behold the third, the same who rules you now,
Fall, shamed to sudden ruin?—Do I seem
To tremble and quail before your modern gods?
Far be it from me!—For thyself, depart,
Re-tread thy steps in haste! To all thou hast asked,
I answer nothing.

Hermes.   Such a wind of pride
Impelled thee of yore full sail upon these rocks.

Prometheus.   I would not barter—learn   thou
      soothly that!—
My suffering for thy service!   I maintain
It is a nobler thing to serve these rocks
Than live a faithful slave to father Zeus—
Thus upon scorners I retort their scorn.

Hermes.   It seems that thou dost glory in thy
      despair.

Prometheus. I, glory! would, my foes did glory so,
And I stood by to see them!—Naming whom
Thou art not unremembered.

Hermes.   Dost thou charge
Me also with the blame of thy mischance?

30

Prometheus.　　I tell thee I loathe the universal
　　gods,
Who for the good I gave them rendered back
The ill of their injustice.
　　Hermes.　　　　　　　Thou art mad—
I hear thee raving, Titan, at the fever-height.
　　Prometheus.　If it be madness to abhor my foes,
May I be mad!
　　Hermes.　　　　　　If thou wert prosperous,
Thou wouldst be unendurable.
　　Prometheus.　　　　　　　Alas!
　　Hermes.　Zeus knows not that word.
　　Prometheus.　　　　　　But maturing time
Doth teach all things.
　　Hermes.　　　　　Howbeit, thou hast not learnt
The wisdom yet, thou needest.
　　Prometheus.　　　　　　　If I had,
I should not talk thus with a slave like thee.
　　Hermes.　No answer thou vouchsafest, I be-
　　lieve,
To the great Sire's requirement.
　　Prometheus.　　　　　　　Verily
I owe him grateful service,—and should pay it.
　　Hermes.　Why thou dost mock me, Titan, as I
　　stood
A child before thy face.
　　Prometheus.　　　　No child, forsooth,
But yet more foolish than a foolish child,
If thou expect that I should answer aught
Thy Zeus can ask.　No torture from his hand
Nor any machination in the world
Shall force mine utterance, ere he loose, himself,
These cankerous fetters from me!　For the rest,
Let him now hurl his blanching lightnings down.

And with his white-winged snows, and mutterings
    deep
Of subterranean thunders, mix all things;
Confound them in disorder! None of this
Shall bend my sturdy will, and make me speak
The name of his dethroner who shall come.
    Hermes. Can this avail thee? Look to it!
    Prometheus.   Long ago
It was looked forward to,—precounselled of.
    Hermes. Vain god, take righteous courage!—
    dare for once
To apprehend and front thine agonies
With a just prudence!
    Prometheus.   Vainly dost thou chafe
My soul with exhortation, as yonder sea
Goes beating on the rock. Oh! think no more
That I, fear-struck by Zeus to a woman's mind,
Will supplicate him, loathed as he is
With feminine upliftings of my hands,
To break these chains! Far from me be the
    thought!
    Hermes. I have indeed, methinks, said much in
    vain,—
For still thy heart, beneath my showers of prayers,
Lies dry and hard!—nay, leaps like a young horse
Who bites against the new bit in his teeth,
And tugs and struggles against the new-tried rein,—
Still fiercest in the feeblest thing of all,
Which sophism is,—since absolute will disjoined
From perfect mind is worse than weak. Behold,
Unless my words persuade thee, what a blast
And whirlwind of inevitable woe
Must sweep persuasion through thee! For at first

The Father will split up this jut of rock
With the great thunder and the bolted flame,
And hide thy body where a hinge of stone
Shall catch it like an arm!—and when thou hast
        passed
A long black time within, thou shalt come out
To front the sun, while Zeus's winged hound,
The strong carniverous eagle, shall wheel down
To meet thee,—self-called to a daily feast,
And set his fierce beak in thee, and tear off
The long rags of thy flesh, and batten deep
Upon thy dusky liver!   Do not look
For any end moreover to this curse,
Or ere some god appear, to accept thy pangs
On his own head vicarious, and descend
With unreluctant step the darks of hell
And gloomy abysses around Tartarus!
Then ponder this!—this threat is not a growth
Of vain invention : it is spoken and meant!
King Zeus's mouth is impotent to lie,
Consummating the utterance by the act—
So, look to it, thou!—take heed!—and nevermore
Forget good counsel, to indulge self-will!

    Chorus.   Our Hermes suits his reasons to the
        times—
At least I think so !—since he bids thee drop
Self-will for prudent counsel.   Yield to him !
When the wise err, their wisdom makes their
        shame.

    Prometheus.   Unto me the foreknower, this man-
        date of power
        He cries, to reveal it.
What's strange in my fate, if I suffer from hate
        At the hour that I feel it ?

Let the locks of the lightning, all bristling and
        whitening,
        Flash, coiling me round!
While the æther goes surging 'neath thunder and
        scourging
        Of wild winds unbound!
Let the blast of the firmament whirl from its place
        The earth rooted below,
And the brine of the ocean, in rapid emotion,
        Be it driven in the face
Of the stars up in heaven, as they walk to and fro!
Let him hurl me anon, into Tartarus—on—
        To the blackest degree,
With Necessity's vortices strangling me down!
But he cannot join death to a fate meant for *me!*

  Hermes.   Why the words that he speaks and the
        thoughts that he thinks,
        Are maniacal—add,
If the Fate who hath bound him, should loose not
        the links,
        He were utterly mad.
    Then depart ye who groan with him,
    Leaving to moan with him—
Go in haste! lest the roar of the thunder anearing
Should blast you to idiocy, living and hearing.

  Chorus.   Change thy speech for another, thy
        thought for a new,
If to move me and teach me, indeed be thy care!
For thy words swerve so far from the loyal and
        true,
    That the thunder of Zeus seems more easy to bear.
How! couldst teach me to venture such vileness?
        Behold!
    I *choose,* with this victim, this anguish foretold!

30*   Z

I recoil from the traitor in hate and disdain,—
And I know that the curse of the treason is worse
      Than the pang of the chain.
    Hermes. Then remember, O nymphs, what I tell
      you before,
    Nor, when pierced by the arrows that Até will
      throw you,
Cast blame on your fate, and declare evermore
    That Zeus thrust you on anguish he did not fore-
      show you.
Nay, verily, nay! for ye perish anon
    For your deed—by your choice!—by no blind-
      ness of doubt,
No abruptness of doom!—but by madness alone,
    In the great net of Até, whence none cometh out,
      Ye are wound and undone!
    Prometheus. Ay! in act, now—in word, now, no
      more!
      Earth is rocking in space!
And the thunders crash up with a roar upon roar—
    And the eddying lightnings flash fires in my face
And the whirlwinds are whirling the dust round and
    round—
    And the blasts of the winds universal, leap free
And blow each upon each, with a passion of
    sound,
    And æther goes mingling in storm with the sea!
Such a curse on my head, in a manifest dread,
    From the hand of your Zeus has been hurtled
      along!
O my mother's fair glory! O, Æther, enringing,
All eyes, with the sweet common light of thy
    bringing.
      Dost thou see how I suffer this wrong?

A LAMENT FOR ADONIS.

FROM BION.

I.

I MOURN for Adonis—Adonis is dead!
  Fair Adonis is dead, and the Loves are lamenting.
Sleep, Cypris, no more on thy purple-strewed bed!
  Arise, wretch stoled in black,—beat thy breast
      unrelenting,
And shriek to the worlds, 'Fair Adonis is dead.'

II.

I mourn for Adonis—the Loves are lamenting.
  He lies on the hills, in his beauty and death,—
The white tusk of a boar has transfixed his white
      thigh;
  Cytherea grows mad at his thin gasping breath,
While the black blood drips down on the pale ivory,
  And his eye-balls lie quenched with the weight of
      his brows,
The rose fades from his lips, and upon them just
      parted
  The kiss dies the goddess consents not to lose,
Though the kiss of the Dead cannot make her glad-
      hearted—
  He knows not who kisses him dead in the dews.

III.

I mourn for Adonis—the Loves are lamenting.
    Deep, deep in the thigh, is Adonis's wound;
But a deeper, is Cypris's bosom presenting—
    The youth lieth dead while his dogs howl around,
And the nymphs weep aloud from the mists of the
        hill,
    And the poor Aphrodite, with tresses unbound,
All dishevelled, unsandalled, shrieks mournful and
        shrill
    Through the dusk of the groves. The thorns,
        tearing her feet,
Gather up the red flower of her blood which is holy,
    Each footstep she takes; and the valleys repeat
The sharp cry she utters, and draw it out slowly.
    She calls on her spouse, her Assyrian; on him
Her own youth; while the dark blood spreads over
        his body—
    The chest taking hue from the gash in the limb,
And the bosom once ivory, turning to ruddy.

IV.

Ah, ah, Cytherea! the Loves are lamenting:
    She lost her fair spouse, and so lost her fair smile—
When he lived she was fair by the whole world's
        consenting,
    Whose fairness is dead with him! woe worth the
        while!
All the mountains above and the oaklands below
    Murmur, ah, ah Adonis! the streams overflow
Aphrodite's deep wail,—river-fountains in pity
    Weep soft in the hills; and the flowers as they
        blow,

Redden outward with sorrow; while all hear her go
    With the song of her sadness, through mountain
        and city.

V.

Ah, ah, Cytherea! Adonis is dead:
    Fair Adonis is dead—Echo answers, Adonis!
Who weeps not for Cypris, when bowing her head,
    She stares at the wound where it gapes and as-
        tonies?
—When, ah, ah!—she saw how the blood ran away
    And empurpled the thigh; and, with wild hands
        flung out,
Said with sobs, 'Stay, Adonis! unhappy one, stay,
    Let me feel thee once more—let me ring thee
        about
With the clasp of my arms, and press kiss into kiss!
    Wait a little, Adonis, and kiss me again,
For the last time, beloved; and but so much of this
    That the kiss may learn life from the warmth of
        the strain!
—Till thy breath shall exude from thy soul to my
        mouth;
    To my heart; and, the love-charm I once more
        receiving,
May drink thy love in it, and keep of a truth
    That one kiss in the place of Adonis the living.
Thou fliest me, mournful one, fliest me far,
    My Adonis; and seekest the Acheron portal,—
To Hell's cruel King goest down with a scar,
    While I weep and live on like a wretched im-
        mortal,
And follow no step;—O Persephone, take him,
    My husband!—thou'rt better and brighter than I

So all beauty flows down to thee! *I* cannot make him
    Look up at my grief; there's despair in my cry,
Since I wail for Adonis, who died to me .. died to
        me ..
    —Then, I fear *thee!*—Art thou dead, my Adored?
Passion ends like a dream in the sleep that's denied
        to me.—
    Cypris is widowed; the Loves seek their lord
All the house through in vain! Charm of cestus
        has ceased
    With thy clasp!—O too bold in the hunt, past
        preventing;
Ay, mad: thou so fair ... to have strife with a
        beast!' —
    Thus the goddess wailed on—and the Loves are
        lamenting.

VI.

Ah, ah, Cytherea! Adonis is dead.
She wept tear after tear, with the blood which was
        shed;
And both turned into flowers for the earth's garden-
        close;
Her tears, to the wind-flower,—his blood, to the rose.

VII.

I mourn for Adonis—Adonis is dead.
    Weep no more in the woods, Cytherea, thy lover!
So, well; make a place for his corse in thy bed,
    With the purples thou sleepest in, under and over.
He's fair though a corse—a fair corse .. like a
        sleeper—
    Lay him soft in the silks he had pleasure to fold,

When, beside thee at night, holy dreams deep and
    deeper
Enclosed his young life on the couch made of gold!
Love him still, poor Adonis! cast on him together
    The crowns and the flowers! since he died from
      the place,
Why let all die with him—let the blossoms go
    wither;
    Rain myrtles and olive-buds down on his face:
Rain the myrrh down, let all that is best fall a-
    pining,
    For the myrrh of his life from thy keeping is
      swept!—
—Pale he lay, thine Adonis, in purples reclining,—
    The Loves raised their voices around him and wept.
They have shorn their bright curls off to cast on
    Adonis:
One treads on his bow,—on his arrows, another,—
One breaks up a well-feathered quiver; and one is
    Bent low at a sandal, untying the strings;
    And one carries the vases of gold from the
      springs,
While one washes the wound; and behind them a
    brother
    Fans down on the body sweet air with his wings.

VIII.

Cytherea herself, now, the Loves are lamenting.
    Each torch at the door Hymenæus blew out;
And the marriage-wreath dropping its leaves as
    repenting,
    No more 'Hymen, Hymen,' is chanted about,
But the *ai ai* instead— 'ai alas' is begun
    For Adonis, and then follows 'ai Hymenæus!'

The Graces are weeping for Cinyris' son
   Sobbing low, each to each, ' His fair eyes cannot
      see us!'—
Their wail strikes more shrill than the sadder
      Dione's;
The Fates mourn aloud for Adonis, Adonis,
Deep chanting! he hears not a word that they say:
   He *would* hear, but Persephone has him in keep-
      ing.
—Cease moan, Cytherea—leave pomps for to-day,
   And weep new when a new year refits thee for
      weeping.

BERTHA IN THE LANE.

PUT the broidery-frame away,
   For my sewing is all done !
The last thread is used to-day,
   And I need not join it on.
   Though the clock stands at the noon
   I am weary ! I have sewn,
   Sweet, for thee, a wedding-gown

Sister, help me to the bed,
   And stand near me, Dearest-sweet !
Do not shrink nor be afraid,
   Blushing with a sudden heat !
   No one standeth in the street ?—
   By God's love I go to meet,
   Love I thee with love complete.

Lean thy face down ! drop it in
   These two hands, that I may hold
'Twixt their palms thy cheek and chin,
   Stroking back the curls of gold.
   'Tis a fair, fair face, in sooth—
   Larger eyes and redder mouth
   Than mine were in my first youth !

31

Thou art younger by seven years—
   Ah !—so bashful at my gaze,
That the lashes, hung with tears,
   Grow too heavy to upraise ?
    I would wound thee by no touch
    Which thy shyness feels as such—
    Dost thou mind me, Dear, so much ?

Have I not been nigh a mother
   To thy sweetness—tell me, Dear ?
Have we not loved one another
   Tenderly. from year to year,
    Since our dying mother mild
    Said with accents undefiled,
' Child, be mother to this child !'

Mother, mother, up in heaven,
   Stand up on the jasper sea,
And be witness I have given
   All the gifts required of me,—
    Hope that blessed me, bliss that crowned,
    Love, that left me with a wound,
    Life itself, that turneth round !

Mother, mother, thou art kind,
   Thou art standing in the room,
In a molten glory shrined,
   That rays off into the gloom !
    But thy smile is bright and bleak
    Like cold waves—I cannot speak ;
    I sob in it, and grow weak.

Ghostly mother, keep aloof
   One hour longer from my soul—
For I still am thinking of
   Earth's warm-beating joy and dole :
   On my finger is a ring
   Which I still see glittering,
   When the night hides everything.

Little sister, thou art pale !
   Ah, I have a wandering brain—
But I lose that fever-bale,
   And my thoughts grow calm again.
   Lean down closer—closer still !
   I have words thine ear to fill,—
   And would kiss thee at my will.

Dear, I heard thee in the spring,
   Thee and Robert—through the trees,—
When we all went gathering
   Boughs of May-bloom for the bees.
   Do not start so ! think instead
   How the sunshine overhead
   Seemed to trickle through the shade.

What a day it was, that day !
   Hills and vales did openly
Seem to heave and throb away
   At the sight of the great sky.
   And the Silence, as it stood
   In the Glory's golden flood,
   Audibly did bud—and bud

Through the winding hedgerows green,
   How we wandered, I and you,—
With the bowery tops shut in,
   And the gates that showed the view—
  How we talked there ! thrushes soft
   Sang our pauses out —or oft
   Bleatings took them, from the croft.

Till the pleasure grown too strong
   Left me muter evermore ;
And, the winding road being long,
   I walked out of sight, before,
   And so, wrapt in musings fond,
   Issued (past the wayside pond)
   On the meadow-lands beyond.

I sate down beneath the beech
   Which leans over to the lane,
And the far sound of your speech
   Did not promise any pain ;
   And I blessed you full and free,
   With a smile stooped tenderly
   O'er the May-flowers on my knee.

But the sound grew into word
   As the speakers drew more near—
Sweet, forgive me that I heard
   What you wished me not to hear.
   Do not weep so—do not shake—
   Oh,—I heard thee, Bertha, make
   Good true answers for my sake.

Yes, and HE too! let him stand
　In thy thoughts, untouched by blame
Could he help it, if my hand
　He had claimed with hasty claim?
　That was wrong perhaps—but then
　Such things be—and will, again!
　Women cannot judge for men.

Had he seen thee, when he swore
　He would love but me alone
Thou wert absent,—sent before
　To our kin in Sidmouth town.
　When he saw thee who art best
　Past compare, and loveliest,
　He but judged thee as the rest.

Could we blame him with grave words,
　Thou and I, Dear, if we might?
Thy brown eyes have looks like birds,
　Flying straightway to the light:
　Mine are older.—Hush!—look out—
　Up the street!　Is none without?
　How the poplar swings about!

And that hour—beneath the beech,
　When I listened in a dream,
And he said, in his deep speech,
　That he owed me all *esteem*,—
　Each word swam in on my brain
　With a dim, dilating pain,
　Till it burst with that last strain—

31*

I fell flooded with a Dark,
  In the silence of a swoon—
When I rose, still cold and stark,
  There was night,—I saw the moon:
  And the stars, each in its place,
  And the May-blooms on the grass,
  Seemed to wonder what I was.

And I walked as if apart
  From myself when I could stand—
And I pitied my own heart,
  As if I held it in my hand,
  Somewhat coldly,—with a sense
  Of fulfilled benevolence,
  And a ' Poor thing ' negligence.

And I answered coldly too,
  When you met me at the door;
And I only *heard* the dew
  Dripping from me to the floor:
  And the flowers I bade you see,
  Were too withered for the bee,—
  As my life, henceforth, for me.

Do not weep so—Dear—heart-warm!
  It was best as it befell!
If I say he did me harm,
  I speak wild,—I am not well.
  All his words were kind and good—
  He esteemed me!   Only blood
  Runs so faint in womanhood.

Then I always was too grave,—
    Liked the saddest ballads sung,—
With that look, besides, we have
    In our faces, who die young.
    I had died, Dear, all the same—
    Life's long, joyous, jostling game
    Is too loud for my meek shame.

We are so unlike each other,
    Thou and I ; that none could guess
We were children of one mother,
    But for mutual tenderness.
    Thou art rose-lined from the cold,
    And meant, verily, to hold
    Life's pure pleasures manifold.

I am pale as crocus grows
    Close beside a rose-tree's root !
Whosoe'er would reach the rose,
    Treads the crocus underfoot—
    I, like May-bloom on thorn tree—
    Thou, like merry summer-bee !
    Fit, that *I* be plucked for *thee*.

Yet who plucks me ?—no one mourns—
    I have lived my season out,
And now die of my own thorns
    Which I could not live without.
    Sweet, be merry !   How the light
    Comes and goes !   If it be night,
    Keep the candles in my sight.

Are there footsteps at the door?
  Look out quickly.   Yea, or nay?
Some one might be waiting for
  Some last word that I might say.
  Nay?   So best!—So angels would
  Stand off clear from deathly road,
  Not to cross the sight of God.

Colder grow my hands and feet—
  When I wear the shroud I made,
Let the folds lie straight and neat,
  And the rosemary be spread,
  That if any friend should come,
  (To see *thee*, sweet!) all the room
  May be lifted out of gloom.

And, dear Bertha, let me keep
  On my hand this little ring,
Which at nights, when others sleep,
  I can still see glittering.
  Let me wear it out of sight,
  In the grave,—where it will light
  All the Dark up, day and night

On that grave, drop not a tear!
  Else, though fathom-deep the place,
Through the woollen shroud I wear
  I shall feel it on my face.
  Rather smile there, blessed one,
  Thinking of me in the sun—
  Or forget me—smiling on!

Art thou near me ? nearer ? so .
    Kiss me close upon the eyes,
That the earthly light may go
      Sweetly as it used to rise,
      When I watched the morning-gray
      Strike, betwixt the hills, the way
      He was sure to come that day.

So,—no more vain words be said !
    The hosannas nearer roll—-
Mother, smile now on thy Dead,
      I am death-strong in my soul.
      Mystic Dove alit on cross,
      Guide the poor bird of the snows
      Through the snow-wind above loss '

Jesus, Victim, comprehending
    Love's divine self-abnegation,
Cleanse my love in its self-spending,
      And absorb the poor libation !
      Wind my thread of life up higher,
      Up, through angels' hands of fire !--
      I aspire while I expire !

THAT DAY.

I STAND by the river where both of us stood,
And there is but one shadow to darken the flood ;
And the path leading to it, where both used to pass,
Has the step but of one, to take dew from the grass,—
One forlorn since that day.

The flowers of the margin are many to see,
For none stoops at my bidding to pluck them for me ;
The bird in the alder sings loudly and long,
For my low sound of weeping disturbs not his song,
As thy vow did that day!

I stand by the river—I think of the vow—
Oh, calm as the place is, vow-breaker, be *thou!*
I leave the flower growing—the bird, unreproved.—
Would I trouble *thee* rather than *them*, my beloved
And my lover that day?

Go ! be sure of my love —by that treason forgiven;
Of my prayers—by the blessings they win thee from
    Heaven ;
Of my grief—(guess the length of the sword by the
    sheath's)
By the silence of life, more pathetic than death's !
Go,—be clear of that day !

LIFE AND LOVE.

I.

Fast this life of mine was dying,
　　Blind already and calm as death;
Snowflakes on her bosom lying
　　Scarcely heaving with the breath.

II.

Love came by, and, having known her
　　In a dream of fabled lands,
Gently stooped, and laid upon her
　　Mystic chrism of holy hands;

III.

Drew his smile across her folded
　　Eyelids, as the swallow dips,
Breathed as finely as the cold did,
　　Through the locking of her lips.

IV.

So, when Life looked upward, being
　　Warmed and breathed on from above,
What sight could she have for seeing,
　　Evermore . . . but only Love?

THE RUNAWAY SLAVE

AT PILGRIM'S POINT.

I.

I STAND on the mark beside the shore
　Of the first white pilgrim's bended knee,
Where exile turned to ancestor,
　And God was thanked for liberty.
I have run through the night, my skin is as dark
I bend my knee down on this mark . .
　I look on the sky and the sea.

II.

O pilgrim souls, I speak to you!
　I see you come out proud and slow
From the land of the spirits pale as dew . .
　And round me and round me ye go!
O pilgrims, I have gasped and run
All night long from the whips of one
　Who in your names works sin and woe.

III.

And thus I thought that I would come
　And kneel here where ye knelt before,
And feel your souls around me hum
　In undertone to the ocean's roar;

And lift my black face, my black hand.
Here, in your names, to curse this land
   Ye blessed in freedom's evermore.

IV.

I am black, I am black ;
   And yet God made me, they say.
But if He did so, smiling back
   He must have cast his work away
Under the feet of his white creatures,
With a look of scorn,—that the dusky features
   Might be trodden again to clay.

V.

And yet He has made dark things
   To be glad and merry as light.
There's a little dark bird, sits and sings ;
   There's a dark stream ripples out of sight ;
And the dark frogs chant in the safe morass,
And the sweetest stars are made to pass
   O'er the face of the darkest night.

VI.

But *we* who are dark, we are dark !
   Ah God, we have no stars !
About our souls in care and cark
   Our blackness shuts like prison-bars ·
The poor souls crouch so far behind,
That never a comfort can they find
   By reaching through the prison-bars.

32

VII.

Indeed we live beneath the sky,
  That great smooth Hand of God stretched out
On all His children fatherly,
  To save them from the dread and doubt
Which would be, if, from this low place,
All opened straight up to His face
  Into the grand eternity.

VIII.

And still God's sunshine and His frost.
  They make us hot, they make us cold,
As if we were not black and lost :
  And the beasts and birds, in wood and fold,
Do fear and take us for very men !
Could the weep-poor-will or the cat of the glen
  Look into my eyes and be bold ?

IX.

I am black, I am black !—
  But, once, I laughed in girlish glee ;
For one of my colour stood in the track
  Where the drivers drove, and looked at me—
And tender and full was the look he gave :
Could a slave look *so* at another slave ?—
  I look at the sky and the sea.

X.

And from that hour our spirits grew
  As free as if unsold, unbought :

Oh. strong enough, since we were two,
   To conquer the world, we thought!
The drivers drove us day by day;
We did not mind, we went one way
   And no better a freedom sought.

XI.

In the sunny ground between the canes,
   He said ' I love you ' as he passed:
When the shingle-roof rang sharp with the rains,
   I heard how he vowed it fast:
While others shook he smiled in the hut
As he carved me a bowl of the cocoa-nut
   Through the roar of the hurricanes.

XII.

I sang his name instead of a song;
   Over and over I sang his name—
Upward and downward I drew it along
   My various notes; the same, the same!
I sang it low, that the slave-girls near
Might never guess from aught they could hear,
   It was only a name—a name.

XIII.

I look on the sky and the sea—
   We were two to love, and two to pray,—
Yes, two, O God, who cried to Thee,
   Though nothing didst Thou say.
Coldly Thou sat'st behind the sun !
And now I cry who am but one,
   Thou wilt not speak to-day.—

XIV.

We were black, we were black!
    We had no claim to love and bliss:
What marvel, if each went to wrack?
    They wrung my cold hands out of his,—
They dragged him .. where? .. I crawled to touch
His blood's mark in the dust! .. not much,
    Ye pilgrim-souls, .. though plain as *this!*

XV.

Wrong, followed by a deeper wrong!
    Mere grief's too good for such as I.
So the white men brought the shame ere long
    To strangle the sob of my agony.
They would not leave me for my dull
Wet eyes!—it was too merciful
    To let me weep pure tears and die.

XVI.

I am black, I am black!
    I wore a child upon my breast ..
An amulet that hung too slack,
    And, in my unrest, could not rest:
Thus we went moaning, child and mother
One to another, one to another,
    Until all ended for the best:

XVII.

For hark! I will tell you low .. low ..
    I am black, you see,—

And the babe who lay on my bosom so,
  Was far too white . . too white for me;
As white as the ladies who scorned to pray
Beside me at church but yesterday;
  Though my tears had washed a place for my knee

XVIII.

My own, own child! I could not bear
  To look in his face, it was so white.
I covered him up with a kerchief there;
  I covered his face in close and tight:
And he moaned and struggled, as well might be,
For the white child wanted his liberty—
  Ha, ha! he wanted the master right.

XIX.

He moaned and beat with his head and feet,
  His little feet that never grew—
He struck them out, as it was meet,
  Against my heart to break it through.
I might have sung and made him mild—
But I dared not sing to the white-faced child
  The only song I knew.

XX.

I pulled the kerchief very close:
  He could not see the sun, I swear
More, then, alive, than now he does
  From between the roots of the mango ... where?
. I know where. Close! a child and mother
Do wrong to look at one another,
  When one is black and one is fair.

32*

XXI.

Why, in that single glance I had
　　Of my child's face, . . I tell you all,
I saw a look that made me mad . .
　　The *master's* look, that used to fall!
On my soul like his lash . . or worse !—
And so, to save it from my curse,
　　I twisted it round in my shawl.

XXII.

And he moaned and trembled from foot to head,
　　He shivered from head to foot;
Till, after a time, he lay instead
　　Too suddenly still and mute.
I felt beside a stiffening cold . .
I dared to lift up just a fold, . .
　　As in lifting a leaf of the mango-fruit.

XXIII.

But *my* fruit . . ha. ha!—there, had been
　　(I laugh to think on't at this hour ! . .)
Your fine white angels, who have seen
　　Nearest the secret of God's power, . .
And plucked my fruit to make them wine,
And sucked the soul of that child of mine,
　　As the humming-bird sucks the soul of the
　　　flower.

XXIV.

Ha, ha, the trick of the angels white !
　　They freed the white child's spirit so.
I said not a word, but, day and night,
　　I carried the body to and fro ;

And it lay on my heart like a stone . . as chill.
—The sun may shine out as much as he will:
  I am cold, though it happened a month ago.

XXV.

From the white man's house, and the black man's
      hut,
  I carried the little body on.
The forest's arms did round us shut,
  And silence through the trees did run:
They asked no question as I went,—
They stood too high for astonishment,—
  They could see God sit on his throne.

XXVI.

My little body, kerchiefed fast,
  I bore it on through the forest . . on:
And when I felt it was tired at last,
  I scooped a hole beneath the moon.
Through the forest-tops the angels far,
With a white sharp finger from every star,
  Did point and mock at what was done.

XXVII.

Yet when it was all done aright, . .
  Earth, 'twixt me and my baby, strewed, . .
All, changed to black earth, . . nothing white, .
  A dark child in the dark,—ensued
Some comfort, and my heart grew young:
I sate down smiling there and sung
  The song I learnt in my maidenhood.

XXVIII.

And thus we two were reconciled,
    The white child and black mother, thus:
For, as I sang it soft and wild
    The same song, more melodious,
Rose from the grave whereon I sate!
It was the dead child singing that,
    To join the souls of both of us.

XXIX.

I look on the sea and the sky!
    Where the pilgrims' ships first anchored lay,
The free sun rideth gloriously;
    But the pilgrim-ghosts have slid away
Through the earliest streaks of the morn.
My face is black, but it glares with a scorn
    Which they dare not meet by day.

XXX.

Ah!—in their 'stead, their hunter sons!
    Ah, ah! they are on me—they hunt in a ring—
Keep off! I brave you all at once—
    I throw off your eyes like snakes that sting!
You have killed the black eagle at nest, I think:
Did you never stand still in your triumph, and
        shrink
    From the stroke of her wounded wing?

XXXI.

(Man, drop that stone you dared to lift!—)
    I wish you who stand there five a-breast,

Each, for his own wife's joy and gift,
  A little corpse as safely at rest
As mine in the manglos!—Yes, but *she*
May keep live babies on her knee,
  And sing the song she liketh best.

XXXII.

I am not mad: I am black.
  I see you staring in my face—
I know you staring, shrinking back—
  Ye are born of the Washington-race:
And this land is the free America:
And this mark on my wrist . . (I prove what I say)
  Ropes tied me up here to the flogging-place.

XXXIII.

You think I shrieked then? Not a sound!
  I hung, as a gourd hangs in the sun.
I only cursed them all around,
  As softly as I might have done
My very own child!—From these sands
Up to the mountains, lift your hands,
  O slaves, and end what I begun!

XXXIV.

Whips, curses; these must answer those!
  For in this UNION, you have set
Two kinds of men in adverse rows,
  Each loathing each: and all forget
The seven wounds in Christ's body fair;
While HE sees gaping everywhere
  Our countless wounds that pay no debt.

XXXV.

Our wounds are different. Your white men
    Are, after all, not gods indeed,
Nor able to make Christs again
    Do good with bleeding. *We* who bleed
(Stand off!) *we* help not in our loss!
We are too heavy for our cross,
    And fall and crush you and your seed.

XXXVI.

I fall, I swoon! I look at the sky:
    The clouds are breaking on my brain;
I am floated along, as if I should die
    Of liberty's exquisite pain—
In the name of the white child waiting for me
In the death-dark where we may kiss and agree
White men, I leave you all curse-free
    In my broken heart's disdain!

HECTOR IN THE GARDEN.

I.

NINE years old! The first of any
    Seem the happiest years that come:
    Yet when *I* was nine, I said
    No such word!—I thought instead
That the Greeks had used as many
    In besieging Ilium.

II.

Nine green years had scarcely brought me
    To my childhood's haunted spring:
    I had life, like flowers and bees
    In betwixt the country trees;
And the sun the pleasure taught me
    Which he teacheth every thing.

III.

If the rain fell, there was sorrow;
    Little head leant on the pane,
    Little finger drawing down it
    The long trailing drops upon it,
And the ' Rain, rain, come to-morrow, '
    Said for charm against the rain.

IV.

Such a charm was right Canidian,
   Though you meet it with a jeer!
   If I said it long enough,
   Then the rain hummed dimly off,
And the thrush with his pure Lydian
   Was left only to the ear:

V.

And the sun and I together
   Went a-rushing out of doors:
   We, our tender spirits, drew
   Over hill and dale in view,
Glimmering hither, glimmering thither,
   In the footsteps of the showers.

VI

Underneath the chestnuts dripping,
   Through the grasses wet and fair,
   Straight I sought my garden-ground,
   With the laurel on the mound,
And the pear-tree oversweeping
   A side-shadow of green air.

VII.

In the garden lay supinely
   A huge giant wrought of spade!
   Arms and legs were stretched at length
   In a passive giant strength,—
And the meadow turf, cut finely,
   Round them laid and interlaid.

VIII.

Call him Hector, son of Priam !
   Such his title and degree.
   With my rake I smoothed his brow ;
   Both his cheeks I weeded through :
But a rhymer such as I am,
   Scarce can sing his dignity.

IX.

Eyes of gentianellas azure,
   Staring, winking at the skies ;
   Nose of gillyflowers and box ;
   Scented grasses put for locks—
Which a little breeze, at pleasure,
   Set a-waving round his eyes.

X.

Brazen helm of daffodillies,
   With a glitter toward the light ;
   Purple violets for the mouth,
   Breathing perfumes west and south ;
And a sword of flashing lilies,
   Holden ready for the fight.

XI.

And a breastplate made of daisies,
   Closely fitting, leaf by leaf;
   Periwinkles interlaced
   Drawn for belt about the waist ;
While the brown bees, humming praises,
   Shot their arrows round the chief.

33

XII.

And who knows, (I sometimes wondered,)
  If the disembodied soul
  Of old Hector, once of Troy,
  Might not take a dreary joy
Here to enter—if it thundered,
  Rolling up the thunder-roll?

XIII.

Rolling this way from Troy-ruin,
  In this body rude and rife
  He might enter, and take rest
  'Neath the daisies of the breast—
They, with tender roots. renewing
  His heroic heart to life.

XIV.

Who could know? I sometimes started
  At a motion or a sound!
  Did his mouth speak—naming Troy,
  With an οτοτοτοτοι?
Did the pulse of the Strong-hearted
  Make the daisies tremble round?

XV.

It was hard to answer, often :
  But the birds sang in the tree—
  But the little birds sang bold
  In the pear-tree green and old;
And my terror seemed to soften
  Through the courage of their glee.

XVI.

Oh, the birds, the tree, the ruddy
  And white blossoms, sleek with rain
Oh, my garden, rich with pansies!
  Oh, my childhood's bright romances!
All revive, like Hector's body,
  And I see them stir again!

XVII.

And despite life's changes—chances,
  And despite the deathbell's toll,
They press on me in full seeming!
  Help, some angel! stay this dreaming!
As the birds sang in the branches,
  Sing God's patience through my soul!

XVIII.

That no dreamer, no neglecter
  Of the present's work unsped,
I may wake up and be doing,
  Life's heroic ends pursuing,
Though my past is dead as Hector,
  And though Hector is twice dead

CONFESSIONS.

I.

FACE to face in my chamber, my silent chamber,
    I saw her!
God and she and I only, . . there, I sate down to
    draw her
Soul through the clefts of confession. . . Speak, I
    am holding thee fast,
As the angels of resurrection shall do it at the last.
       ' My cup is blood-red
        With my sin,' she said,
    'And I pour it out to the bitter lees,
As if the angels of judgment stood over me strong
    at the last,
       Or as thou wert as these!'

II.

When God smote His hands together, and struck
    out thy soul as a spark
Into the organised glory of things, from deeps of
    the dark,—
Say, didst thou shine, didst thou burn, didst thou
    honour the power in the form,
As the star does at night, or the fire-fly, or even the
    little ground-worm?

CONFESSIONS. 389

'I have sinned,' she said,
'For my seed-light shed
Has smouldered away from His first decrees!
The cypress praiseth the fire-fly, the ground-leaf
praiseth the worm:
. I am viler than these!'

III.

When God on that sin had pity, and did not
trample thee straight
With His wild rains beating and drenching thy
light found inadequate;
When He only sent thee the north-winds, a little
searching and chill,
To quicken thy flame .. didst thou kindle and flash
to the heights of His will?
'I have sinned,' she said,
'Unquickened, unspread
My fire dropt down; and I wept on my knees!
I only said of His winds of the north as I shrank
from their chill, ..
What delight is in these?'

IV.

When God on that sin had pity, and did not meet
it as such,
But tempered the wind to thy uses, and softened
the world to thy touch;
At least thou wast moved in thy soul, though un-
able to prove it afar,
Thou couldst carry thy light like a jewel, not giving
it out like a star?

33*

'I have sinned,' she said,
'And not merited
The gift He gives, by the grace He sees!
The mine-cave praiseth the jewel, the hill-side
praiseth the star:
I am viler than these.'

v.

Then I cried aloud in my passion, . . unthankful and
impotent creature,
To throw up thy scorn unto God through the rents
in thy beggarly nature!
If He, the all-giving and loving, is served so unduly,
what then
Hast thou done to the weak and the false, and the
changing, . . thy fellows of men?
'I have *loved*,' she said,
(Words bowing her head
As the wind the wet acacia-trees!)
'I saw God sitting above me,—but I . . I sate among
men,
And I have loved these.'

VI.

Again with a lifted voice, like a choral trumpet that
takes
The lowest note of a viol that trembles, and triumph-
ing breaks
On the air with it solemn and clear,—'Behold! I
have sinned not in this!
Where I loved, I have loved much and well,—I have
verily loved not amiss.

Let the living,' she said,
'Enquire of the Dead,
In the house of the pale-fronted Images,
My own true dead will answer for me, that I have
not loved amiss
In my love for all these.

VII.

'The least touch of their hands in the morning, I
keep it by day and by night:
Their least step on the stair, at the door, still throbs
through me, if ever so light:
Their least gift, which they left to my childhood, far
off, in the long-ago years,
Is now turned from a toy to a relic, and seen through
the crystals of tears.
Dig the snow,' she said
'For my churchyard bed;
Yet I, as I sleep, shall not fear to freeze,
If one only of these my beloveds, shall love me with
heart-warm tears,
As I have loved these!

VIII.

'If I angered any among them, from thenceforth my
own life was sore;
If I fell by chance from their presence, I clung to
their memory more:
Their tender I often felt holy, their bitter I sometimes
called sweet;
And whenever their heart has refused me, I fell down
straight at their feet.

I have loved,' she said,—
    ' Man is weak, God is dread;
Yet the weak man dies with his spirit at ease,
Having poured such an unguent of love but once on
        the Saviour's feet,
    As I lavished for these.'

IX.

Go, I cried, thou hast chosen the Human, and left
    the Divine!
Then, at least, have the Human shared with thee
    their wild berry-wine?
Have they loved back thy love, and when strangers
    approached thee with blame,
Have they covered thy fault with their kisses, and
    loved thee the same?
        But she shrunk and said,
        ' God, over my head,
    Must sweep in the wrath of His judgment seas,
If *He* deal with me sinning, but only indeed the
    same
        And no gentler than these.'

A VALEDICTION.

God be with thee my beloved,—God be with thee!
    Else alone thou goest forth,
    Thy face unto the north,
Moor and pleasance all around thee and beneath thee
    Looking equal in one snow!
    While I who try to reach thee,
    Vainly follow, vainly follow,
    With the farewell and the hollo,
    And cannot reach thee so.
    Alas! I can but teach thee.
God be with thee my beloved,—God be with thee!

Can I teach thee, my beloved—can I teach thee?
    If I said, Go left or right,
    The counsel would be light,
The wisdom, poor of all that could enrich thee!
    My right would show like left;
    My raising would depress thee,
    My choice of light would blind thee,
    Of way, would leave behind thee,
    Of end, would leave bereft!
    Alas! I can but bless thee —
May God teach thee my beloved,—may God teach
      thee!

Can I bless thee, my beloved,—can I bless thee?
>   What blessing word can I,
>   From mine own tears, keep dry?
What flowers grow in my field wherewith to dress
        thee?
>   My good reverts to ill;
>   My calmnesses would move thee,
>   My softnesses would prick thee,
>   My bindings up would break thee,
>   My crownings, curse and kill.
>   Alas! I can but love thee.
May God bless thee my beloved,—may God bless
        thee!

Can I love thee, my beloved,—can I love thee?
>   And is *this* like love, to stand
>   With no help in my hand,
When strong as death I fain would watch above thee?
>   My love-kiss can deny
>   No tears that fall beneath it:
>   Mine oath of love can swear thee
>   From no ill that comes near thee,—
>   And thou diest while I breathe it,
>   And I—*I* can but die!
May God love thee my beloved,—may God love
        thee!

A CHILD'S GRAVE AT FLORENCE.

A. A. E. C.

BORN JULY, 1848. DIED NOVEMBER, 1849.

I.

OF English blood, of Tuscan birth, . .
    What country should we give her?
Instead of any on the earth,
    The civic Heavens receive her.

II.

And here, among the English tombs,
    In Tuscan ground we lay her,
While the blue Tuscan sky endomes
    Our English words of prayer.

III.

A little child!—how long she lived,
    By months, not years, is reckoned:
Born in one July, she survived
    Alone to see a second

IV.

Bright-featured, as the July sun
    Her little face still played in,
And splendours, with her birth begun,
    Had had no time for fading.

V.

So, LILY, from those July hours,
    No wonder we should call her;
She looked such kinship to the flowers
    Was but a little taller.

VI.

A Tuscan Lily,—only white . . .
    As Dante, in abhorrence
Of red corruption, wished aright
    The lilies of his Florence.

VII.

We could not wish her whiter, . . Her
    Who perfumed with pure blossom
The house!—a lovely thing to wear
    Upon a mother's bosom!

VIII.

This July creature thought perhaps
    Our speech not worth assuming:
She sate upon her parents' laps,
    And mimicked the gnat's humming;

IX.

. . Said 'Father,' 'Mother!'—then, left off;
    For tongues celestial, fitter.
Her hair had grown just long enough
    To catch Heaven's jasper-glitter.

X.

Babes! Love could always hear and see
    Behind the cloud that hid them:
'Let little children come to me,
    And do not thou forbid them.'

XI.

So, unforbidding, have we met,
    And gently here have laid her;
Though winter is no time to get
    The flowers that should o'erspread her.

XII.

We should bring pansies quick with spring,
    Rose, violet, daffodilly,
And also, above everything,
    White lilies for our Lily.

XIII.

Nay, more than flowers, this grave exacts . .
    Glad, grateful attestations
Of her sweet eyes and pretty acts,
    With calm renunciations.

34

XIV.

Her very mother with light feet
   Should leave the place too earthy,
Saying, 'The angels have thee, sweet,
   Because we are not worthy.'

XV.

But winter kills the orange-buds,
   The gardens in the frost are;
And all the heart dissolves in floods,
   Remembering we have lost her!

XVI.

Poor earth, poor heart!—too weak, too weak,
   To miss the July shining!
Poor heart!—what bitter words we speak,
   When God speaks of resigning!

XVII.

Sustain this heart in us that faints,
   Thou God, the self-existent!
We catch up wild at parting saints,
   And feel thy Heaven too distant!

XVIII.

The wind that swept them out of sin,
   Has ruffled all our vesture:
On the shut door that let them in,
   We beat with frantic gesture;

XIX.

To us, us also—open straight!
    The outer life is chilly—
Are *we* too, like the earth, to wait
    Till next year for our Lily?

XX.

—Oh, my own baby on my knees,
    My leaping, dimpled treasure,
At every word I write like these,
    Clasped close, with stronger pressure!

XXI.

Too well my own heart understands . . .
    At every word beats fuller . . .
My little feet, my little hands,
    And hair of Lily's colour!

XXII.

—But God gives patience, Love learns strength,
    And Faith remembers promise;
And Hope itself can smile at length
    On other hopes gone from us.

XXIII.

Love, strong as Death, shall conquer Death,
    Through struggle, made more glorious:
This mother stills her sobbing breath,
    Renouncing, yet victorious.

XXIV.

Arms, empty of her child, she lifts,
    With spirit unbereaven—
' God will not all take back His gifts:
    My Lily's mine in Heaven !

XXV.

Still mine !   maternal rights serene
    Not given to another !
The crystal bars shine faint between
    The souls of child and mother.

XXVI.

' Meanwhile, ' the mother cries, ' content !
    Our love was well divided ;
Its sweetness following where she went,
    Its anguish stayed where I did.

XXVII.

Well done of God, to halve the lot,
    And give her all the sweetness !
To us, the empty room and cot,—
    To her, the Heaven's completeness :

XXVIII.

' To us, this grave—to her, the rows
    The mystic palm-trees spring in :
To us, the silence in the house,—
    To her, the choral singing !

XXIX.

' For her, to gladden in God's view,—
  For us, to hope and bear on !—
Grow, Lily, in thy garden new,
  Beside the Rose of Sharon.

XXX.

' Grow fast in Heaven, sweet Lily clipped,
  In love more calm than this is,—
And may the angels dewy-lipped
  Remind thee of our kisses !

XXXI.

' While none shall tell thee of our tears,
  These human tears now falling ;
Till, after a few patient years,
  One home shall take us all in ;

XXXII.

' Child, father, mother—who, left out ?
  Not mother, and not father !—
And when, their dying couch about,
  The natural mists shall gather,

XXXIII.

' Some smiling angel close shall stand
  In old Correggio's fashion,
And bear a LILY in his hand,
  For death's ANNUNCIATION. '
34*

SONNETS FROM THE PORTUGUESE.

I.

I THOUGHT once how Theocritus had sung
Of the sweet years, the dear and wished for years,
Who each one in a gracious hand appears
To bear a gift for mortals, old or young:
And, as I mused it in his antique tongue,
I saw, in gradual vision through my tears,
The sweet, sad years, the melancholy years,
Those of my own life, who by turns had flung
A shadow across me.   Straightway I was 'ware,
So weeping, how a mystic Shape did move
Behind me, and drew me backward by the hair;
And a voice said in mastery while I strove, . .
'Guess now who holds thee?'—'Death!' I said
     But, there,
The silver answer rang . . 'Not Death, but Love.'

II.

But only three in all God's universe
Have heard this word thou hast said; Himself, beside
Thee speaking and me listening! and replied
One of us . . *that* was God! . . and laid the curse
So darkly on my eyelids as to amerce
My sight from seeing thee,—that if I had died,
The deathweights, placed there, would have signified
Less absolute exclusion.   'Nay' is worse
From God than from all others, O my friend!
Men could not part us with their worldly jars,
Nor the seas change us, nor the tempests bend:
Our hands would touch for all the mountain-bars;—
And, heaven being rolled between us at the end,
We should but vow the faster for the stars.

III.

Unlike are we, unlike, O princely Heart!
Unlike our uses and our destinies.
Our ministering two angels look surprise
On one another, as they strike athwart
Their wings in passing.   Thou, bethink thee, art
A guest for queens to social pageantries,
With gages from a hundred brighter eyes
Than tears even can make mine, to ply thy part
Of chief musician.   What hast *thou* to do
With looking from the lattice-lights at me,
A poor, tired, wandering singer? . . singing through
The dark, and leaning up a cypress tree?
The chrism is on thine head,—on mine, the dew,—
And Death must dig the level where these agree.

IV.

Thou hast thy calling to some palace floor,
Most gracious singer of high poems! where
The dancers will break footing from the care
Of watching up thy pregnant lips for more.
And dost thou lift this house's latch too poor
For hand of thine? and canst thou think and bear
To let thy music drop here unaware
In folds of golden fulness at my door?
Look up and see the casement broken in,
The bats and owlets builders in the roof!
My cricket chirps against thy mandolin.
Hush! call no echo up in further proof
Of desolation! there's a voice within
That weeps .. as thou must sing .. alone, aloof.

V.

I LIFT my heavy heart up solemnly,
As once Electra her sepulchral urn,
And, looking in thine eyes, I overturn
The ashes at thy feet. Behold and see
What a great heap of grief lay hid in me,
And how the red wild sparkles dimly burn
Through the ashen greyness. If thy foot in scorn
Could tread them out to darkness utterly,
It might be well perhaps. But if instead
Thou wait beside me for the wind to blow
The grey dust up, ... those laurels on thine head,
O My beloved, will not shield thee so,
That none of all the fires shall scorch and shred
The hair beneath. Stand farther off then! Go.

VI.

Go from me.   Yet I feel that I shall stand
Henceforward in thy shadow.   Nevermore
Alone upon the threshold of my door
Of individual life, I shall command
The uses of my soul, nor lift my hand
Serenely in the sunshine as before,
Without the sense of that which I forbore, . .
Thy touch upon the palm.   The widest land
Doom takes to part us, leaves thy heart in mine
With pulses that beat double.   What I do
And what I dream include thee, as the wine
Must taste of its own grapes.   And when I sue
God for myself, He hears that name of thine,
And sees within my eyes, the tears of two

VII.

THE face of all the world is changed, I think,
Since first I heard the footsteps of thy soul
Move still, oh, still, beside me ; as they stole
Betwixt me and the dreadful outer brink
Of obvious death, where I who thought to sink
Was caught up into love and taught the whole
Of life in a new rhythm.   The cup of dole
God gave for baptism, I am fain to drink,
And praise its sweetness, sweet, with thee anear.
The names of country, heaven, are changed away
For where thou art or shalt be, there or here ;
And this . . this lute and song . . loved yesterday,
(The singing angels know) are only dear,
Because thy name moves right in what they say.

VIII.

WHAT can I give thee back, O liberal
And princely giver, . . who has brought the gold
And purple of thine heart, unstained, untold,
And laid them on the outside of the wall
For such as I to take or leave withal,
In unexpected largesse? Am I cold,
Ungrateful, that for these most manifold
High gifts, I render nothing back at all?
Not so. Not cold!—but very poor instead!
Ask God who knows! for frequent tears have run
The colours from my life, and left so dead
And pale a stuff, it were not fitly done
To give the same as pillow to thy head.
Go farther! Let it serve to trample on.

IX.

CAN it be right to give what I can give?
To let thee sit beneath the fall of tears
As salt as mine, and hear the sighing years
Re-sighing on my lips renunciative
Through those infrequent smiles which fail to live
For all thy adjurations? O my fears,
That this can scarce be right! We are not peers,
So to be lovers; and I own and grieve
That givers of such gifts as mine are, must
Be counted with the ungenerous. Out, alas!
I will not soil thy purple with my dust,
Nor breathe my poison on thy Venice-glass,
Nor give thee any love . . . which were unjust.
Beloved, I only love thee! let it pass.

X.

YET, love, mere love, is beautiful indeed
And worthy of acceptation.   Fire is bright,
Let temple burn, or flax!   An equal light
Leaps in the flame from cedar-plank or weed.
And love is fire: and when I say at need
I love thee . . mark! . . *I love thee!* . . in thy sight
I stand transfigured, glorified aright,
With conscience of the new rays that proceed
Out of my face toward thine.   There's nothing low
In love, when love the lowest: meanest creatures
Who love God, God accepts while loving so.
And what I *feel*, across the inferior features
Of what I *am*, doth flash itself, and show
How that great work of Love enhances Nature's.

XI.

AND therefore if to love can be desert,
I am not all unworthy.   Cheeks as pale
As these you see, and trembling knees that fail
To bear the burden of a heavy heart,
This weary minstrel-life that once was girt
To climb Aornus, and can scarce avail
To pipe now 'gainst the valley nightingale
A melancholy music! . . why advert
To these things? O Beloved, it is plain
I am not of thy worth nor for thy place:
And yet because I love thee, I obtain
From that same love this vindicating grace,
To live on still in love and yet in vain, . .
To bless thee yet renounce thee to thy face.

XII.

INDEED this very love which is my boast,
And which, when rising up from breast to brow,
Doth crown me with a ruby large enow
To draw men's eyes and prove the inner cost, . .
This love even, all my worth, to the uttermost,
I should not love withal, unless that thou
Hadst set me an example, shown me how,
When first thine earnest eyes with mine were crossed,
And love called love.   And thus, I cannot speak
Of love even, as a good thing of my own.
Thy soul hath snatched up mine all faint and weak,
And placed it by thee on a golden throne,—
And that I love, (O soul, we must be meek!)
Is by thee only, whom I love alone.

XIII.

AND wilt thou have me fashion into speech
The love I bear thee, finding words enough,
And hold the torch out, while the winds are rough,
Between our faces, to cast light on each?—
I drop it at thy feet.   I cannot teach
My hand to hold my spirit so far off
From myself . . me . . that I should bring thee proof
In words, of love hid in me out of reach.
Nay, let the silence of my womanhood
Commend my woman-love to thy belief,—
Seeing that I stand unwon, however wooed,
And rend the garment of my life, in brief,
By a most dauntless, voiceless fortitude,
Lest one touch of this heart convey its grief

XIV.

IF thou must love me, let it be for nought
Except for love's sake only.   Do not say
' I love her for her smile . . her look . . her way
Of speaking gently, . . for a trick of thought
That falls in well with mine, and certes brought
A sense of pleasant ease on such a day '—
For these things in themselves, Beloved, may
Be changed, or change for thee,—and love so wrought,
May be unwrought so.   Neither love me for
Thine own dear pity's wiping my cheeks dry,
A creature might forget to weep, who bore
Thy comfort long, and lose thy love thereby.
But love me for love's sake, that evermore
Thou may'st love on through love's eternity.

XV.

ACCUSE me not, beseech thee, that I wear
Too calm and sad a face in front of thine;
For we two look two ways, and cannot shine
With the same sunlight on our brow and hair.
On me thou lookest, with no doubting care,
As on a bee shut in a crystalline,—
For sorrow hath shut me safe in love's divine,
And to spread wing and fly in the outer air
Were most impossible failure, if I strove
To fail so.   But I look on thee . . on thee . .
Beholding, besides love, the end of love,
Hearing oblivion beyond memory . . .
As one who sits and gazes from above,
Over the rivers to the bitter sea.

35

XVI.

And yet, because thou overcomest so,
Because thou art more noble and like a king,
Thou canst prevail against my fears and fling
Thy purple round me, till my heart shall grow
Too close against thine heart, henceforth to know
How it shook when alone.   Why, conquering
May prove as lordly and complete a thing
In lifting upward as in crushing low :
And as a vanquished soldier yields his sword
To one who lifts him from the bloody earth,—
Even so, Beloved, I at last record,
Here ends my strife.   If *thou* invite me forth,
I rise above abasement at the word.
Make thy love larger to enlarge my worth.

XVII.

My poet, thou canst touch on all the notes
God set between His After and Before,
And strike up and strike off the general roar
Of the rushing worlds, a melody that floats
In a serene air purely.   Antidotes
Of medicated music, answering for
Mankind's forlornest uses, thou canst pour
From thence into their ears.   God's will devotes
Thine to such ends, and mine to wait on thine!
How, Dearest, wilt thou have me for most use?
A hope, to sing by gladly ? . . or a fine
Sad memory. with thy songs to interfuse ?
A shade. in which to sing . . . of palm or pine ?
A grave. on which to rest from singing ? . . Choose

XVIII.

I NEVER gave a lock of hair away
To a man, Dearest, except this to thee,
Which now upon my fingers thoughtfully
I ring out to the full brown length and say
' Take it.' My day of youth went yesterday;
My hair no longer bounds to my foot's glee,
Nor plant I it from rose or myrtle-tree,
As girls do, any more. It only may
Now shade on two pale cheeks, the mark of tears,
Taught drooping from the head that hangs aside
Through sorrow's trick. I thought the funeral-shears
Would take this first; but Love is justified:
Take it thou, . . finding pure, from all those years,
The kiss my mother left here when she died.

XIX.

THE soul's Rialto hath its merchandise;
I barter curl for curl upon that mart;
And from my poet's forehead to my heart,
Receive this lock which outweighs argosies,—
As purply black, as erst to Pindar's eyes
The dim purpureal tresses gloomed athwart
The nine white Muse-brows. For this counterpart,.
The bay-crown's shade, Beloved, I surmise,
Still lingers on thy curl, it is so black!
Thus, with a fillet of smooth-kissing breath,
I tie the shadow safe from gliding back,
And lay the gift where nothing hindereth,
Here on my heart as on thy brow, to lack
No natural heat till mine grows cold in death.

XX.

BELOVED, my Beloved, when I think
That thou wast in the world a year ago,
What time I sate alone here in the snow
And saw no footprint, heard the silence sink
No moment at thy voice, . . but link by link
Went counting all my chains as if that so
They never could fall off at any blow
Struck by thy possible hand . . . . why, thus I drink
Of life's great cup of wonder. Wonderful,
Never to feel thee thrill the day or night
With personal act or speech,—nor ever cull
Some prescience of thee with the blossoms white
Thou sawest growing! Atheists are as dull,
Who cannot guess God's presence out of sight.

XXI.

SAY over again and yet once over again
That thou dost love me. Though the word repeated
Should seem 'a cuckoo-song,' as thou dost treat it.
Remember never to the hill or plain,
Valley and wood, without her cuckoo-strain,
Comes the fresh Spring in all her green completed!
Beloved, I, amid the darkness greeted
By a doubtful spirit-voice, in that doubt's pain
Cry . . speak once more . . thou lovest! Who can fear
Too many stars, though each in heaven shall roll—
Too many flowers, though each shall crown the year?
Say thou dost love me, love me, love me—toll
The silver iterance!—only minding, Dear,
To love me also in silence, with thy soul.

XXII.

WHEN our two souls stand up erect and strong,
Face to face, silent, drawing nigh and nigher,
Until the lengthening wings break into fire
At either curvèd point,—what bitter wrong
Can the earth do to us, that we should not long
Be here contented?   Think.   In mounting higher,
The angels would press on us, and aspire
To drop some golden orb of perfect song
Into our deep, dear silence.   Let us stay
Rather on earth, Beloved,—where the unfit
Contrarious moods of men recoil away
And isolate pure spirits, and permit
A place to stand and love in for a day,
With darkness and the death-hour rounding it.

XXIII.

Is it indeed so?   If I lay here dead,
Would'st thou miss any life in losing mine,
And would the sun for thee more coldly shine,
Because of grave-damps falling round my head?
I marvelled, my Beloved, when I read
Thy thought so in the letter.   I am thine—
But .. *so* much to thee?   Can I pour thy wine
While my hands tremble?   Then my soul, instead
Of dreams of death, resumes life's lower range!
Then, love me, Love! look on me .. breathe on me!
As brighter ladies do not count it strange,
For love, to give up acres and degree,
I yield the grave for thy sake, and exchange
My near sweet view of Heaven, for earth with thee!
35*

XXIV.

LET the world's sharpness like a clasping knife
Shut in upon itself and do no harm
In this close hand of Love, now soft and warm;
And let us hear no sound of human strife
After the click of the shutting. Life to life—
I lean upon thee, Dear, without alarm
And feel as safe as guarded by a charm,
Against the stab of worldlings who if rife
Are weak to injure. Very whitely still
The lilies of our lives may reassure
Their blossoms from their roots! accessible
Alone to heavenly dews that drop not fewer;
Growing straight, out of man's reach, on the hill.
God only, who made us rich, can make us poor.

XXV.

A HEAVY heart, Beloved, have I borne
From year to year until I saw thy face,
And sorrow after sorrow took the place
Of all those natural joys as lightly worn
As the stringed pearls . . each lifted in its turn
By a beating heart at dance-time. Hopes apace
Were changed to long despairs, . . till God's own grace
Could scarcely lift above the world forlorn
My heavy heart. Then *thou* didst bid me bring
And let it drop adown thy calmly great
Deep being! Fast it sinketh, as a thing
Which its own nature doth precipitate,
While thine doth close above it mediating
Betwixt the stars and the unaccomplished fate.

XXVI.

I LIVED with visions for my company
Instead of men and women, years ago,
And found them gentle mates, nor thought to know
A sweeter music than they played to me.
But soon their trailing purple was not free
Of this world's dust,—their lutes did silent grow,
And I myself grew faint and blind below
Their vanishing eyes.   Then THOU didst come . . to *be*,
Beloved, what they *seemed*.   Their shining fronts,
Their songs, their splendours . . (better, yet the
    same,
As river-water hallowed into fonts . .)
Met in thee, and from out thee overcame
My soul with satisfaction of all wants—
Because God's gifts put man's best dreams to shame.

XXVII.

My own Beloved, who hast lifted me
From this drear flat of earth where I was thrown,
And in betwixt the languid ringlets, blown
A life-breath, till the forehead hopefully
Shines out again, as all the angels see,
Before thy saving kiss!   My own, my own,
Who camest to me when the world was gone,
And I who looked for only God, found *thee!*
I find thee: I am safe, and strong, and glad.
As one who stands in dewless asphodel
Looks backward on the tedious time he had
In the upper life . . so I, with bosom-swell,
Make witness here between the good and bad,
That Love, as strong as Death, retrieves as well.

My letters! all dead paper, . . mute and white!--
And yet they seem alive and quivering
Against my tremulous hands which loose the string
And let them drop down on my knee to-night.
This said, . . he wished to have me in his sight
Once, as a friend: this fixed a day in spring
To come and touch my hand . . . a simple thing,
Yet I wept for it!—this, . . the paper's light . .
Said, *Dear, I love thee:* and I sank and quailed
As if God's future thundered on my past:
This said, *I am thine*—and so its ink has paled
With lying at my heart that beat too fast:
And this . . . O Love, thy words have ill availed,
If, what this said, I dared repeat at last!

I THINK of thee!—my thoughts do twine and bud
About thee, as wild vines about a tree,
Put out broad leaves, and soon there's nought to see
Except the straggling green which hides the wood.
Yet, O my palm-tree, be it understood
I will not have my thoughts instead of thee
Who art dearer, better! Rather instantly
Renew thy presence! As a strong tree should,
Rustle thy boughs and set thy trunk all bare,
And let these bands of greenery which insphere thee,
Drop heavily down, . . burst, shattered, everywhere!
Because, in this deep joy to see and hear thee
And breathe within thy shadow a new air,
I do not think of thee—I am too near thee.

I SEE thine image through my tears to-night,
And yet to-day I saw thee smiling. How
Refer the cause?—Beloved, is it thou
Or I? Who makes me sad? The acolyte
Amid the chanted joy and thankful rite,
May so fall flat, with pale insensate brow,
On the altar-stair. I hear thy voice and vow
Perplexed, uncertain, since thou'rt out of sight,
As he, in his swooning ears, the choir's amen!
Beloved, dost thou love? or did I see all
The glory as I dreamed, and fainted when
Too vehement light dilated my ideal
For my soul's eyes? Will that light come again,
As now these tears come . . . falling hot and real?

XXXI

THOU comest! all is said without a word.
I sit beneath thy looks, as children do
In the noon-sun, with souls that tremble through
Their happy eyelids from an unaverred
Yet prodigal inward joy. Behold, I erred
In that last doubt! and yet I cannot rue
The sin most, but the occasion . . . that we two
Should for a moment stand unministered
By a mutual presence. Ah, keep near and close,
Thou dovelike help! and, when my fears would rise,
With thy broad heart serenely interpose!
Brood down with thy divine sufficiencies
These thoughts which tremble when bereft of those,
Like callow birds left desert to the skies.

XXXII.

THE first time that the sun rose on thine oath
To love me, I looked forward to the moon
To slacken all those bonds which seemed too soon
And quickly tied to make a lasting troth.
Quick-loving hearts, I thought, may quickly loathe;
And, looking on myself, I seemed not one
For such man's love!—more like an out of tune
Worn viol, a good singer would be wroth
To spoil his song with, and which, snatched in haste,
Is laid down at the first ill-sounding note.
I did not wrong myself so, but I placed
A wrong on *thee*.   For perfect strains may float
'Neath master-hands, from instruments defaced,—
And great souls, at one stroke, may do and doat.

XXXIII.

YES, call me by my pet-name! let me hear
The name I used to run at, when a child,
From innocent play, and leave the cowslips piled,
To glance up in some face that proved me dear
With the look of its eyes.   I miss the clear
Fond voices, which, being drawn and reconciled
Into the music of Heaven's undefiled,
Call me no longer.   Silence on the bier,
While *I* call God . . call God!—So let thy mouth
Be heir to those who are now exanimate:
Gather the north flowers to complete the south,
And catch the early love up in the late!
Yes, call me by that name,—and I, in truth,
With the same heart, will answer, and not wait.

XXXIV.

WITH the same heart, I said, I'll answer thee
As those, when thou shalt call me by my name—
Lo, the vain promise!   Is the same, the same,
Perplexed and ruffled by life's strategy?
When called before, I told how hastily
I dropped my flowers, or brake off from a game,
To run and answer with the smile that came
At play last moment, and went on with me
Through my obedience.   When I answer now,
I drop a grave thought;—break from solitude:—
Yet still my heart goes to thee . . . ponder how . ,
Not as to a single good but all my good!
Lay thy hand on it, best one, and allow
That no child's foot could run fast as this blood.

XXXV.

IF I leave all for thee, wilt thou exchange
And *be* all to me?   Shall I never miss
Home-talk and blessing, and the common kiss
That comes to each in turn, nor count it strange,
When I look up, to drop on a new range
Of walls and floors . . another home than this?
Nay, wilt thou fill that place by me which is
Filled by dead eyes too tender to know change!
That's hardest!   If to conquer love, has tried,
To conquer grief tries more . . . as all things prove
For grief indeed is love and grief beside.
Alas, I have grieved so I am hard to love—
Yet love me—wilt thou?   Open thine heart wide,
And fold within, the wet wings of thy dove.

XXXVI.

WHEN we met first and loved, I did not build
Upon the event with marble.   Could it mean
To last, a love set pendulous between
Sorrow and sorrow ?   Nay, I rather thrilled,
Distrusting every light that seemed to gild
The onward path, and feared to overlean
A finger even.   And, though I have grown serene
And strong since then, I think that God has willed
A still renewable fear . . O love, O troth . .
Lest these enclasped hands should never hold,
This mutual kiss drop down between us both
As an unowned thing, once the lips being cold.
And Love be false ! if *he*, to keep one oath,
Must lose one joy by his life's star foretold.

XXXVII.

PARDON, oh, pardon, that my soul should make
Of all that strong divineness which I know
For thine and thee, an image only so
Formed of the sand, and fit to shift and break.
It is that distant years which did not take
Thy sovranty, recoiling with a blow,
Have forced my swimming brain to undergo
Their doubt and dread, and blindly to forsake
Thy purity of likeness, and distort
Thy worthiest love to a worthless counterfeit.
As if a shipwrecked Pagan, safe in port,
His guardian sea-god to commemorate,
Should set a sculptured porpoise, gills a-snort,
And vibrant tail, within the temple-gate.

XXXVIII.

First time he kissed me, he but only kissed
The fingers of this hand wherewith I write,
And ever since it grew more clean and white, . . .
Slow to world-greetings . . quick with its ' Oh, list,'
When the angels speak.   A ring of amethyst
I could not wear here plainer to my sight,
Than that first kiss.   The second passed in height
The first, and sought the forehead, and half missed,
Half falling on the hair.   O beyond meed!
That was the chrism of love, which love's own crown,
With sanctifying sweetness, did precede.
The third upon my lips was folded down
In perfect, purple state! since when, indeed,
I have been proud and said, 'My Love, my own.'

XXXIX.

Because thou hast the power and own'st the grace
To look through and behind this mask of me,
(Against which years have beat thus blanchingly
With their rains!) and behold my soul's true face,
The dim and weary witness of life's race :—
Because thou hast the faith and love to see,
Through that same soul's distracting lethargy,
The patient angel waiting for his place
In the new Heavens : because nor sin nor woe,
Nor God's infliction, nor death's neighbourhood,
Nor all which others viewing, turn to go, . .
Nor all which makes me tired of all, self-viewed, . .
Nothing repels thee, . . Dearest, teach me so
To pour out gratitude, as thou dost, good !

XL.

On, yes! they love through all this world of ours!
I will not gainsay love, called love forsooth.
I have heard love talked in my early youth,
And since, not so long back but that the flowers
Then gathered, smell still.   Mussulmans and Giaours
Throw kerchiefs at a smile, and have no ruth
For any weeping.   Polypheme's white tooth
Slips on the nut, if after frequent showers
The shell is over-smooth; and not so much
Will turn the thing called love, aside to hate,
Or else to oblivion.   But thou art not such
A lover, my Beloved! thou canst wait
Through sorrow and sickness, to bring souls to touch,
And think it soon when others cry 'Too late.'

XLI.

I THANK all who have loved me in their hearts,
With thanks and love from mine.   Deep thanks to all
Who paused a little near the prison-wall,
To hear my music in its louder parts,
Ere they went onward, each one to the mart's
Or temple's occupation, beyond call.
But thou, who in my voice's sink and fall,
When the sob took it, thy divinest Art's
Own instrument didst drop down at thy foot,
To hearken what I said between my tears, . .
Instruct me how to thank thee!—Oh, to shoot
My soul's full meaning into future years,
That *they* should lend it utterance, and salute
Love that endures! with Life that disappears!

XLII.

How do I love thee?   Let me count the ways.
I love thee to the depth and breadth and height
My soul can reach, when feeling out of sight
For the ends of Being and Ideal Grace.
I love thee to the level of everyday's
Most quiet need, by sun and candlelight.
I love thee freely, as men strive for Right;
I love thee purely, as they turn from Praise;
I love thee with the passion put to use
In my old griefs, and with my childhood's faith;
I love thee with a love I seemed to lose
With my lost saints,—I love thee with the breath
Smiles, tears, of all my life!—and, if God choose.
I shall but love thee better after death.

XLIII.

Beloved, thou hast brought me many flowers
Plucked in the garden, all the summer through
And winter, and it seemed as if they grew
In this close room, nor missed the sun and showers.
So, in the like name of that love of ours,
Take back these thoughts which here unfolded too,
And which on warm and cold days I withdrew
From my heart's ground.   Indeed, those beds and
        bowers
Be overgrown with bitter weeds and rue,
And wait thy weeding: yet here's eglantine,
Here's ivy!—take them, as I used to do
Thy flowers, and keep them where they shall not pine;
Instruct thine eyes to keep their colours true,
And tell thy soul, their roots are left in mine.

XLIV.

My future will not copy fair my past.
I wrote that once; and, thinking at my side
My ministering life-angel justified
The word by his appealing look upcast
To the white throne of God, I turned at last.
And there, instead, saw *thee;* not unallied
To angels in thy soul!   Then I, long tried
By natural ills, received the comfort fast,
While budding at thy sight, my pilgrim's staff
Gave out green leaves with morning dews impearled.
—I seek no copy now of life's first half!
Leave here the pages with long musing curled,
And write me new my future's epigraph,
New angel mine, unhoped for in the world!

TRANSLATIONS.

36*

THESE Translations were only intended, many years ago, to accompany and explain certain Engravings after ancient Gems, in the projected work of a friend, by whose kindness they are now recovered; but as two of the original series (the "Adonis," of Bion, and "Song to the Rose," from Achilles Tatius) are already included in these volumes, it is presumed that the remainder may not improperly follow. A single recent version is added.

PARAPHRASE ON THEOCRITUS.

THE CYCLOPS.

(Idyll XL)

AND so an easier life our Cyclops drew,
    The ancient Polyphemus, who in youth
Loved Galatea, while the manhood grew
    Adown his cheeks and darkened round his mouth.
No jot he cared for apples, olives, roses ;
    Love made him mad : the whole world was neg-
        lected,
The very sheep went backward to their closes
    From out the fair green pastures, self-directed.
      And singing Galatea, thus, he wore
      The sunrise down along the weedy shore,
And pined alone, and felt the cruel wound
    Beneath his heart, which Cypris' arrow bore,
With a deep pang ; but, so, the cure was found ;
      And sitting on a lofty rock he cast
      His eyes upon the sea, and sang at last :—
' O whitest Galatea, can it be
    That thou shouldst spurn me off who love thee
      so ?

More white than curds, my girl, thou art to see,
More meek than lambs, more full of leaping glee
   Than kids, and brighter than the early glow
On grapes that swell to ripen,—sour like thee!
Thou comest to me with the fragrant sleep,
   And with the fragrant sleep thou goest from me;
 Thou fliest . . fliest, as a frightened sheep
   Flies the gray wolf!—yet Love did overcome me,
So long;—I loved thee, maiden, first of all
   When down the hills (my mother fast beside thee)
I saw thee stray to pluck the summer-fall
   Of hyacinth bells, and went myself to guide thee:
And since my eyes have seen thee, they can leave
     thee
   No more, from that day's light! But thou . . by
     Zeus,
Thou wilt not care for *that*, to let it grieve thee!
   I know thee, fair one, why thou springest loose
From my arm round thee. Why? I tell thee,
     Dear!
   One shaggy eyebrow draws its smudging road
Straight through my ample front, from ear to ear,—
   One eye rolls underneath; and yawning, broad
Flat nostrils feel the bulging lips too near.
Yet . . ho, ho!—*I*,—whatever I appear,—
   Do feed a thousand oxen! When I have done,
I milk the cows, and drink the milk that's best!
   I lack no cheese, while summer keeps the sun;
And after, in the cold, it's ready prest!
   And then, I know to sing, as there is none
Of all the Cyclops can, . . a song of thee,
Sweet apple of my soul, on love's fair tree,
And of myself who love thee . . till the West
Forgets the light, and all but I have rest.

I feed for thee, besides, eleven fair does,
  And all in fawn ; and four tame whelps of bears.
Come to me, Sweet ! thou shalt have all of those
  In change for love !   I will not halve the shares.
Leave the blue sea, with pure white arms extended
  To the dry shore ; and, in my cave's recess,
Thou shalt be gladder for the noonlight ended,—
  For here be laurels, spiral cypresses,
Dark ivy, and a vine whose leaves enfold
Most luscious grapes ; and here is water cold,
  The wooded Ætna pours down through the trees
From the white snows,—which gods were scarce too
      bold
  To drink in turn with nectar.   Who with these
  Would choose the salt wave of the lukewarm
      seas ?
Nay, look on me !   If I am hairy and rough,
  I have an oak's heart in me ; there's a fire
In these gray ashes which burns hot enough ;
  And when I burn for *thee*, I grudge the pyre
No fuel . . not my soul, nor this one eye,—
Most precious thing I have, because thereby
I see thee, Fairest !   Out, alas ! I wish
My mother had borne me finnéd like a fish,
That I might plunge down in the ocean near thee,
  And kiss thy glittering hand between the weeds,
If still thy face were turned ; and I would bear thee
  Each lily white, and poppy fair that bleeds
Its red heart down its leaves !—one gift, for hours
  Of summer, . . one, for winter ; since, to cheer
      thee,
I could not bring at once all kinds of flowers.
Even now, girl, now, I fain would learn to swim,
  If stranger in a ship sailed nigh, I wis, —

That I may know how sweet a thing it is
To live down with you, in the Deep and Dim!
Come up, O Galatea, from the ocean,
   And having come, forget again to go!
As I, who sing out here my heart's emotion,
   Could sit for ever. Come up from below!
Come, keep my flocks beside me, milk my kine,—
   Come, press my cheese, distrain my whey and
       curd!
Ah, mother! she alone . . that mother of mine . .
   Did wrong me sore! I blame her!—Not a word
Of kindly intercession did she address
Thine ear with for my sake; and ne'ertheless
   She saw me wasting, wasting, day by day!
   Both head and feet were aching, I will say,
All sick for grief, as I myself was sick!
   O Cyclops, Cyclops, whither hast thou sent
   Thy soul on fluttering wings? If thou wert bent
On turning bowls, or pulling green and thick
   The sprouts to give thy lambkins,—thou wouldst
      make thee
   A wiser Cyclops than for what we take thee.
Milk dry the present! Why pursue too quick
That future which is fugitive aright?
   Thy Galatea thou shalt haply find,—
   Or else a maiden fairer and more kind;
For many girls do call me through the night,
   And, as they call, do laugh out silverly.
I, too, am something in the world, I see!'

   While thus the Cyclops love and lambs did fold,
   Ease came with song, he could not buy with gold.

PARAPHRASES ON APULEIUS.

PSYCHE GAZING ON CUPID.

(METAMORPH., Lib. IV.)

THEN Psyche, weak in body and soul, put on
    The cruelty of Fate, in place of strength :
She raised the lamp to see what should be done,
    And seized the steel, and was a man at length
In courage, though a woman! Yes, but when
    The light fell on the bed whereby she stood
To view the '*beast*' that lay there,—certes, then,
    She saw the gentlest, sweetest beast in wood—
Even Cupid's self, the beauteous god! more beau-
        teous
    For that sweet sleep across his eyelids dim!
The light, the lady carried as she viewed,
    Did blush for pleasure as it lighted him,
The dagger trembled from its aim unduteous;
    And *she* . . oh, *she*—amazed and soul distraught,
And fainting in her whiteness like a veil,
    Slid down upon her knees, and, shuddering thought
To hide—though in her heart—the dagger pale!
She would have done it, but her hands did fail
    To hold the guilty steel, they shivered so,—

And feeble, exhausted, unawares she took
To gazing on the god,—till, look by look
    Her eyes with larger life did fill and glow.
She saw his golden head alight with curls,—
    She might have guessed their brightness in the
        dark
    By that ambrosial smell of heavenly mark !
She saw the milky brow, more pure than pearls,
    The purple of the cheeks, divinely sundered
By the globed ringlets, as they glided free,
Some back, some forwards,—all so radiantly,
    That, as she watched them there, she never won-
        dered
    To see the lamplight, where it touched them, trem
        ble ;
On the god's shoulders, too, she marked his wings
    Shine faintly at the edges and resemble
A flower that's near to blow.   The poet sings
    And lover sighs, that Love is fugitive ;
And certes, though these pinions lay reposing,
    The feathers on them seemed to stir and live
As if by instinct, closing and unclosing.
    Meantime the god's fair body slumbered deep,
    All worthy of Venus, in his shining sleep ;
    While at the bed's foot lay the quiver, bow,
And darts,—his arms of godhead.   Psyche gazed
    With eyes that drank the wonders in,—said—' Lo,
Be these my husband's arms?'—and straightway
        raised
    An arrow from the quiver-case, and tried
Its point against her finger,—trembling till
    She pushed it in too deeply (foolish bride !)
And made her blood some dewdrops small distil,
And learnt to love Love, of her own goodwill.

PSYCHE WAFTED BY ZEPHYRUS.

(METAMORPH., Lib. IV.)

WHILE Psyche wept upon the rock forsaken,
  Alone, despairing, dreading,—gradually
By Zephyrus she was enwrapt and taken
  Still trembling,—like the lilies planted high,—
Through all her fair white limbs.   Her vesture
      spread,
  Her very bosom eddying with surprise,—
He drew her slowly from the mountain-head,
  And bore her down the valleys with wet eyes,
And laid her in the lap of a green dell
  As soft with grass and flowers as any nest,
With trees beside her, and a limpid well:
  Yet Love was not far off from all that Rest.

PSYCHE AND PAN.

(METAMORPH., Lib. V.)

THE gentle River, in her Cupid's honor,
  Because he used to warm the very wave,
Did ripple aside, instead of closing on her,
  And cast up Psyche, with a refluence brave,
Upon the flowery bank,—all sad and sinning.
Then Pan, the rural god, by chance was leaning
  37

Along the brow of waters as they wound,
Kissing the reed-nymph till she sank to ground,
And teaching, without knowledge of the meaning,
To run her voice in music after his
Down many a shifting note ; (the goats around.
In wandering pasture and most leaping bliss,
Drawn on to crop the river's flowery hair).
And as the hoary god beheld her there,
The poor, worn, fainting Psyche !—knowing all
The grief she suffered, he did gently call
Her name, and softly comfort her despair :—

'O wise, fair lady, I am rough and rude,
And yet experienced through my weary age !
And if I read aright, as soothsayer should,
Thy faltering steps of heavy pilgrimage,
Thy paleness, deep as snow we cannot see
The roses through,—thy sighs of quick returning,
Thine eyes that seem, themselves, two souls in mourn
     ing,—
Thou lovest, girl, too well, and bitterly !
But hear me : rush no more to a headlong fall! :
Seek no more deaths ! leave wail, lay sorrow down,
And pray the sovran god ; and use withal
Such prayer as best may suit a tender youth,
Well-pleased to bend to flatteries from thy mouth
And feel them stir the myrtle of his crown.'

—So spake the shepherd-god ; and answer none
Gave Psyche in return : but silently
She did him homage with a bended knee,
And took the onward path.—

PSYCHE PROPITIATING CERES.

(METAMORPH., Lib. VI.)

THEN mother Ceres from afar beheld her,
  While Psyche touched, with reverent fingers meek,
The temple's scythes; and with a cry compelled her:
  'O wretched Psyche, Venus roams to seek
Thy wandering footsteps round the weary earth,
Anxious and maddened, and adjures thee forth
  To accept the imputed pang, and let her wreak
Full vengeance with full force of deity!
  Yet *thou*, forsooth, art in my temple here,
Touching my scythes, assuming my degree,
  And daring to have thoughts that are not fear!'
—But Psyche clung to her feet, and as they moved
  Rained tears along their track, tear dropped on
    tear,
And drew the dust on in her trailing locks,
  And still, with passionate prayer, the charge dis-
    proved :—
'Now, by thy right hand's gathering from the shocks
Of golden corn,—and by thy gladsome rites
Of harvest,—and thy consecrated sights
Shut safe and mute in chests,—and by the course
Of thy slave-dragons,—and the driving force
Of ploughs along Sicilian glebes profound,—
By thy swift chariot,—by thy steadfast ground,—
By all those nuptial torches that departed
  With thy lost daughter,—and by those that shone
Back with her, when she came again glad-hearted,—
  And by all other mysteries which are done
In silence at Eleusis,—I beseech thee,

O Ceres, take some pity, and abstain
From giving to my soul extremer pain
Who am the wretched Psyche!   Let me teach thee
  A little mercy, and have thy leave to spend
A few days only in thy garnered corn,
  Until that wrathful goddess, at the end,
Shall feel her hate grow mild, the longer borne,—
Or till, alas!—this faintness at my breast
  Pass from me, and my spirit apprehend
From life-long woe a breath-time hour of rest!'
—But Ceres answered, ' I am moved indeed
  By prayers so moist with tears, and would defend
The poor beseecher from more utter need :
  But where old oaths, anterior ties, commend,
  I cannot fail to a sister, lie to a friend,
As Venus is to *me*.   Depart with speed !'

PSYCHE AND THE EAGLE.

(Metamorph., Lib. VI.)

But sovran Jove's rapacious bird, the regal
High percher on the lightning, the great eagle
Drove down with rushing wings ; and,—thinking
      how,
By Cupid's help, he bore from Ida's brow
A cup-boy for his master,—he inclined
To yield, in just return, an influence kind ;
The god being honored in his lady's woe.
And thus the bird wheeled downward from the track,
Gods follow gods in, to the level low
Of that poor face of Psyche left in wrack.

—'Now fie, thou simple girl!' the Bird began;
' For if thou think to steal and carry back
A drop of holiest stream that ever ran,
No simpler thought, methinks, were found in man.
What! know'st thou not these Stygian waters be
Most holy, even to Jove? that as, on earth,
Men swear by gods, and by the thunder's worth,
Even so the heavenly gods do utter forth
Their oaths by Styx's flowing majesty?
And yet, one little urnful, I agree
To grant thy need!'   Whereat, all hastily,
He takes it, fills it from the willing wave,
And bears it in his beak, incarnadined
By the last Titan-prey he screamed to have;
And, striking calmly out, against the wind,
Vast wings on each side,—there, where Psyche stands,
He drops the urn down in her lifted hands.

PSYCHE AND CERBERUS.

(Metamorph., Lib. VI.)

A mighty Dog with three colossal necks,
　　And heads in grand proportion; vast as fear,
With jaws that bark the thunder out that breaks
　　In most innocuous dread for ghosts anear,
Who are safe in death from sorrow: he reclines
Across the threshold of queen Proserpine's
Dark-sweeping halls, and, there, for Pluto's spouse,
Doth guard the entrance of the empty house.
　37*

When Psyche threw the cake to him, once amain
He howled up wildly from his hunger-pain,
And was still, after.—

PSYCHE AND PROSERPINE.

(METAMORPH., Lib. VI.)

THEN Psyche entered in to Proserpine
In the dark house, and straightway did decline
With meek denial the luxurious seat,
   The liberal board for welcome strangers spread,
But sate down lowly at the dark queen's feet,
   And told her tale, and brake her oaten bread.
And when she had given the pyx in humble duty,
   And told how Venus did entreat the queen
To fill it up with only one day's beauty
   She used in Hades, star-bright and serene,
To beautify the Cyprian, who had been
   All spoilt with grief in nursing her sick boy,—
Then Proserpine, in malice and in joy,
   Smiled in the shade, and took the pyx, and put
   A secret in it; and so, filled and shut,
   Gave it again to Pysche.   Could she tell
   It held no beauty, but a dream of hell?

PSYCHE AND VENUS.

(METAMORPH., Lib. VI.)

AND Psyche brought to Venus what was sent
By Pluto's spouse; the paler, that she went
So low to seek it, down the dark descent.

MERCURY CARRIES PSYCHE TO OLYMPUS.

(METAMORPH., Lib. VI.)

THEN Jove commanded the god Mercury
To float up Psyche from the earth.   And she
Sprang at the first word, as the fountain springs,
And shot up bright and rustling through his wings.

MARRIAGE OF PSYCHE AND CUPID.

(METAMORPH., Lib. VI.)

AND Jove's right-hand approached the ambrosial bow
    To Psyche's lips, that scarce dared yet to smile,—
'Drink, O my daughter, and acquaint thy soul
    With deathless uses, and be glad the while!
No more shall Cupid leave thy lovely side;
    Thy marriage-joy begins for never-ending.'

While yet he spake,—the nuptial feast supplied,—
   The bridegroom on the festive couch was bending
O'er Psyche in his bosom—Jove, the same,
   On Juno, and the other deities,
Alike ranged round.   The rural cup-boy came
   And poured Jove's nectar out with shining eyes,
While Bacchus, for the others, did as much,
   And Vulcan spread the meal; and all the Hours,
   Made all things purple with a sprinkle of flowers,
Or roses chiefly, not to say the touch
   Of their sweet fingers; and the Graces glided
Their balm around, and the Muses, through the air
   Struck out clear voices, which were still divided
By that divinest song Apollo there
   Intoned to his lute; while Aphroditè fair
Did float her beauty along the tune, and play
   The notes right with her feet.   And thus, the day
Through every perfect mood of joy was carried,
   The Muses sang their chorus; Satyrus
   Did blow his pipes; Pan touched his reed;—and
     thus
At last were Cupid and his Psyche married.

PARAPHRASES ON NONNUS.

HOW BACCHUS FINDS ARIADNE SLEEPING.

(Dionysiaca. Lib. XLVII.)

WHEN Bacchus first beheld the desolate
And sleeping Ariadne, wonder straight
Was mixed with love in his great golden eyes;
He turned to his Bacchantes in surprise,
And said with guarded voice,—'Hush! strike no more
Your brazen cymbals; keep those voices still
Of voice and pipe; and since ye stand before
Queen Cypris, let her slumber as she will!
And yet the cestus is not here in proof.
A Grace, perhaps, whom sleep has stolen aloof:
In which case, as the morning shines in view,
Wake this Aglaia!—yet in Naxos, who
Would veil a Grace so? Hush! And if that she
Were Hebe, which of all the gods can be
The pourer-out of wine? or if we think
She's like the shining moon by ocean's brink,
The guide of herds,—why, could she sleep without
Endymion's breath on her cheek? or if I doubt
Of silver-footed Thetis, used to tread
These shores,—even she (in reverence be it said)
Has no such rosy beauty to dress deep

With the blue waves.   The Loxian goddess might
Repose so from her hunting-toil aright
Beside the sea, since toil gives birth to sleep,
But who would find her with her tunic loose,
Thus? Stand off, Thracian! stand off ' Do not leap,
Not this way! Leave that piping, since I choose,
O dearest Pan, and let Athene rest!
And yet if she be Pallas . . truly guessed . .
Her lance is—where? her helm and ægis—where?'
—As Bacchus closed, the miserable Fair
Awoke at last, sprang upward from the sands,
And gazing wild on that wild throng that stands
Around, around her, and no Theseus there!—
Her voice went moaning over shore and sea,
Beside the halcyon's cry; she called her love;
She named her hero, and raged maddeningly
Against the brine of waters; and above,
Sought the ship's track and cursed the hours she slept;
And still the chiefest execration swept
Against queen Paphia, mother of the ocean;
And cursed and prayed by times in her emotion
The winds all round.   .   .   .

       .   .   .   .   .   .
Her grief did make her glorious; her despair
Adorned her with its weight.   Poor wailing child!
She looked like Venus when the goddess smiled
At liberty of godship, debonair;
Poor Ariadne! and her eyelids fair
Hid looks beneath them lent her by Persuasion
And every Grace, with tears of Love's own passion.
She wept long: then she spake:—' Sweet sleep did
        come
While sweetest Theseus went.   O, glad and dumb,
I wish he had left me still! for in my sleep

I saw his Athens, and did gladly keep
My new bride-state within my Theseus' hall;
And heard the pomp of Hymen, and the call
Of 'Ariadne, Ariadne,' sung
In choral joy; and there, with joy I hung
Spring-blossoms round love's altar!—ay, and wore
A wreath myself; and felt *him* evermore,
Oh, evermore beside me, with his mighty
Grave head bowed down in prayer to Aphroditè!
Why, what a sweet, sweet dream! *He* went with it,
And left me here unwedded where I sit!
Persuasion help me! The dark night did make me
  A brideship, the fair morning takes away;
My Love had left me when the Hour did wake me;
  And while I dreamed of marriage, as I say,
And blest it well, my blessèd Theseus left me:
And thus the sleep, I loved so, has bereft me.
Speak to me, rocks, and tell my grief to-day,
Who stole my love of Athens?' . . . .

HOW BACCHUS COMFORTS ARIADNE.

(DIONYSIACA, Lib. XLVII.)

THEN Bacchus' subtle speech her sorrow crossed:—
'O maiden, dost thou mourn for having lost
The false Athenian heart? and dost thou still
Take thought of Theseus, when thou may'st at will
Have Bacchus for a husband? Bacchus bright
A god in place of mortal! Yes, and though
The mortal youth be charming in thy sight,
That man of Athens cannot strive below,

In beauty and valor, with my deity!
Thou'lt tell me of the labyrinthine dweller,
The fierce man-bull, he slew: I pray thee, be,
Fair Ariadne, the true deed's true teller,
And mention thy clue's help! because, forsooth,
Thine armed Athenian hero had not found
A power to fight on that prodigious ground,
Unless a lady in her rosy youth
Had lingered near him: not to speak the truth
Too definitely out till names be known—
Like Paphia's—Love's—and Ariadne's own.
Thou wilt not say that Athens can compare
With Æther, nor that Minos rules like Zeus,
Nor yet that Gnossus has such golden air
As high Olympus.   Ha! for noble use
We came to Naxos!   Love has well intended
To change thy bridegroom!   Happy thou, defended
From entering in thy Theseus' earthly hall,
That thou mayst hear the laughters rise and fall
Instead, where Bacchus rules!   Or wilt thou choose
A still-surpassing glory?—take it all,—
A heavenly house, Kronion's self for kin,—
A place where Cassiopea sits within
Inferior light, for all her daughter's sake,
Since Perseus, even amid the stars, must take
Andromeda in chains ætherial!
But *I* will wreathe *thee*, sweet, an astral crown,
And as my queen and spouse thou shalt be known—
Mine, the crown-lover's!'   Thus, at length, he proved
His comfort on her; and the maid was moved;
And casting Theseus' memory down the brine,
She straight received the troth of her divine
Fair Bacchus; Love stood by to close the rite:
The marriage-chorus struck up clear and light,

Flowers sprouted fast about the chamber green,
And with spring-garlands on their heads, I ween,
The Orchomenian dancers came along,
And danced their rounds in Naxos to the song.
A Hamadryad sang a nuptial dit
Right shrilly: and a Naiad sate beside
A fountain, with her bare foot shelving it,
And hymned of Ariadne, beauteous bride,
Whom thus the god of grapes had deified.
Ortygia sang out, louder than her wont,
An ode which Phœbus gave her to be tried,
And leapt in chorus, with her steadfast front,
While prophet Love, the stars have called a brother,
Burnt in his crown, and twined in one another,
His love-flower with the purple roses, given
In type of that new crown assigned in heaven.

PARAPHRASE ON HESIOD.

BACCHUS AND ARIADNE.

(THEOG., 947.)

THE golden-hairëd Bacchus did espouse
  That fairest Ariadne, Minos' daughter,
And made her wifehood blossom in the house;
  Where such protective gifts Kronion brought her,
Nor Death nor Age could find her when they sought
    her.

38

PARAPHRASE ON EURIPIDES.

ANTISTROPHE.

(TROADES. 853.)

LOVE, Love who once didst pass the Dardan portals
      Because of Heavenly passion !
Who once didst lift up Troy in exultation,
To mingle in thy bond the high Immortals !—
      Love, turned from his own name
        To Zeus's shame,
      Can help no more all.
And Eos' self, the fair, white-steeded Morning,—
Her light which blesses other lands, returning,
      Has changed to a gloomy pall !
She looked across the land with eyes of amber,—
      She saw the city's fall,—
      She, who, in pure embraces,
Had held there, in the hymeneal chamber,
Her children's father, bright Tithonus old,
Whom the four steeds with starry brows and paces
Bore on, snatched upward, on the car of gold,
And with him, all the land's full hope of joy !
The love-charms of the gods are vain for Troy.

NOTE.—Rendered after Mr. Burges's reading, in some respects not quite all.

PARAPHRASES ON HOMER.

HECTOR AND ANDROMACHE.

(ILIAD, Lib. VI.)

SHE rushed to meet him : the nurse following
Bore on her bosom the unsaddened child,
A simple babe, prince Hector's well-loved son,
Like a star shining when the world is dark.
Scamandrius, Hector called him , but the rest
Named him Astyanax, the city's prince,
Because that Hector only, had saved Troy.
He, when he saw his son, smiled silently ;
While, dropping tears, Andromache pressed on,
And clung to his hand, and spake, and named his
    name.

' Hector, my best one,—thine own nobleness
Must needs undo thee.   Pity hast thou none
For this young child, and this most sad myself,
Who soon shall be thy widow—since that soon
The Greeks will slay thee in the general rush—
And then, for me, what refuge, 'reft of *thee*,
But to go graveward ?   Then, no comfort more
Shall touch me, as in the old sad times thou know'st—
Grief only—grief!   I have no father now,

No mother mild !   Achilles the divine.
He slew my father, sacked his lofty Thebes,
Cilicia's populous city, and slew its king,
Eëtion—father !--did not spoil the corse,
Because the Greek revered him in his soul,
But burnt the body with its dædal arms,
And   · ed the dust out gently.   Round that tomb
The Oreads, daughters of the goat-nursed Zeus,
Tripped in a ring, and planted their green elms.
There were seven brothers with me in the house,
Who all went down to Hades in one day,—
For *he* slew all, Achilles the divine,
Famed for his swift feet,—slain among their herds
Of cloven-footed bulls and flocking sheep !
My mother too, who queened it o'er the woods
Of Hippoplacia, he, with other spoil,
Seized,—and, for golden ransom, freed too late,—
Since, as she went home, arrowy Artemis
Met her and slew her at my father's door.
But—oh, my Hector,—thou art still to me
Father and mother !—yes, and brother dear,
O thou, who art my sweetest spouse beside !
Come now, and take me into pity !   Stay
I' the town here with us !   Do not make thy child
An orphan, nor a widow, thy poor wife !
Call up the people to the fig-tree, where
The city is most accessible, the wall
Most easy of assault !—for thrice thereby
The boldest Greeks have mounted to the breach,—
Both Ajaxes, the famed Idomeneus
Two sons of Atreus, and the noble one
Of Tydeus,—whether taught by some wise seer,
Or by their own souls prompted and inspired.'

Great Hector answered :—'Lady, for these things
It is my part to care.   And *I* fear most
My Trojans, and their daughters, and their wives,
Who through their long veils would glance scorn at
          me,
If, coward-like, I shunned the open war.
Nor doth my own soul prompt me to that end !
I learnt to be a brave man constantly,
And to fight foremost where my Trojans fight,
And vindicate my father's glory and mine—
Because I know, by instinct and my soul,
The day comes that our sacred Troy must fall,
And Priam and his people.   Knowing which,
I have no such grief for all my Trojans' sake,
For Hecuba's, for Priam's, our old king,
Not for my brothers', who so many and brave
Shall bite the dust before our enemies,—
As, sweet, for *thee !*—to think some mailëd Greek
Shall lead thee weeping and deprive thy life
Of the free sun-sight—that, when gone away
To Argos, thou shalt throw the distaff there,
Not for thy uses—or shalt carry instead
Upon thy loathing brow, as heavy as doom,
The water of Greek wells—Messeis' own,
Or Hyperea's !—that some stander-by,
Marking thy tears fall, shall say, " This is she,
The wife of that same Hector who fought best
Of all the Trojans, when all fought for Troy—'
Ay !—and, so speaking, shall renew thy pang
That, 'reft of him so named, thou shouldst survive
To a slave's life !   But earth shall hide my corse
Ere that shriek sound, wherewith thou art dragged
          from Troy.'
          38*

Thus Hector spake, and stretched his arms to his
    child.
Against the nurse's breast, with childly cry,
The boy clung back, and shunned his father's face,
And feared the glittering brass and waving hair
Of the high helmet, nodding horror down.
The father smiled, the mother could not choose
But smile too. Then he lifted from his brow
The helm, and set it on the ground to shine :
Then, kissed his dear child—raised him with both
    arms,
And thus invoked Zeus and the general gods :—

'Zeus, and all godships ! grant this boy of mine
To be the Trojans' help, as I myself,—
To live a brave life and rule well in Troy !
Till men shall say, ' The son exceeds the sire
By a far glory.' Let him bring home spoil
Heroic, and make glad his mother's heart.'

With which prayer, to his wife's extended arms
He gave the child ; and she received him straight
To her bosom's fragrance—smiling up her tears.
Hector gazed on her till his soul was moved ;
Then softly touched her with his hand and spake.
' My best one—'ware of passion and excess
In any fear. There's no man in the world
Can send me to the grave apart from fate,—
And no man . . Sweet, I tell thee . . can fly fate—
No good nor bad man. Doom is self-fulfilled.
But now, go home, and ply thy woman's task
Of wheel and distaff ! bid thy maidens haste
Their occupation. War's a care for men—
For all men born in Troy, and chief for me.'

Thus spake the noble Hector, and resumed
His crested helmet, while his spouse went home;
But as she went, still looked back lovingly,
Dropping the tears from her reverted face.

THE DAUGHTERS OF PANDARUS.

(ODYSS., Lib. XX.)

AND so these daughters fair of Pandarus,
The whirlwinds took.   The gods had slain their kin:
They were left orphans in their father's house.
And Aphroditè came to comfort them
With incense, luscious honey, and fragrant wine;
And Here gave them beauty of face and soul
Beyond all women ; purest Artemis
Endowed them with her stature and white grace;
And Pallas taught their hands to flash along
Her famous looms.   Then, bright with deity,
Toward far Olympus, Aphroditè went
To ask of Zeus (who has his thunder-joys
And his full knowledge of man's mingled fate)
How best to crown those other gifts with love
And worthy marriage: but, what time she went,
The ravishing Harpies snatched the maids away,
And gave them up, for all their loving eyes,
To serve the Furies who hate constantly.

ANOTHER VERSION.

So the storms bore the daughters of Pandarus out
    into thrall—
The gods slew their parents; the orphans were left in
    the hall.
And there came, to feed their young lives, Aphroditè
    divine,
With the incense, the sweet-tasting honey, the sweet-
    smelling wine ;
Herè brought them her wit above woman's, and
    beauty of face ;
And pure Artemis gave them her stature, that form
    might have grace :
And Athenè instructed their hands in her works of
    renown ;
Then, afar to Olympus, divine Aphroditè moved on :
To complete other gifts, by uniting each girl to a
    mate,
She sought Zeus, who has joy in the thunder and
    knowledge of fate,
Whether mortals have good chance or ill ! But the
    Harpies alate
In the storm came, and swept off the maidens, and
    gave them to wait,
With that love in their eyes, on the Furies who con-
    stantly hate.

PARAPHRASE ON ANACREON.

———

ODE TO THE SWALLOW.

Thou indeed, little Swallow,
A sweet yearly comer,
Art building a hollow
New nest every summer,
And straight dost depart
Where no gazing can follow,
Past Memphis, down Nile!
Ay! but love all the while
Builds his nest in my heart,
Through the cold winter-weeks:
And as one Love takes flight,
Comes another, O Swallow,
In an egg warm and white,
And another is callow.
And the large gaping beaks
Chirp all day and all night:
And the Loves who are older
Help the young and the poor Loves,
And the young Loves grown bolder
Increase by the score Loves—
Why, what can be done?
If a noise comes from one,
Can I bear all this rout of a hundred and more Loves?

PARAPHRASES ON HEINE.

[THE LAST TRANSLATION.]

ROME, 1860.

I.

I.

OUT of my own great woe
I make my little songs,
Which rustle their feathers in throngs,
And beat on her heart even so.

II.

They found the way, for their part,
Yet come again, and complain,
Complain, and are not fain
To say what they saw in her heart.

II.

I.

ART thou indeed so adverse?
Art thou so changed indeed?
Against the woman who wrongs me
I cry to the world in my need.

II.

O recreant lips unthankful,
How could ye speak evil, say,
Of the man who so well has kissed you
On many a fortunate day?

III.

I.

My child, we were two children,
Small, merry by childhood's law;
We used to crawl to the hen-house,
And hide ourselves in the straw.

II.

We crowed like cocks, and whenever
The passers near us drew—
Cock-a-doodle! they thought
'Twas a real cock that crew.

III.

The boxes about our courtyard
We carpeted to our mind,
And lived there both together—
Kept house in a noble kind.

IV.

The neighbor's old cat often
Came to pay us a visit;
We made her a bow and curtsey,
Each with a compliment in it.

V.

After her health we asked,
Our care and regard to evince—
(We have made the very same speeches
To many an old cat since).

VI.

We also sate and wisely
Discoursed, as old folks do,
Complaining how all went better
In those good times we knew,—

VII.

How love and truth and believing
Had left the world to itself,
And how so dear was the coffee,
And how so rare was the pelf.

VIII.

The children's games are over,
The rest is over with youth—
The world, the good games, the good times,
The belief, and the love, and the truth.

IV.

I.

Thou lovest me not, thou lovest me not!
'Tis scarcely worth a sigh :
Let me look in thy face, and no king in his place
Is a gladder man than I.

II.

Thou hatest me well, thou hatest me well—
  Thy little red mouth has told :
Let it reach me a kiss, and, however it is,
  My child, I am well consoled.

V.

I.

My own sweet Love, if thou in the grave,
  The darksome grave, wilt be,
Then will I go down by the side, and crave
  Love-room for thee and me.

II.

I kiss and caress and press thee wild,
  Thou still, thou cold, thou white !
I wail, I tremble, and weeping mild,
  Turn to a corpse at the right.

III.

The Dead stand up, the midnight calls,
  They dance in airy swarms—
We two keep still where the grave-shade falls,
  And I lie on in thine arms.

IV.

The Dead stand up, the Judgment-day
  Bids such to weal or woe—
But nought shall trouble us where we stay
  Embraced and embracing below.

39

VI.

I.

THE years they come and go,
The races drop in the grave,
Yet never the love doth so,
Which here in my heart I have.

II.

Could I see thee but once, one day
And sink down so on my knee,
And die in thy sight while I say,
' Lady, I love but thee !'